Also by Bernice Rubens in Abacus:

BIRDS OF PASSAGE
BROTHERS
THE ELECTED MEMBER
A FIVE YEAR SENTENCE
I SENT A LETTER TO MY LOVE
MADAME SOUSATZKA
MR WAKEFIELD'S CRUSADE
THE PONSONBY POST
SPRING SONATA
SUNDAY BEST
MATE IN THREE
SET ON EDGE

Bernice Rubens

OUR FATHER

AN ABACUS BOOK

First published in Great Britain by Hamish Hamilton Ltd 1987
Published in Abacus by Sphere Books Ltd 1988
Reprinted 1990

Printed and bound in Great Britain by
Richard Clay Ltd, Bungay, Suffolk

ISBN 0 349 12904 5

Sphere Books Ltd
A Division of
Macdonald & Co. (Publishers) Ltd
Orbit House, 1 New Fetter Lane, London EC4A 1AR
A member of Maxwell Macmillan Pergamon Publishing Corporation

For Moris and Nina Farhi

Chapter One

Veronica Smiles was crossing the Sahara desert, minding her own business, when she ran into God.

She had seen His shadow before. Or, rather, shadows. For God was a man of parts, ubiquitous, unavoidable. Often the shadows loomed large; at times they dogged her like children. She did not know their gender. She was too wary to inspect. They did not worry her, those shadows. At least, not very much. She dared not let them harass her, otherwise she would have to go home and do what she had to do to make sure that she would never see them again. She preferred to think that they were tricks of the light; the desert optics could fashion strange patterns on the rock and sand. Every desert traveller had seen them, or at least she assumed they had, though no one had ever spoken of them to her. Perhaps they all thought that the shadows were personal secrets that might bring ill luck if revealed. She didn't talk about them either. Often she would shut her eyes when she saw them, but then other visions would sear the retina, images of terrible recall, and it was a relief to open her eyes again and face those strange menacing ghosts on the sand. She tried not to hate them. Though knowing their identities, she wondered at the same time, and in utter innocence, who on earth they were, those spectres that splintered her mind that, in every second of fearful recall, were both familiars and strangers in the instant.

She knew exactly who they were, yet with equal clarity they were aliens, lodged by accident in her head with all their frightful baggage.

So that when, that afternoon, minding her own business, she ran into God, she felt an enormous relief, for in that moment she understood the shadows. They were His, all of them, and there in front of her was the living proof. They were only God, after all, and she could cope with Him, with that solidity that stood in front of her. God was entitled to cast shadows, and the position of the sun determined their size. She was abundantly grateful that at last those ghosts had found their rationale.

A little nervous, she attempted a smile at Him. After all, it's not every day one runs into God. She braced herself for some momentous pronouncement. It was a brief encounter and, later on, when she recalled it, she could not help but be needled by its sheer banality. One would have thought that talking to God, or having God talk to one, would be an experience not to be trifled with. That one would feel, not to put too fine a point on it, a certain earthquake in one's soul, or, if one were not too greedy, then at least a small tremor in one's spirit. But not a bit of it. Veronica might just as well have run into her milkman in Surbiton – that surly suburb where she was cosily domiciled – for all the enrichment she had felt after their meeting. For God had talked to her about the weather. Not exactly the kind of topic suitable for the Sahara, for in such terrain it was open to so little variation. The weather anywhere is a pretty desperate subject for dialogue, but if, as in the desert, it is fairly constant and predictable, it is a topic of conversation exhausted before its launch. However, God had seen fit to comment on it.

"Looks at though we're in for a sand-storm," He had said.

"Don't you *know*?" she asked. After all, He was supposed to be in charge of such things. And if He had a sand-storm in mind, He could easily have arranged one.

"Perhaps not," Veronica added. "We might be lucky."

She wondered whether God knew about luck, whether that eventuality was part of His scheme of things. Probably not. Whatever was not arrangeable, God had no hand in.

"I think there'll be a sand-storm," He said, and passed on

His way. No salute, no salaam, no goodbye, no form of leave-taking in any culture, and He should have been aware of them all, since enough of them had bid adieu to Him in their time.

Veronica looked after Him and thought He was very rude indeed. She got quickly back into her jeep, thought about offering Him a lift, but decided against it. If He was arranging a sand-storm, He could jolly well weather it. In any case she couldn't afford to waste time with God. Her plane for London left at midnight. She drove back to her quarters and picked up her bags. Thence to the local station where the one train of the week would take her to Dakar in time for the plane to Heathrow.

She arrived in London the following morning, and made her way to Victoria station for the last leg of her journey to Surbiton. But even after all those road, rail and plane hours, she could not shake off her irritation with the banality of her God-encounter. She had rightly expected from God some discourse of a highly intelligent nature, some opinion perhaps on the theory of relativity, or an assessment of the Razamovsky quartets. But perhaps God had never heard of Einstein or Beethoven. It was possible, ever since the sixth day, that He hadn't kept up with things. His Sabbath had been eternal. All He wanted was to be loved. Didn't we all, for God's sake, Veronica thought. But that didn't stop us from keeping abreast of things. It was all very confusing.

She was glad when the train shunted into the station. Its arrival allowed her to busy herself with her luggage and thus take her mind off her confusion. Not that Veronica sported much baggage. Despite three months of travel through the cities and deserts of Africa, her possessions were minimal. Two rucksacks, the smaller for clothes and the larger for equipment.

Veronica Smiles was the kind of woman for whom the word "intrepid" was coined. Moreover, she came from a long line of intrepidity. Whereas Veronica specialized in deserts, her mother had tended towards mountains and in her time had been the first woman to scale the Matterhorn. After a short lifetime of mountaineering, a desperate half-climb of the Himalayas was her final achievement. She was never seen again. Buried in snow, she was already half way to heaven. Veronica's grandmother, a woman of questionable propriety, had scorned the mountains and the sand and had gone below earth, potholing, an unlikely pursuit for a Victorian gentlelady. On her last expedition, somewhere in the Mendips, she had chosen not to surface ever again and, already half way to hell, she, like her daughter, had saved her relatives all the vexing paraphernalia of funeral. Between them, those three generations, they had carved up the universe, on it, above it, and below. Intrepid indeed. Each one of them.

Unlike her mother and grandmother before her, Veronica Smiles was unmarried. Not that either of her predecessors had been over-aware of their marital status. Her father and grandfather were bewildered figures who had stood in doorways waiting for their wives to come home, waiting to be fleetingly greeted, to be left once more. No shadow would be in Veronica's Surbiton doorway. She was thirty-seven years old, and men had played little part in her life. None had approached her and she, on her part, had done little to encourage them. The only man who'd ever picked her up was God. Perhaps she should have been grateful. But gratitude in that quarter was not a viable proposition. Gratitude was reserved for the discovery of a sudden desert snail or a dazzling sand-sea. For such things she would give thanks in abundance. No other area of her life was worthy of any feeling of obligation. She regarded men as peripheral, much as she viewed cut flowers or haute couture. One of them was sitting opposite her now. She sensed his stare and quickly looked across at him, then, in Pavlovian response, lowered her eyes and, with them fixed on her lap, she recalled how, in the desert, she had broken that life-long habit and stared God straight in the eye. But she didn't want to think of that. Soon she would be back in Surbiton and the encounter would be behind her.

"Been away?" she heard.

The words travelled across the space between them and could have been addressed only to herself, since no one sat beside either of them. She studied the frayed seam on her khaki shorts and nodded her head. She was giving nothing away. But he persevered.

"Far?" he asked.

The monosyllable echoed across the space and reached her as if from a thousand miles. Without raising her head, she looked obliquely past him and saw her person wholly reflected in the glass of the window by his side. She was seeing herself as this man, should he be curious enough, would view her. Central to his line of vision would be her parting. Immaculate, she was happy to observe. No single hair astray. Yet it was not taut. Her fair hair hung loose to her shoulders and turned up slightly at the ends as if loath to touch the collar of her khaki shirt. That symmetry pleased her. About an inch or so above the ends was a slight indentation running round the perimeter and he would rightly guess that normally her hair was tied back in a tail. What he saw now was her relaxed presentation and he must be wondering what occupation she pursued when plaited. She supposed that her khaki outfit was a clue of sorts. It pointed to the outdoors and the visible tan on her legs, arms and neck indicated a long spell in the sun. He must be aware that hers was a special kind of tan, clearly distinguishable from that which is hastily acquired on a fortnight's package tour, that deep brownish pigmentation that threatens to peel before it reaches Surbiton, before, indeed, one can organize the wine and cheese party to show it off. No, he must know that the tan had come upon her gracefully and evenly while she was in the course of doing other things. But the reflection in the glass gave no hint as to what those things might be. She looked back at her knees and covertly studied him.

With her lowered head, her vision was blinkered. She had caught a quick glance of his face when she had first entered the carriage. About forty, she guessed. An educated face. Not the night-school type of do-it-yourself learning, but one which had passed with ease through formal education, a passage fuelled by money and background, and which was utterly taken for granted. She surmised all this simply from the classical layout of his features, an unreliable deduction, she knew, but it was confirmed by the sight of his educated shoes, hand-crafted and polished, clearly many years old and probably initialled on the tongue. She imagined his personal last, catalogued on a shelf in the basement at Lobbs. So, too, his chart of measurements in storage somewhere on Saville Row, from which specifications his suit was built. A light grey flannel of offensive durability. His hands lay on his lap. Were the sleeves a little too short? Was the suit a possible hand-down from an elder brother, or a father perhaps? There was an upper-crust shabbiness about his person that gave off an undoubted whiff of British aristocracy. She looked at his hands. Educated, too. The crests of his cuticles were exactly half-moon, born in that shape, with never an intention of a reduced quarter. The nails likewise, with the whiter-than-white rim, which, even after gardening, would return so. She guessed that he was a gentleman of leisure who knew well how profitably to use his time.

"How far are you going?"

His words bounced across the space between.

This man is trying to pick me up, Veronica thought. Two in a week. Not bad going. She looked up at him, as she had ventured to look at God, and she hoped that the ensuing conversation would be more edifying.

"Surbiton," she said.

He smiled. "I'm bound for Esher. The stop after yours."

So far, so banal.

"D'you actually live in Esher?" she asked. She was emboldened to give their conversation every chance.

"My mother does," he said. "I live in London. I visit her now and then. It's her seventieth birthday tomorrow."

It was a clue as to his own age. He was possibly the youngest sibling of his family, the result of a mother's accidental flowering.

"We'll all be there, my two brothers and I."

No sisters, Veronica thought, and she wondered whether this represented a loss in a man's understanding of women. She herself was an only child. Perhaps, had she had a brother she would, with greater ease, have been able to hold a man's look in the eye. So he was forty, she suddenly categorically decided and she, almost thirty-seven. Then she wondered why she had made such a preposterous juxta-position. It worried her. She was not her usual self. The holy encounter in the desert had done her little good. This unaccustomed mood of hers would pass, she hoped. Then why did she pursue this conversation when her silence would have eased its passing?

"It must be wonderful to be seventy," she said, "and surrounded by family."

He smiled again and she noticed that, despite the creases of laughter around his eyes and about his mouth, his face looked far younger than in the attitude of earnestness with which he had first presented himself. His presence was beginning to disturb her and she lowered her eyes once more.

"Where *have* you been?" he asked.

"The Sahara."

This to her lap, her eyes once again on the frayed seams of her khaki. I must sew them, she thought to herself, before my next trip. Then suddenly the thought crossed her mind that she would never go to the desert again. She did not wish to risk another God-encounter. She would be safer staying in Surbiton. God was no suburb crawler. He wandered in barren places where no witness could testify that He was ever there. He would not enter any place where He could be cornered, pressed for His identity and charged for His loitering. But what should she do in Surbiton? Although she had lived there most of her life, she knew little about the area. Apart from primary schooling, her education had been in Scotland and Oxford and her adult years had been spent in the sundry deserts of the world. Was it only fear of another God-encounter that occasioned the thought that she might remain Surbiton-bound? Or was there some other reason that vaguely had to do with that man who sat across from her, that un-orphan who, unlike herself, had little notion of mortality? She kept her eyes on her lap.

"What's your name?" she said, then wondered what had prompted such an audacious question. She was not herself at all.

"Edward," he said. "Edward Boniface."

She looked at him and laughed aloud. It seemed a natural response to such a handle.

Edward laughed too, as if glad of her responsiveness. "And yours?" he said.

"Veronica. Veronica Smiles."

"With our names," he said, "we are what is known as a happy couple."

It was a flimsy enough reason for marriage, Veronica thought, but on the other hand it was adequate enough and with such a thought she again wondered what on earth had come over her.

"I'd like to hear more about the desert," Edward said.

"Deserts are private things," she said quickly, suddenly being herself.

"I know," he said. "That's why I'm curious."

The train stopped at Berrylands. Surbiton was next. Normally at this stop, on her way home from expeditions, she had grown excited, longing to be home, to acknowledge singly every familiar object in her rooms, to consolidate herself in that base that she would shortly leave again. At this stop, she would rise and assemble her luggage and make her way down the aisle to the exact exit door that, on arrival, would align her with the platform bridge that would lead her to the taxi-rank. But this time, she made no move, stiffening herself as if to will the train not to move forward. All of a sudden she didn't want to reach her stop, and to have to say goodbye to this man, this first man in her life to whom she had actually volunteered conversation.

"I'd like to see you again," she heard him say. "We don't have to speak about the desert."

"I'd like that," she said, and rose from her seat, knowing now that it would be safe to gather her rucksacks. "I'll give you my phone number," she said. She watched him take a pen from his briefcase. A gold Parker that was filled with real ink and had probably been used by his father and grandfather before him. She felt safe inside his pedigree. "401 2219," she said, and he wrote it neat and large on the back of his cheque-book.

"May I ring you soon?" he said.

She nodded and struggled into her rucksacks.

"I'll carry those," he offered.

"I can manage," she said. Now, having secured another meeting, she was anxious to be away from him and she practically fled down the aisle, arriving at the exit door as the train pulled into the station. When she alighted, she put down

8

her rucksacks and turned to wave to him, to offset the swiftness of her departure. He saw her through the glass window and waved in response. Then she hurried over the bridge and into a taxi, anxious to get home and wait for the telephone to ring.

She waited for a week. She was loath to go out at all and when she had to, she would make her errands quick, and leave the phone off the hook while she was away from home. She became obsessed with the telephone, loath to use it herself for her own business, in fear that she might interrupt his dialling. She had been without bread for four days. She was reluctant to make the journey to the bakery which was a good mile from her house. But on the fifth morning, aching for fresh bread, she set out to catch the baker, an early bird who opened his doors at seven. She did not leave the phone off the hook, assured that Edward was far too civilized to call at the crack of dawn. Her car refused to start, so she ran all the way, collected the first loaf that came out of the oven and sprinted out of the shop. The streets were deserted. It would be an hour before the first trains left for the city. She savoured her aloneness as she savoured it in the desert, that appetite of hers that had first lured her to the solitary wastes of the world. So she was slightly irritated to see a figure approach her from the opposite direction. As she ran towards him, nibbling on the crust of the hot bread, she saw that he was God. She pulled up sharply as she reached Him.

"What are you doing in Surbiton?" she asked crossly.

"I am everywhere," He said.

Everywhere, she thought, as long as there's not a soul around to witness it. "Then I'll see you in the market on Thursday," she said. "Twelve o'clock under the tower." Let Him get out of that one. "I'll be there," she threatened, "so you'd better show up." And she left Him, without a look behind her, nibbling on her bread and pretending that she'd met nobody.

She was home before the clock struck eight, and she went straight to the phone to examine it, as if it might, in its texture or stance, carry some trace of disturbance. She knew that her behaviour was bordering on the strange, but preferred to think of it as a schoolgirl infatuation, for any alternative was

9

inadmissible. As was her God-encounter. She set about making preparations for breakfast to take her mind off things. She was hungry and she convinced herself that all would be well once she was fed. To this end she ate far more than was her custom then felt over-full and more out of countenance than before. She decided that this day she would unpack her desert clothes, something she never did after an expedition. For she would leave them in the rucksack, apart, ready for cleaning, once the date of her next safari was settled. Unpacking them now was by way of deciding never to use them again. And it was not even to avoid a meeting with God, who clearly was now abroad in Surbiton. Let Him wait till Thursday, she thought, and see how the crowds will gather.

She unpacked the rucksack, and washed and put the clothes away. Then her notebooks, laying them neatly on her desk. She was glad to have something positive to do while waiting for the phone to ring. To do nothing, while waiting, was to nurture expectation, with its inbuilt possibility of disappointment. But once the clothes were hung and the notebooks arranged, there was little to do except settle down to the writing-up of her expedition, collating her notes into a publishable form. But her restless heart was not in it. Besides, since she was thinking of remaining in Surbiton, there seemed little point in pursuing a work that was never likely to be finished. But what should she do in Surbiton? If it was her decision to remain, she must gather together those few and intermittent friends, and consider them now as more permanent than stopover. She would give a small party, she decided, as a gesture towards announcing herself more frequently available.

She sat at her desk and drew up a list, but half way through she paused, thinking again of Boniface, and in the rôle of guest of honour. She would wait, she decided. She would give him another week. There was time, she told herself. But, for the first time in her life, she seriously counted up her years and shuddered at the thought that there was no time at all. I'll prepare the list anyway, she decided, and a tentative date. I might even get the wine in and all the non-perishables. But that thought disturbed her, for she didn't want to go out. She could, of course, order the wine by telephone. She reckoned on twelve guests and listed her requirements. Then she dialled her local merchant.

Hullo, she heard. *The shop is closed at this time. Our opening hours are between ten am. and six pm. Please leave your name and number and we will contact you.*

She stared at the receiver. "Thank you," she said, in sudden gratitude for the idea that the machine had inspired. The solution to her house-bound Boniface expectation. An answering machine would free her, allow her to brave the streets, at any hour, and as far and as long as she wished. Why, she might even return to the Sahara. She would arrange for its installation immediately.

The yellow pages offered an infinite choice and she chose that supplier who would most quickly deliver. They would be there within the hour, they promised her. And they were. By lunchtime, all the wires were connected and tested, and her own message recorded loud and clear on the twenty-second tape. In her new-found freedom, she overtipped the engineers and, as soon as they were gone, prepared herself for her first carefree sortie since her return from the desert. She hurried, as if anxious to fulfil some duty. She felt obliged to leave the machine alone, to let it get on with its own business, a business that in her presence, it might find embarrassing to pursue.

She drove to the market square and could not resist the telephone box on the corner. She dialled her number and listened in wonder to her own voice. But when the tone sounded, signalling her to leave a message, she was at a loss to deliver. She giggled. "It's only me," she said. "I'm testing you, just to see if you're working." She giggled again, then was suddenly full of words and she emptied them into the phone. "So at least I can be sure my little red light will be on when I get home and at least number one on the call-counter." She paused, breathless, then said, "Goodbye," needing some kind of sign-off that would distinguish her message from the next. For she was sure that there would be another one. That's what the machine was for. It was new, after all, and there was no doubt that it was in tip-top condition. It needed time, that was all, and there would be plenty of that, for she intended to spend many hours out of the house in order to allow the machine its privacy.

She went first to the wine store to place her order. She dallied there, strolling along the racks, not in order to pay attention to the bottle labels, but rather to give the machine time. The slow perusal of each large bin would allow for one phone-call, and a similar examination of the whole cellar would furnish her with listening matter for the rest of the day. She had reached the end of the first line of bins when she heard footsteps behind her. She feared it was God again and turned, trembling. But to her relief, it was only the shop assistant.

"Have you decided?" he asked, ever so politely.

"I'll leave it to you," she said. "Twelve people, not heavy drinkers." She could not be sure of Boniface, but her Surbiton friends were sober enough. "Half red and half white, I should think. And not too expensive," she added.

He led her back to the counter and introduced her to their house wines. "Would you like to taste?" he asked.

Why not? she thought. Time for at least one more telephone call.

He poured her a little of the white and held the glass to the light.

"Good colour," he said, then he sniffed at it. "And a pretty fair nose," he added.

Veronica did not know what he was talking about, but she nodded in acknowledgement of his expertise. Then she took the glass from his hand and drank it in one gulp. She noticed his look of disapproval.

"That's fine," she said. "I'll take your advice."

He did the same with a sample of red, offering her first a piece of bread to clear her palate. But his commentary was the same and Veronica wondered whether he ever varied it for different vintages. But this time she sipped slowly, in deference to his unlikely connoisseurship. "Lovely," she said.

"A case and a half I think, would be plenty," he assessed her needs. Though Veronica thought that it was too great a quantity, unless of course Boniface was an alcoholic, she agreed with him, and he offered to load the order in the boot of her car.

That done, she took herself to the supermarket for the rest

of the imperishables. She took her time, secure in the knowledge that the real business of her life was being attended to. When she had stacked her trolley, she joined the longest queue at the check-outs and even allowed two middle-aged women to pass in front of her, seeing their scarcely-filled baskets of food. She studied them, the baskets that is, and each of them was a savage pointer to the life style of its carrier. Not that they were dissimilar, for each basket had sundry items in common. The bottle of sweet sherry lay hopelessly ill-concealed beneath a packet of frozen peas. A small tin of peaches was common to each. And there the resemblance ended. But the differences were unstartling. The first basket held a packet of two lamb chops, while the second satisfied itself with mince meat. The difference was not in price, Veronica noticed, nor even in taste, but in real and false teeth, a surmise borne out by the packet of porridge oats, which lay at the mince's side. She looked up at its owner, who gave her a dentured smile.

"Just had to pick up a few extras," she said, as if in apology for her sparse basket, for Veronica's loaded trolley was painful to view.

"Is that a good sherry?" Veronica asked, not wishing to know, but by way of her own apology for her extravagance.

"I wouldn't know that," the woman said quickly. "It's for my husband. He likes his drop, of an evening." Then quickly she clenched her ringless hand and hid it in the folds of her coat. Veronica shivered at the gesture and only half-knew why. The queue shuffled along slowly. Veronica was anxious for more conversation with the woman.

"My husband prefers dry sherry," she said, not even bothering to hide her ringless hand.

"Each to his own," the woman said, then looked at Veronica straight in the eye and actually winked at her, as if in acknowledgement of their mutual duplicity.

Thereafter only silence was possible between them. Veronica was confused. She could not understand what had prompted such a fantasy on her part and it vaguely disturbed her. The queue moved along once again and she would be glad to get to the end of it, when the two sparse baskets would be gone. During the wait, she consoled herself with the thought of clocking up another phone-call, but even that thought did not ease her impatience and she began to resent that she had allowed the two baskets, so chock-a-block empty, to precede her. At last their turn came and their few contents were quickly disposed of. Each woman offered the exact change for her purchases, dropping it from a clenched fist on to the counter, as if that exact amount had been precisely earmarked for the occasion. That gesture depressed Veronica even more. She began to offload her trolley onto the counter.

"Having a party then?"

A man's voice behind her seemed eager for conversation. Veronica turned. His old mouth dribbled with expectation. He was clearly fishing for a party invitation.

"No," Veronica said quickly. "Just stocking up."

"Stocking up on crisps and serviettes?" He did not intend to believe her.

"Why not?" she said, then wondered why she had to apologize to this total stranger for her husbandry.

"Tinned stuff I would understand. But crisps? I do like a good get together, though."

The man was relentless. He placed his basket next to a mound of crisps, the closest he would ever get to the party. Veronica viewed its contents with little surprise. With the exception of a packet of throwaway razors, they were exactly the same as the woman's before her. In old age, she surmised, the edges of gender are blurred, a razor's edge perhaps. The common factor of aging overtakes all previous differences.

She stacked her purchases in a box and carried them to her car. She looked at her watch. Her machine had been diligently at work for over an hour. She didn't want to overtax it. It was, after all, its first day of operation. She decided to go home, but slowly, taking the long route around the outskirts of the town, then working back towards the centre. Another two phone calls at least.

When she reached her home, she did not go straight to her study. She was confident that the little red light was shining. It was the number on the call-counter that would be the exciting surprise. So she delayed. She off-loaded and unpacked her purchases, and only when all was put away did she venture into the study. From the door she could see the red light, but the call-counter required closer inspection. She inched her way towards the desk, her eyes shut. She felt the outline of the machine and stood herself squarely in front of it. Then she opened her eyes. The small square of the call-counter was filled with the number '2'.

She trembled with disappointment, then gave the machine a shake, convinced that the counter was stuck. But the offensive number was firm. She sat down. A mere '2', and '1', her own, that would hold no surprises at all. Yet there was a small excitement at the second one and since there was only one call that she was truly waiting for, one that she was so desperately afraid to miss, it might well be that that unknown second was the voice of Boniface which, even backwards, and at high speed, would be decipherable. She pressed the rewind button. The duration of the message was short, but it was clearly in a male voice. This she confirmed as she heard her own backward message in high squeak reverberation. When she reached the beginning of the tape, she switched to playback and heard her own voice loud and clear. Her message bored her with its silliness and, when she came to its end, she switched off the machine to give herself pause, better to savour the unknown message that would follow. Then, holding her breath, she switched on.

Hullo, she heard. The voice had a familiar ring, but its recall was faintly irksome. *Hullo,* the man said again. *This is God. I'm just ringing to remind you of our meeting on Thursday*. Then a click. And that was all. The tape ran on, soundless, while Veronica put her head in her hands and wondered whether she shouldn't go and have herself seen to.

Chapter Two

Over the next few days, a number of friends rang to welcome her home. Veronica had left the machine running so that the offensive message could be erased. When Thursday came, she woke in two minds as to whether or not she should keep her appointment in the market-place. She was cross with God on two accounts. The fact that He was there at all and the even more irritating fact that He kept reminding her of His existence. She did not know how to deal with Him. Avoidance, even if it were possible, she knew was no solution. She would meet Him in the market-place, she decided, and there confront Him, collar Him by His non-dog collar and demand to know why He haunted her. She would not dress for the occasion. From what people said about Him, He was not one impressed by chic or style. He would be more likely to view a sackcloth with favour. With her, He would have to make do with jeans and sweater.

She reached the square as the clock struck twelve. She was glad that it was crowded, that hundreds of people would bear witness to their strange encounter. She found an orange crate next to a vegetable stall and stood on it to view the market-place and to pinpoint His position. She had no doubt that He would show up and she was unsurprised to spot Him almost immediately, standing alone between a fish and a bread stall, an apt juxtaposition, she thought, for whatever sermon He was about to deliver. She made a beeline in His direction. A few yards-away from Him, she stopped, finding a small space for herself in the throng. A space through which she could view Him, could, for the first time, seriously consider His face, His figure, His clothing and His mien. She sensed that one day she might be called upon to describe Him. But as she stared at His face and began a slow and detailed examination of each of His features, He spotted her, and at once turned on His sandalled feet and moved, as if invisibly propelled, through the crowd. Her last sight of Him was of His turning off the square.

She ran, pushing her way through the shoppers. She was angry in the extreme, angry at His cowardice, that He could not stomach witnesses. At the corner of the square, she saw Him slink into an arcade.

"God," she yelled after Him.

A few passers-by stared at her with pity. For God's sake, she thought, He's there for all to see if only they would look, and she heard herself thinking like a Christian. She recalled such platitudes from church, where as a child, her father had brought her in her mother's frequent absences, possibly to divert God's attention from his wife's lack of faith. Secretly Veronica had sided with her mother, though she loved her father and pitied him too for his loneliness. Now she saw how naive he was to look to God for comfort, that ubiquitous spirit that at this very moment was slinking through an arcade, witness-shy and hunted. Veronica watched Him with contempt.

"You," she yelled after Him. He surely was not entitled to divine appellation. But He knew it was He whom she'd called. He turned. "God," she shouted, acknowledging Him. "I love you." That's what He wanted, she thought. That's what He was always bleating for. That's what His servants endlessly adjured you to do. With all your heart. With all your soul. Perhaps now He'd get off her back.

She turned towards the market-place. She was aware that people were staring at her, but that did not faze her. Indeed, she felt somewhat elated. She had had her say, laying her cards firmly on the table. Now He could seek elsewhere for loving. But by the time she returned home and viewed the unlit bulb on her answering-machine, the euphoria had waned and, in its place, the slow gatherings of a depression. She tried to put from her mind the sensible consideration of having herself seen to. In any case, how could she begin to explain to anybody what was happening to her?

"Well it's like this, Doctor," she rehearsed. "Wherever I go, I keep running into God."

"Tell me about it," the doctor would say, and she would sit down, or probably lie on a sofa he'd offer her and she'd tell him about the desert and the early bread call, the market-place and, for good measure, she'd throw in His message on the answering-machine.

"Oh yes," he would say, gently and unbelieving, and would probably straightway certify her rather than delve into the years of confusion and mismanagement that were always a preamble to such God-encounters. She could save herself a journey. In any case, to go for help would be to acknowledge that her encounters were a mere figment of her imagination. It would be like admitting to lunacy. She had no doubt about her own stability. She *had* met God, and on more than one occasion. He had presented Himself to her in His flesh and blood. If she'd wanted to exercise her imagination, it would be directed to a more worthy target. It was God who needed treatment, she decided, to understand what motivation drove Him to haunt her. This reasoning satisfied her a little and helped to reassure her that she would not run into Him again.

She felt the need to do something positive. She would no longer wait for Boniface's call. She would arrange a date for her party and soon, she thought, else even the imperishables would perish. She decided on two weeks hence, then set about writing the invitations. She gathered together twelve guests. They were friends of long standing. Despite a nine-year exile from Surbiton when her Aunt Cissy in Scotland had care of her, their friendship had weathered her absence. All of them knew and remembered her parents. Indeed, now that in hindsight she thought about it, she realized that that factor must have been an unconscious criterion for choosing and holding her friends, as if remembrance were too great a burden for an only child to bear. Most had been with her to primary school, had shared her mother-less after-school teas and homework, had shared too the legend of granny-underground and mother-head-in-air. They, too, and their parents had shared the mournings, with no bodies to show for their tears. Above all, they had shared her father's loneliness. When she thought of such things, Veronica was glad that her desert explorations caused no one any pain or sense of deprivation. Yet such thoughts also gave rise to a melancholy of a kind. No one hovered in the doorway for her desert return. But, in that figure of no one, she did not envisage a husband, but rather a father with a child at his side, as she herself had stood, awaiting her mother's return. She tried not to think about such things, yet in doing so, she had to count her years. More, she thought, than were left to her and, as a woman, far too many. She shivered and thought of God, He to whom she had declared her love, and she felt that He owed her. Miracles were His department. Sarah, after all, when she birthed Isaac at ninety-one years, was no chicken. Next time Veronica ran into God, she would ask for payment for her love. Or else withdraw it. That would teach Him. Nothing is for nothing, she would tell Him, but she had a strong suspicion that God, with his acute sense of vengeance, would know that already. She wondered where and when their next meeting would take place, and now she began to look forward to it. Perhaps He would come back to the market-place, or run into her at early morning bread. She understood that the early morning encounter would be easier for him. He clearly didn't like a lot of people around. Very un-Godlike, she thought. But she was now anxious not to embarrass Him in any way. She would go every morning for the bread.

And she did, and for a whole week long, as well as walking across the common and availing herself to encounter at every lonely corner. But there was no sign of Him. He had taken her love and vanished, so like any male of the species. His Son was the same, promising to come back and then never showing up. It ran in the family.

She needed to see Him again and this need irritated her. All her self-sufficient life, her needs had been confined to bed and board, but never other people. She was weakening, she thought, and blamed God for it, for having presented Himself in the first place. So she cursed Him and wished Him in hell, whatever or wherever that might be, but not before He'd met her just one more time.

In her Boniface-expectant days, she was disinclined to leave the house. Now she was reluctant to stay indoors in case God was abroad and she missed the opportunity of running into Him. But to cover herself and all eventualities, she left a new message on her machine. And this is what she recorded.

Hello, this is Veronica Smiles. If that's you God, I've got a party on Saturday week, the 14th, at eight o'clock. Please come. If you're not God, leave a message after the tone.

She left the house well-satisfied, and kerb-crawled Surbiton, looking for Him.

She did not give up hope of seeing Him again. He was simply playing hard-to-get. She would bide her time and when He finally relented she would use Him for her own purposes and then discard Him. Each day she returned home and went straight to her machine. Almost always it was lit, and with sundry messages, all of them affirmative and delighted replies to her party invitation. One day, on her return from the God-hunt, the machine recorded that there had been one call. There was a short message on the tape.

I'll be there, it said.

His voice was friendly, caressing almost, as if her declared love had softened Him. She thrilled to His coming. She had read of parties studded with celebrities and of how hosts vied with each other for a bigger and better star. And here in a little suburban drawing-room, with a mere spinster as host, the greatest star of all would put in an appearance and she didn't even have to rent Him. God is coming to my party, she told herself, and to confirm it, she replayed His message over and over again. I won't warn anyone of His coming, she decided. I'll just introduce Him casually when He arrives. She wondered how He wished to be addressed. Should she say, "This is God, I'd like you to meet so-and-so?" Or, "This is our Lord? Or "The Almighty?" Some called Him Yahweh, or Adonai, forbidding names that would send everybody wiping their feet and minding their manners. Perhaps she should just call Him Fred, a cosy name that would unnerve nobody. Then they could all settle down and accommodate Him according to their will and ability. During the course of the evening, she would get Him in a corner and turn the conversation to the subject of Sarah. She hoped He wouldn't think it rude. Birthing was hardly a subject for a Surbiton drawing room. She would couch it in other terms, masking it in a treatise on procreation. She wondered what He ate. He was no doubt a vegetarian, reserving meat for sacrifice. She would prepare an avocado dish. He would like that, having grown them himself in the Garden of Eden. But the apple tart she had planned for dessert must now give way to a less offensive confection. He would not be comforted with apples. Honey would please Him perhaps. Or figs. She would accommodate Him. Thus, with her star as her guiding light, she re-fashioned her party menu. By the same token, she re-chose her party dress, discarding the flimsy bare-backed silk, and, in its place, putting out an ill-chosen, but well-meant gift from Emily, a little black dress that oozed reliability, honesty and innocence, the latter through the addition of a white lace collar.

In the few remaining days before the party, she kept to the house. There was now no need for God-hunt and, if Boniface should ring, she would be there for his call, though lately God had overtaken the Boniface excitement and she almost did not care whether he rang or not. She saw her future entailed by her God-encounters, her salvation almost, though she must not think in those terms for fear of becoming a Christian. Her mother and grandmother would have taken a dim view of such a belief. They who had scoured the mountains and potholes would have found such faith an impediment, a diminishment of their own struggle, a factor which would have endowed a mountain with more than its height and a pothole with more than its chasm. There was no divine mystery about either; only the man-made miracle of scaling the one and plumbing the depths of the other.

The days dragged until Saturday. Sometimes Veronica hoped it would never come, or the calendar would skip a day unnoticed. Yet sometimes she counted the hours to her party, fearful that she was setting such high hopes on her star. She spent most of Friday preparing the party food. She arranged the table buffet-fashion, but set a single place discreetly apart from the others. A celebrity required special treatment. At His place too, she positioned the silver candlesticks. She would surround Him with light and glory. Those words too were perilously loaded and at once she thought again of Boniface, who was a far safer encounter and who, at the least, evoked a vocabulary without nuance or threat.

On Saturday morning she awoke in fear, considering for the first time how her other guests would receive God. She knew that most of them, like herself, were rarely disturbed by the notion of belief. She hoped they wouldn't be rude to Him. Perhaps she could pass Him off as someone else, but she couldn't rely on Him to keep His big mouth shut. With luck they might simply ignore Him and possibly would, since He was a man of little conversation and what he offered was mundane in the extreme. She hoped He would just bore them all away, then she could have Him for herself.

At six o'clock she started on her toilette. She meant to look her best for Him. But as she powdered and scented herself, she wondered why she was going to so much trouble. God had proved time and time again that He didn't like women very much. He was piggish to Delilah and faintly unpleasant in the matter of Jael, though both women were in the business of loving. And what He did to poor Lot's wife didn't bear thinking about. He favoured the men. No doubt about it. Between Abraham and Zephania lay an alphabet of blue-eyed boys. It was no wonder He was haunting her, as He had probably haunted her mother and underground granny. He resented their heathen investigations, their lack of respect for His works. Their crass assumption that a mountain simply grew, that a pothole simply split, that a desert simply laid itself waste. Had He come to her mother on her final summit and to her grandmother in the lower depths, and whispered softly to them, in their death-throes, "I told you so," as He might indeed whisper to her one day as she lay in the sand? Tonight she would ask Him about her forebears. At least it would be a topic of conversation.

She was ready long before the appointed time. Over and over again, she checked on the food and the seating arrangements and then she sat quietly and waited, having no idea of what she was waiting for.

Arriving late for a party is not a Surbiton practice and, on the stroke of eight, practically the whole guest-list was gathered on Veronica's doorstep. She opened the door, She was glad He was not amongst them. She could trust Him not to come in a crowd. He would arrive alone and, without even a summons, He would make His solitary entry into her world.

She welcomed her friends, safe in their familiarity. Hilary'n'John, May'n'Alec, Wendy'n'Jim, Pat'n'Peter. As she pronounced them in greeting, she wondered whether they were eight or four. And a small resentment crept upon her at their oneness, their togetherness, their oh-so-stable statement of dynasty. She would not ask after their children. She wondered how they regarded her. Outwardly it was with admiration, respect, perhaps even a little envy. But pity too? She wished that God would come. The bell rang once more, with Tony'n'Gemma, Paul'n'Emily and Carol'n'Charles, all panting on the doorstep and, at two minutes past eight, apologizing profusely for their late arrival.

Veronica plied them with drinks and the imperishables and the talk was of children and domestic matters. In due course, when each had seen to each others' business, they would turn to Veronica and ask her to tell of her latest expedition. They would listen intently as they always did at every reunion, or at least they would look as if they were listening though Veronica wondered what thoughts in fact lay behind their attention.

"The usual things," she heard herself saying, but with little enthusiasm. "Sand and rock. Rock and sand."

They noticed her lack of excitement.

"Did you meet anybody?" This from Wendy, Veronica's newest and least familiar friend, who did not know which questions must not be asked. The others would have wished to change the subject, but changing it would only draw attention to what Wendy's subject was all about. Subtitled, it was a simple enquiry as to whether Veronica had met a man on her travels, a long-term mate perhaps, a possible 'n, who would neatly append himself to their host's name. All of them wished her well, thinking that 'well' was like themselves.

Veronica hesitated. Should she tell them about God, that man who'd picked her up, bold as brass, on the desert wastes?

"I did meet someone," she said softly, and Wendy's question

seemed suddenly less gauche and Wendy herself was seen to climb almost visibly in their esteem.

"Tell us," Tony said, and the others chorused with him, for now, no holds were barred. Their time-honoured discretion could be cast aside, their erstwhile sensitivity blunted. Veronica was on the way to becoming one of them.

She was silent. They were not, however, indisposed by her reticence. Indeed, they were glad of it, for it pointed to a seriousness of which she did not wish to speak. In her own good time she would tell them. They would ask no more questions.

"He's coming tonight," she ventured. Then regretted it. For what if He failed to show up? Or worse, arrived and fled yet again at the sight of witnesses? Either way she would be humiliated. If He doesn't come, she thought to herself, I'll scour Surbiton for Him and kill Him.

She plied them with more drinks. Perhaps if they were drunk enough, they wouldn't notice His non-arrival. Now she regretted that she hadn't ordered more wine. Should she wait before serving the food? She glanced at her watch. It was almost nine o'clock and she noticed how some of her guests had wandered towards the buffet-table, and had there taken up a mute stand. "I'll kill Him," she muttered to herself.

"Oh how wonderful the salmon looks," Paul'n'Emily said, for tact had been discarded along with discretion. Those who were not already at the table now gravitated towards it to ascertain the veracity of Paul'n'Emily's declaration. And they all agreed and looked at Veronica. It was undisputably her move.

"Are you hungry?" she asked needlessly.

"D'you want us to wait?" Gemma said kindly.

"No, not at all," Veronica was over-emphatic. "He may be late, or . . . well, he may not even come at all. He travels a lot," she added, and its sorry truth somehow gave it no authenticity. She giggled and they stifled their pity. "Help yourself," she said.

And then the door-bell rang.

The room froze. Forks hovered in mid-air and glasses trembled. Veronica was rooted, but no one understood the nature of her fear. Or of her joy. Or of her panic. But whatever it looked like, or seemed to them to be, Veronica knew it solely as terror. Terror is the no-man's-land between knowing and not knowing, between doubts and certainties, between an absence of evidence on the one hand and infallible proof on the other. Veronica had often thought of having herself seen to and just as often she had concluded that she was not a suitable case for treatment. If she opened the door and allowed God to enter, allowed Him to be witnessed and accounted for, could she then pass as sane? But if only *she* saw God in her drawing room and the others gazed on her with wonder, was she then certifiable? She wondered which outcome would give her more comfort. She felt her guests eyeing her as the echo of God's summons still lingered in the silent room.

She hesitated, wishing now that she hadn't asked Him to come. Now He rang again, with a certain insistence, demanding entry and she began to hate Him.

"Shall I answer the door?" Peter's offer was gently made, as if he understood her nervousness and frailty. But he didn't know the half of it. No one could measure the courage it required to answer the door to God, to be faced with the proof of one's sanity, or proof, perhaps, that one was undeniably round the bend. "I'll go," she heard herself saying, and she listened to the silence that she left behind her as she crossed through the hall.

She saw His silhouette through the frosted glass. He had shrunk a little, she thought. His shadowed stance was one of apology and she was glad of it. His arrogance was not an endearing quality. "Hullo God," she rehearsed under her breath, as she hesitated at the door. Then opened it, the greeting still trembling on her lips.

Boniface stood there, a half-smile on his face, but quizzical, as if questioning his right of entry.

Her relief was sublime and so enveloping that there was no room to wonder what he was doing there.

"I heard the message on your machine," he said, "so I thought I'd surprise you."

"Come in," she said, still confused.

"D'you really know someone called God?" he was saying.

Then suddenly it was all clear. "Godfrey," she improvised

quickly. "God's for short. He's moved and I don't know his number. I thought he might phone, so I left him a message." She marvelled at her invention and, in her delight and relief, she welcomed him.

"Is it all right?" he asked, needing reassurance. "My coming to your party?"

He would never know how all right it was, she thought. Boniface was the someone she had met. Boniface was the someone on whom she would not elaborate. It is true she had not met him in the desert, but nobody had specified that venue. He was a someone, and he would do. She practically dragged the living proof of him into the drawing room.

She found them all hovering, silent, expectant. Edward Boniface would have the impression that he was much waited for, which indeed he was, but in another guise.

"This is Edward," Veronica said. "Edward Boniface."

A single thought would have shot through each paired mind. "Ted'n'Veronica." It would do very nicely.

They were all at pains to make him feel at home, all of them hosts and Boniface the single guest. Edward might have been overwhelmed by their friendliness, but he seemed too ingenuous to be suspicious of its motive. Veronica idled on the sidelines, adjusting herself to her relief and her surprise. With Edward's coming, she had a feeling that she would never run into God again. The connection between them, between God and Boniface, was only a vague one, yet there was something disturbing about it. Whatever she thought pointed equally well to her sanity or its contrary. She shivered with confusion.

He was approaching her, a glass of wine in his hand. The other guests served themselves discreetly and talked amongst themselves. They had no way of measuring Boniface against other suitors, for as long as they could remember he was the only man ever seen in Veronica's single company. So nothing about him surprised them, except the mere fact that he existed at all. Yet they feared for its outcome. Veronica was unused to company. She had lived and worked alone for so long that possibly she had become unfit to live with. Moreover she did not suffer fools, even temporarily. She was brilliant, they knew. An enviable thing in a woman. But a bright intelligence was threatening to a man, unless it had the wit to hide itself. Now, as they watched him, he was raising his glass in a toast. If only she would smile, they thought.

But they were mistaken. Edward was raising his glass merely to eye its colour against the light. And Veronica looked stern in deference to the seriousness of his gesture. For it was professional. He was a wine-merchant, he now told her, and his profession was second nature. She was glad that their conversation could not be overheard. If, as she had told them, she had "met" somebody, then they would expect her to know the basic facts about him, his method of earning a living being one of them. She wondered what other facts they would have considered basic. His availability, certainly, whether he had ever been married or, God forbid, that he still was. Divorced perhaps? Separated? Children? These questions they would ask her later. She wished he would circulate amongst them so that they could ask him themselves. And this she engineered by taking his arm ever so lightly and guiding him to the buffet table, where sundry guests served him with supper. For a while she hovered on the fringes of the room and went occasionally to the kitchen, ostensibly to prepare more food. And in her absence they did exactly as she had hoped from them so that shortly they knew Boniface far better than she herself. But more than that. Boniface too was subtly investigating and soon he knew how Veronica had come by her even tan, the subject of the books she had written, her lack of marital status, information donated with some bewilderment by the guests, but all of it generous and promotional. Veronica moved amongst them and eavesdropped on her own biography, and it pleased her for she was unwilling to talk about herself. When, some half an hour later, she found herself alone with Boniface, she was aware of a new intimacy and she knew that he was aware of it too.

"When are you going away again?" was his first question.

"I don't know," she said. "Perhaps never. Sometimes, I feel I never want to set eyes on a desert again. But then there's a pull. Always a pull. My mother was the same, but with mountains."

"And your granny with potholes," he laughed.

"What *don't* you know about me?" she asked.

"I know nothing," he said. "Only from hearsay, and that's the same as nothing. Whatever *you* tell me I shall know. I shall discover. That's really what knowing is all about. Discovery." Veronica looked at him and with little difficulty dismissed any connection he might have with God. His conversation was far superior. But she herself could find no words for him. Gender intruded and she was callow, green and gauche. He touched her arm. "They will tell you I am forty years old, never married, no children, a wine shipper. But you will still know nothing about me."

"Why didn't you phone me?" she asked. Although her question was a non-sequitur, it seemed to her at that time to be most relevant.

"I've been away," he said. "Bordeaux. I stayed longer than I expected. I phoned you immediately on my return and got the message that was clearly not meant for me. Who is this Godfrey?" he asked.

She felt herself blushing from her own deception, but she knew how he would misread it. "No one really," she said quickly. "Just a friend I haven't seen for a long time. In fact it's his wife who's really my friend." She wanted to reassure him.

"It's risky, advertising a party like that," he said. "Anyone could come."

"Like you," she said, "and I'm glad." She felt her declaration too bold and she was anxious that they rejoin the other guests.

He followed her to the table and was quickly set upon by the couples. Veronica helped herelf to food and eavesdropped once again. But they weren't investigating any more. They were telling him about themselves. She hoped that he would find them interesting. It was important to her that he liked her friends and then she feared that she was investing too much expectation in him and, in spite of herself, she counted her years yet again. Suddenly, she wanted the party to end. She had an urge to get to her study, to her notebooks, and relive once more her continual search for the addax, that rare antelope of the desert. She felt her work suddenly threatened, her stability shaken. She did not know what she wanted. All she knew was that she wanted nothing enough.

Her life was suddenly threatened with choice. And choice implied compromise.

He approached her again. "Nice party," he said. "I like your friends. But I'd like to see you on your own. Perhaps next week? D'you ever come up to town?"

"Sometimes," she said, though for years all she had seen of the capital was from the bus on the ride from Victoria Station to Heathrow.

"Would you have dinner with me? Wednesday?"

"Yes," she said quickly and, regretting her eagerness, added, "I'd better check with my diary first," and she fled from the room to her study, there to regain her composure. She hovered at her desk for a while and leafed through the sheaf of photographs that had been delivered that morning, recording her latest journey. Sand and rock, rock and sand, each and every one of them. Barrenness, sterility, mile after endless mile. *Her* element. *Her* choice. She shivered.

"Yes, Wednesday's fine," she said, almost running back to the living room. Thereafter she relaxed and circled amongst her friends, asking after their children and listening too, while they filled her in on their progress during her absence. But none of them spoke of Boniface. Perhaps they smiled at her a little broadly, perhaps their voices were little more than a whisper, despite the lack of secrecy in the topics of their conversation. Yet the smiles and the whispers seemed to be part of a conspiracy, of *their* making, of *their* surmise, and Veronica felt vaguely resentful.

Towards midnight, Pat'n'Peter, professional party-goers – Peter was the local Labour counsellor – set the room in arrangement for charades. It was not a game that Veronica favoured for there was little of the extrovert about her. Besides, she totally lacked any acting skills and her only success was in embarrassing herself. She declared herself a spectator, a role that her friends had, over the years, generously accepted. But when Boniface, too, offered his preference for the sidelines, they were less than willing to accept. But he was adamant. His refusal was final and authoritative. Some of them began to dislike him a little. But Veronica was impressed by his insistence and took her place beside him on the spectators' couch. Now those who would play the game became belligerent almost and went about it with a vengeance, united in a hostility against those who would not join in. So much so, that when Boniface offered a solution to one of their charades he was totally ignored, as if he simply did not exist. Perhaps he felt Veronica's unease, for he surrendered, offering himself to a minor role. As he performed it, they resented him even more, for his acting talent was considerable and pointed to a certain professionalism. At once he became an object of suspicion, an invader of their harmless amateurism.

"Acting helps in my profession," Edward said, in a timid attempt to excuse his talent. "You have to dissemble a little."

This confession did little to endear him to their company. They all played it straight in their life and work. They were teachers and social workers, tax inspectors and bank clerks. Even Jim, of Wendy'n'Jim, the dentist, worked strictly within the National Health programme and took only what was his due. They viewed Edward as a stranger in their midst. In their minds they dropped the 'n' from Veronica and hoped she would find someone more to their taste. So they were surprised and a little displeased to see Veronica rise from the couch and take up her stand at Boniface's side. She said nothing, but it was clearly an alignment. It was an order to them all to accept her choice or to forego her friendship. The charades were quickly dropped as an unsound basis for Veronica's conditions. Now they fell into groups of conversation and, in a little while, the bonhomie returned. Indeed, it was now enhanced. Veronica had, that evening, presented a new face, and there was some excitement among her guests as to the new look of her future.

It was almost three when the party broke up. They left more or less as they had arrived: en masse. Boniface made no move to stay behind and Veronica was glad of it, secure in the knowledge that she would see him in a few days. She saw them to the door and watched them drive off in convoy down the road. Then she lingered a while, watching the gathering light over the distant hills. She heard footsteps and hoped yet feared that Boniface had returned. That his leaving had been discretional but not serious. She trembled a little, but even more so when she saw that the footsteps belonged to God, come yet again without witness, slinking in the shadows. She recalled their last non-meeting and how he had fled like a hunted one.

"You're late," she shouted at Him. "The party's over. It's almost morning."

"The time of the singing of the birds is come," He said, "and the voice of the turtle is heard in the land."

Then she thought of her father and how he would read her into motherless sleep with Bible verses. The turtle was a favourite. The voice of the turtle. Over and over again.

"That's not yours," Veronica said. "It's Solomon's. You stole it."

"All is mine," He told her. "All comes from me."

That arrogance again. She wondered whether she should ask Him inside. Perhaps He would help her with the washing-up. But she decided against it. She felt less need of Him now. Besides, He'd trodden on her motherless dreams with His cheating quotes. At least her father had acknowledged his sources. The voice of the turtle. How he would croon it in her ear. He wanted his child to hear it too, to hear its song of love, inaudible on a mountain-top or far below the earth. Her father was listening for them all.

God had not moved from the shadows, but His voice was like thunder. "The Lord thy God is a jealous God," He said.

Ah, so that was it, Veronica thought. He's jealous of Boniface. That's why He'd gone on about the turtle-dove's song.

"But I told you I loved you," she said. There were different kinds of loving, though what would God know about that? She wanted to go indoors, but she was wary of shutting the door on Him. In any case, He was still thundering on.

". . . visiting the iniquities of the fathers upon the children, until the third and fourth . . ."

"But I have no children," she interrupted Him. "There is no one to inherit my sin."

He laughed. There was no smile on His face, but the laugh was cruelly visible nonetheless. He had caught her out and she didn't even know that she was being baited. She heard the echo of her own words. *There is no one to inherit my sin.* It was she who had spoken them. No other. Yet she had no idea of the sin she had spoken of. She'd spoken not even in a whisper, but aloud and apparently knowing of what that sin was compounded. Her declaration had been like the shadows in the desert. Intimately familiar, yet totally unknown. She heard Him laugh again and then she felt entitled to shut the door on Him. He was mocking her state, He was feeding her fear. Was that His purpose, she wondered, to confirm that which she already half-knew? Where was all that compassion of His that was so widely advertised? She closed the door and lingered behind the glass panel to watch Him steal across the frame. After a while, she heard the faint purrings of a car and she was not surprised to see His fleeting shadow as it folded itself into hiding.

Chapter Three

Veronica had spent what was left of her childhood in Scotland, though there was little enough of it. Indeed, perhaps she'd never had a childhood at all, so early was she burdened with the griefs and confusions of age. When she was nine she was given into the care of her Scottish Aunt Cissy. But the Surbiton house was never sold. Mrs Dale, the housekeeper, was delegated to look after it until Aunt Cissy could sell up in the north. But the move back to the south was postponed over and over again, until Veronica came south anyway and to Oxford University, and was able to fend for herself. But all the while Mrs Dale stayed on and waited, entitled to Veronica on every school holiday, holding the Smiles fort, guarding its grievous secrets. For secrets Mrs Dale chose to consider them. And even though she knew them, deed by terrible deed, it was only in the guise of secrecy that she could accommodate them. And the same went for Veronica.

The secrets were hidden in a chest of three drawers and in those drawers lay the whole of Veronica's childhood. Mrs Dale shut her eyes when she passed the chest and dusted it daily without looking.

Sometimes, when she came down on holiday, Veronica would let her fingers play on the ornate metal handles.

"What's in these drawers?" she would say.

"Just papers." Mrs Dale's voice was squeaking.

And Veronica would not enquire further. Her survival instinct had been nurtured since birth and that instinct prompted her to believe that much of what was inside the drawers was not good for her. For, like Mrs Dale, she knew the secrets too, though with a child's bewilderment and she thought they were mostly fairy tale. But there came a time when the fairy tale option was no longer tenable and when she came down from Oxford Veronica knew that the chest of drawers of her childhood was real and open to perusal, and in all probability held no promise of a happy ending. Slowly she had dared to open them. The first drawer was for papers, the second for photographs. Both of them benign. But the third drawer was not so easily divorced from fairy tale and, unwilling to face it, she had locked it firmly and put the key where no one could find it. Herself included, for its whereabouts was forgotten.

Prior to every departure to the desert, Veronica would sift through the first two drawers. This search had become an imperative before each expedition. In the light of her forebears' history, she assumed that it was on the cards that she would die in the desert and recapping on her childhood, secreted in the drawers, was a way of writing her own obituary. Through the letters and photographs she could record her birth, her schooling, the letter offering a scholarship to Oxford. The final entry in the first drawer was a letter from Aunt Cissy, full of love and reassurance that her favourite niece would be coming to live with her in Scotland. That letter closed the book on her adolescence. Thereafter, all was stored on the shelves of Veronica's memory, undusted and perilously lodged.

In tandem with the contents of the first drawer, Veronica would peruse the photographs in the second, aligning her rompers with her first words and smile, her school reports with the roll-up school assembly. This last she would stretch across the desk, holding down each end with a paperweight and then pick out of the black and white panorama the faces of Emily, her best friend, Hilary, May, Pat, Gemma and Carol. With their recognition came a sense of security that each one of them was still part of her company, despite her many absences and a style of living that was so very different from their own. With the contents of the two drawers, she confirmed her past. Or almost confirmed, for there was always that lingering doubt about the third drawer, that searing omission. But, for a time, those two drawers would do for history. With that in her mind, and her reliable present, she felt free to leave them for the desert. Free, too, never to return, for if one's past and one's present were in order, dying was almost an obligation. Her Will which, since leaving on her first desert safari, had never been amended, lay forever taped to her desk top, to save her inheritors the least trouble. All that she possessed, including future royalties on her books, she bequeathed equally between her friends, ensuring that there would be no acrimony. Apart from these bequests, she stipulated a small sum to be earmarked for the tending of her father's grave. But she tried not to think about that, for such a thought was perilously close to the third drawer.

Such was Veronica's routine on the eve of each departure. But now, a few days before her appointed meeting with Boniface, she felt the urge to rifle the two drawers, although there was no desert in sight. It was as if her rendezvous threatened that same finality as did an expedition, as if she were laying herself open to some new peril. She had to admit that she was somewhat frightened. Not so much of Boniface himself, but of all that his person would threaten. So she went through the two drawers meticulously and, when she left the house early that Wednesday evening, but for the absence of rucksacks, she might well have been going to the Sahara.

He had arranged to meet her at a small French restaurant in Soho. Being only vaguely aware of its location, Veronica took a taxi at Victoria station and arrived a good half hour before the appointed time. She did not want to appear too eager. Her intention was to be five minutes late, not out of any interest in technique, but because she was too shy to sit and wait alone. She decided to walk around Soho, which she had heard was an interesting area, though no one had specified the nature of that interest. A few steps down one side street served to enlighten her. The alley was an unveiling of one strip club after another. In each doorway, a tout urged the passers-by for their custom, promising them a better paradise than the one next door. But Veronica was allowed free passage. She merited an occasional smile from a passer-by who, with a leering look, stripped her for nothing, then passed on his way.

She hurried to the end of the alley, uneasy, and wondered why Boniface had chosen such a venue. In such a place, she thought, she might easily run into God. It would seem a happy hunting ground for Him, this Sodom, to pour forth His wrath, His jealousy and His arrogance. And, indeed, as she turned the corner, she saw His visiting card blazoned on a sandwich board: *The Wages of Sin is Death*. Coward that He was, He had sent a missionary. She looked at the man's feet. God had not even provided him with decent footwear. She wondered whether he received any wages other than those he carried on his board. She stopped outside a newsagents, scanning the headlines of the sundry papers. Her eye caught a notice board and neatly printed offers of services. There was an abundance of French teachers and German, too, though that tongue, for some reason, was often encouraged with a whip. There was a good deal of maid service to be had, with a number of seemingly irrelevant extras thrown in. She was fascinated by the notices and so engrossed was she that she did not feel the presence of a figure behind her and the heat of him as he trembled in her wake. But soon she caught his reflection in the glass and she turned slowly. She took care not to look at his face, but she thought that he was indecently close. At once he put out his hand and fumbled the centre pleat of her skirt and Veronica was rooted there, less in fear than in total astonishment. She actually watched his hand as he fumbled away, noting how filthy it was, its skin encrusted with age-long grime. The sight, however, did not disturb her. She was curious, though, at her own excitement and she watched fascinated, as her knees melted in forbidden joy. She hoped God was looking. It might at least improve His conversation when they next met. She knew instinctively that she must not look at the man's face. Anonymity was a prerequisite for the pleasure she received and perhaps, she thought, even the filth. She straightened herself without looking up, then turned and went on her way, her whole body a-tremble. She walked as swiftly as she was able and at the top of the street dared to look around and, to her horror, she saw that the man was following her. In a panic, she stopped a passing taxi and told the driver to take her to Victoria Station. At least she knew that place, and she needed some small anchorage. Once inside she leaned against the seat, and wondered to what depths she had sunk. But she didn't know, she didn't dare to think. All she knew was that God was not good for her. Since she had met Him, she had tuned into an appetite that had hitherto, in her godless days, lain comfortably dormant. Now she had met with the Devil, but why should that surprise her? If God was lurking, so was the other one. You couldn't run into Dr Jekyll and hope to get away without meeting Mr Hyde.

She had forgotten about her arrangement with Boniface and, when she remembered it, she wondered how she could now face him, so splendidly defiled. God help me, she said to herself, for what I have become.

The clock at the station showed that she was already ten minutes late for her rendezvous. She paid the cab and looked for another and, when one came, instructed the driver to let her down exactly outside the restaurant. She insisted on that, although he had to hold up the traffic to accommodate her. She tipped him well for his pains and his thanks were drowned in the hooting of the line of cars behind him. She noticed how the diners peered through the restaurant window at the din, indecipherable faces, and she hoped that Boniface was not one of them. In the foyer of the restaurant, she composed herself, brushing down her skirt, dismayed at the central creases which she knew no amount of ironing would smoothe, for they were as indelible as the mark of Cain. She asked for Mr Boniface and was shown to his table. She folded her hands in front of her as she walked, lest he noticed the creases and assumed the pleat as a well-used door for anyone's entry. She followed the waiter to a corner of the dining-room and the alcove of his chosen table and, on reaching it, she immediately sat down, even before greetings or apologies for her lateness. Only when she was settled and her sin hidden below the cloth was she able to acknowledge him and to plead a traffic jam for keeping him waiting.

He sat there undisturbed. It had clearly never crossed his mind that she wouldn't come. Indeed, so confident was he that he had already ordered her a drink which the waiter at that moment brought to the table.

"I ordered you a dry Martini. Like mine," Edward said. "I thought you might like that."

Veronica smiled. She would have assented to any aperitif, not knowing what to choose. It struck her that this was the first time in her life that she'd had a date. To be picked up was one thing, to be fumbled at was another – she shivered at the recollection – but a real live rendezvous was something else. She had no idea how to behave. She knew instinctively that she should hide the fact that this was a "first", but she had little talent for subterfuge. She scratched in her mind for something to say, to cover her ineptness with neutral words.

"I spend most of my time in deserts," she blurted out.

"I know," he said. "Your friends told me."

"On my own," she added. "I'm not used to company." She thought she might as well give it to him straightaway, loud and clear.

"There's nothing to be afraid of," he said.

"I'm not afraid," she almost shouted, and she wondered if she were trembling. If she were, it was because of the fumble man. She looked her escort squarely in the face and, in the tingling hangover of that·window-shopping stranger, she knew then that nothing about Edward Boniface would ever make her tremble. And freed from that possibility, she felt suddenly at ease and even laughed a little. He took it for nervousness and hastened to reassure her that there was nothing to fear, even to the extent of laying his hand on her arm. Apart from the print of his hand, she felt nothing. So indifferent was she to his touch that she let it lie and simply looked at it, not even wondering what it was doing there. She continued to look at it as it withdrew and went back to where it came from.

"Is there *anything* that frightens you?" he asked.

"I don't think so," she said, though had she been honest, she might have told him that it was only God who put the fear of God in her. Not so much God, she decided. Of Him she was not afraid. It was all that followed in His wake that frightened her. The strange, the unexpected, the forbidden. Yes, and the madness too. All of that frightened her to death. But how could she spell that out to Boniface? How could she tell him that she had been picked up by God who had lost little time in introducing her to Satan? As if he were part of the family. Perhaps he was. A brother perhaps. Or a close friend, in pain forsaken. And did God have a mother, too, whom she would have to meet by dint of her declared love for her son? There was no end to the Holy Family. But none of them could match Satan, she thought, host in hellfires to fumblers. To see Satan through a newsagent glass darkly was more than good enough for her. Face to face, no matter with whom, was clean, virtuous and pure, without mystery, without secrets and finally unutterably dull. She knew God was not good for her, but He had some very interesting contacts. Edward Boniface, on the other hand, was a face to face man, she thought. His face told all. So she studied it, the shape of him, the texture of his skin, the polite blonde hairs on the backs of his fingers, the shoulders in a continual state of shrug, though seemingly ever at ease. Because of his total and involuntary self-exposure, she felt kindly towards him.

"I'm not afraid of you," she smiled at him. "You put me at my ease."

"Let's drink to that," he said, and he clinked her glass as she held it, touching her little finger with his own.

Again she felt nothing. She knew that it was because she was looking at him, that she could acknowledge his face, that, in her knowing of him, thrill was disallowed. She wondered how people who had seen each other's faces could get married. And, moreover, stay married. Oh, the shame of it, she thought, that one looked at those with whom one sinned. It was little wonder that her mother had fled to the mountains and her granny underground, each going about their arduous business of pure shame. Her own sojourns in the desert were shame of another kind, but she would not think of that, dared not, for such a thought would, against all her animal self-protection, break open the lock on the third drawer.

"What are your books about?" he asked. "Which one should I read first?"

He was threatening her, she thought. He wished to know

39

her wholly. I never want to see him again, she decided. She knew there was madness in her thoughts, yet the madness lured her and she wished herself alone so that she might run into God, or one of his relations perhaps, whose invisibility would unlock that lustful sluice that had so lately engulfed her. She shivered and Edward asked her if she was cold. She smiled at him again. There was something so innocent in his simple equation.

"No," she said quickly. "You asked what books I have written and I thought of the heat of the desert and, sitting here, I shivered."

She considered she'd acquitted herself well enough, but all now threatened to be unhidden between them.

"I've written about the Sahara mainly," she said, "because that's the terrain I know best. But it's all very technical I'm afraid," she said. "I doubt whether you'd find it interesting."

"I'd sooner you told me about it," he said.

So she told him about the dunes and the wind-patterned sand, the plains and the age-long traces of what was once water. She told him about the desert serpents and animals, about her search for the addax, about the ghosts and the silences. She surprised herself with such intimate revelations but, in the light of what she had so recently discovered about herself, she knew that, no matter how private her disclosures, she was telling him nothing about her strange singularity. Edward would think that he knew her wholly, but she knew that he knew her not at all.

Her desert talk saw them through the hors d'oeuvre and as much of the entrée as she could eat. Edward was a good listener and interrupted rarely, and that only for clarification. Then there was a silence between them, broken only by her refusal of dessert and his order for coffee and brandy.

"Now it's your turn," she said after a while.

"I had mumps when I was eighteen," he said. Or rather volunteered, gratuitously, out of the unknown blue, without notice. It was as if he'd stripped for her and laid himself naked on the table. And, for the first time since being with him, her pulse quickened. A new Edward. Not so knowable after all. Yet now, what more was there to know about him? She was puzzled. Was he offering her his sterility or his impotence? Or both perhaps. And offering them too with neither pride, self-pity nor apology. She wondered what he was trying to tell her. 'There is no future for us' perhaps? Or 'Don't be afraid, I will not touch you'? But she wanted to be afraid, and she wanted a future to be afraid in. Fear was the essence of excitement. In all her years of perilous travels, she had never feared the unknown. But a short while ago, at the newsagent's window, that fear had pierced her for the first time and that joy she would not easily relinquish. She didn't know what to say and for a moment she rather resented him for placing her in such embarrassment.

"I'm sorry," she said, knowing that it was the wrong response, for in no way had he asked for her sympathy.

"You are disconcerted," he said, "and for that, *I* am sorry. It was just that you were so honest with me, I felt I had to respond likewise. I said what I said" – it clearly did not bear repetition – "because – well – it explains me. It explains me in full."

In the silence that followed she knew what he wanted to ask her. Did she want to go home? Did she want to forget that the near-nothing that had grown between them was ever anything at all? And, as if he had asked it, she said: "I don't want to go home. I like talking to you."

The relief washed over his face and she wondered how often he had taken that risk, and told his agonizingly brief tale and how many women had reached for their bags and pleaded the lateness of the hour. How many waiters at how many tables had eavesdropped on his impotence and had hurriedly prepared his bill?

"I'd like another brandy," Veronica said, confirming her staying-power.

He touched her hand, acknowledging his reprieve, but he said nothing. He was too well-bred for gratitude.

"I've told you about the desert," she said. "Now you tell me about wine."

Edward was more than willing to dwell on that aspect of his life that was far from failure. It was as if his potency, blocked from its natural channels, had flooded his being elsewhere. She admired him, his knowledge, his enthusiasm, but she could not deny a feeling of disappointment that Edward was not what she sought. She did not want the safety that he offered, nor the barren future. She would return to the desert, to that natural barrenness that she knew, as if she herself were part of it, its meet companion.

She dared now to look at her watch. The last train to Surbiton would leave in twenty minutes. It would not be untoward to suggest they leave. Besides the restaurant was almost empty now and the waiters had begun to hover.

Edward called for the bill and guided her out of the restaurant. Outside he hailed a taxi.

"I'll go with you to the station," he said.

Once inside, he did not look at her and she knew that he was afraid to ask her if he could meet her again.

"When shall I see you again?" she said.

"D'you want to?" His face brightened.

"I'd like that very much."

"I'm going to see my mother at the weekend. May I ring you?"

She nodded. She was glad to leave it open.

At the station he took her to the train and saw her into the carriage.

"I have your telephone number," he said, "But you don't have mine." He handed her a card. Without looking at it, she put it in her bag.

"You can ring me any time," he said. He was shifting the responsibility of their partnership and Veronica was not sure that this pleased her. As the train moved out, he stood on the platform waving. She thought then of her father and how he had stood on platforms with alarming regularity, waving at her departing mother with one hand, while, with the other, he held her own. The memory stabbed her. She watched Edward until the curve of the train hid him from sight and she stayed at the window for a long time. When she sat down, she opened her bag and took out his card. As she had expected from the beginning, he was titled. *Sir Edward Boniface, Bart.*, she read, *Master of Wine*. She was equally unsurprised by his serious address in Knightsbridge.

When she reached Surbiton, God was waiting for her at the station.

"I'll walk you home," he said.

"Why are you always following me? Haven't you any-thing more important to do? What about all the starving in India?"

"I have my eye on them," He said.

"An eye is not enough," she muttered.

He walked by her side.

"Has your conversation improved?" she asked.

He did not answer. He had His pride after all.

"You keep showing up," she said, irritated.

"I only come when I'm bidden."

"Who bids you?"

"You," He said. "From time to time."

She had to think about that one. "You mean I can get rid of you?"

"If that's what you wish."

They were passing the brick wall of a bridge. Graffiti murals. On it was written, not once, but four aggressive times, GOD IS LOVE in large whitewash capitals.

"You're getting pretty good reviews round here," Veronica said.

"I have my fans," He said softly.

She thought He had to be smiling. But His face was as stern as always. She stared at Him. She had no problems in looking at God. She did not need His invisibility. There was no problem in staring virtue in the face. It was the blissful seduction of evil that was unviewable.

"You have no sense of humour at all." She wanted to shake Him. But refrained. Looking was one thing. Touch was something else.

"This is a vale of tears," He said. "Vanity, vanity. All is vanity."

"There you go again," Veronica said. "Quoting. It's no wonder your conversation's so dull. You give your best lines to other people."

She felt Him sulking beside her. In His pouting mood. He was a sullen old bugger, she thought. She was glad when they reached her house.

"Goodbye," she said. "I've no doubt I'll be seeing You around."

"When you wish," He said, and passed by without farewell, as was his rude wont.

Veronica turned the key in her door and went straight to her study. The red light glowed on the machine and the call-counter registered one. She switched on to playback, recognizing a man's voice in its timbre, then paused before listening.

Hullo, the voice said. *This is God. It's eight-ten, and I'm returning your call. I'll pick you up at the station.*

She shivered. Eight-ten, she recalled, was the reading on the clock at Victoria Station, when she realized that she was late for her rendezvous. Perhaps in a panic she had actually said, "God help me," but a million people said that every minute of the day and it need have nothing to do with faith. Nevertheless, it *had* been eight-ten when she had called on Him and He *had* been at the station. "God help me." She muttered an involuntary supplication. It escaped her lips before she realized its possible consequences. She had no doubt that she would run into Him again.

As she lay in bed that night, she considered her day. Momentous, to say the least, she thought, for she had glimpsed the face of the Devil and had found it beautiful. And she had spent time with the barren Edward. The choice was obvious. In the same way as nuns became brides of Christ, she would espouse the Devil and join his harem which, she did not doubt, was many times larger than the Saviour's and much more fun. Tomorrow she would buy herself a brass wedding ring and even a bottle of champagne to celebrate her unhallowed union. God would be jealous, of course. But He was used to that and pretty good at it too. Indeed one might even call Him a specialist. He probably enjoyed it as well, she thought. It certainly inspired some of his best lines. "The ear of jealousy heareth all things," and God had the ears of a grasshopper.

When she awoke, a state of mild euphoria clung to her. She decided to do nothing that would threaten her mood and that possibly to laze the day away lying abed was the safest procedure. But first she rose to wash and make herself a good breakfast. Even in the desert, this was her routine. Today she would bring her breakfast back to bed and consume the day between the sheets. It was really God she wished to avoid, He who never failed to ruffle her temper. She could be pretty sure that He wouldn't show up in her bedroom. It was too rude a location for Him. Nevertheless, since one of His hobby-horses was harlotry, He could not wholly be trusted, so she got up once more and double-locked her door. While out of bed, she thought she might as well turn on her answering-machine. Her day was to be totally undisturbed.

She snuggled back into bed and must have fallen alseep, for when she woke suddenly, the telephone was ringing. She sat up as the ringing stopped and the machine took over, but she could not overcome her curiosity, so she rose and rushed to the study in time to hear the tail-end of her instructions. She thought it might be Edward making sure that she had returned safely. So she was irritated in the extreme to hear God's dreary voice.

This is God, He said, as if she didn't know. *I know that you are there, and I know too that you are thinking about me*.

Then there was a click and He was gone. But where? And more to the point, whence had he come? She was distinctly uneasy with herself. She had spent too long in deserts. Too long, much too long on her own. The solitary life played tricks on one's mind. She remembered her mother telling her that and, with that thought, she remembered Dr Curtis, the mind doctor, that shadowy figure of her childhood, that friend of the family, that slightly menacing after-dinner guest. Each time her mother came home from an expedition, she would, in great haste, pay a visit to Dr Curtis. "He puts my mind back in order," she would say to Veronica's father, and rush out before he could question her. Perhaps, Veronica thought, there was more than a mere professional arrangement between them. She had heard that Dr Curtis was still alive and practising. His address must be amongst her mother's papers. But when she opened that file, she found more than she was looking for, more than she had ever wished to find. Between the leaves of a notebook, there lay a key. She uttered a small cry when she saw it and wished with all her heart that, years ago, she had thrown it clean away. At the time, the hiding-place she had chosen had been seemly. As a dutiful daughter, she had filed and catalogued her mother's leavings. And then she had closed that file with no intention or appetite to open it again. It was her mother's life as she had chosen to lead it and, without judgment, her file could be closed. Now Veronica saw how more than fitting it was that she had hidden the key therein, for it was that file and the being behind that file that had caused the existence of the third drawer in the first place. She held the key in her trembling hand and wondered where now to hide it. Or even, the frightening thought crossed her mind, whether to hide it at all. She knew that to ignore its existence was to cheat on her past and that, to be honestly and fully prepared for death, she must first have opened that third drawer. She must wholly acknowledge it and then, somehow or another, come to terms with its dire burden.

She took the key and with enormous courage fitted it into the third drawer's lock. Her fingers seemed to burn at the commitment and she hurriedly withdrew her hand, and stared at the trap she had laid for herself. She shut her eyes, but the image of the lock was seared on the retina and she ran from the room, trembling. She had enough on her plate. There was the frail Edward, blackmailing with his gentleness; there was the barren desert that beckoned her abdication; above all there was God, who simply refused to get off her back. But there was the Devil, too. All was not black, while the Devil shone. But, like God, he was not in that third drawer, not in that earthquake, not in that fire. All that was in that drawer was she herself, wherein lay the peace that she had not made with her father.

She returned to her study and, with a calm that surprised herself, she turned the key in the lock. She stood far back, as if expecting a detonation as from a time bomb, the moment of which was now ripe, but the silence in the room was as deafening as any explosion. She walked towards the drawer on tip-toe. Surely, on opening it, she would hear a sharp wail of pain? But it was only in her own heart that she heard it and she turned away, leaving the drawer slightly ajar. She regretted its opening. While it lay there, locked and barred, its contents invisible, she scarcely remembered the matter of which she was so afraid. But now, in that moment of unlocking, her mind exploded with the fear of remembrance and she knew that if she looked in the drawer for even a short while, she would begin to recall. She wished that the mind could control memory, could prompt its leisurely unfolding, slowly and gently, chronologically even, until it reached the threshold of what was bearable and then obligingly ceased. But she knew that recall was often a stampede, with no respect for calendar, immune to any system of prompting. Recollection would have its cruel way. No picking, no choosing. It was all or nothing. She touched the drawer again and, trembling, she inched it towards her to a hand's breadth. Not that she intended to put her hand or even her fingers inside, but to squint out of the eye the matter of the paper that lay on top of the pile. A cutting, yellowed with age, from a local newspaper long since defunct. She caught the date. Over thirty years ago. Then she dared to read the headline. *Sunshine drenches Surbiton Common. A picnickers' paradise.*

A gentle headline with not even an undertone that would inspire fear or pain. She whispered a blessing to her father, for it was he who had organized the unfolding of his tale, he who had ordered its origin, climax and dénouement. Her father had been at pains to lighten the burden of his haunting and terrible legacy. She felt safe enough to withdraw the top cutting. A small dose, just to begin with, slowly to measure out her pain as her father had intended. She shut the drawer swiftly. She did not promise herself that she would never open it again. But at least she would conduct the tempo of her adjustment. The quarantine on that memory needed radium for its lifting. A minute, benign dose to begin with, then increasing with greater pain until the blockage was cleared. But Veronica was equally aware that the cure could very well kill her.

She spread the clipping on the desk. "The temperature was well in the eighties yesterday," she read, "when it seemed that the whole of Surbiton turned up on the common to welcome a belated summer. The river bank was crowded with picnickers and the playground area rang with the cries of children having a last fling before returning to school for the Autumn term."

There the announcement ended. It contained nothing to

give rise to alarm. In fact Veronica recalled the event with a certain pleasure. It was a rare occasion of a family outing. A Wednesday, half-day closing at her father's solicitors' office. Her mother had recently returned from an expedition, but would shortly be gone again, as was her wont. Although clothes had always played little part in Veronica's life, she remembered exactly how she was dressed for that picnic outing. Her mother had been climbing in Austria and had brought her back a coloured dirndl skirt with a white embroidered blouse. She felt very pretty that day and happy too, for the event of her parents' rare togetherness. She remembered that her mother was sitting on the grass and actually knitting, laughing to herself at her lack of expertise. Veronica hoped that other children were looking at her, sitting there, hugging her needles, the living proof of a stay-at-home, domesticated mother. The newspaper clipping had not reported that. Her father had taken her to the swings, smoothed out her dirndl over the crossbar and stood in front of her, gently pushing. In the newspaper there was no mention of the little boy beside her on the swing. Even less mention of the child's mother who was pushing him. Nor was there a word about the words that passed between them, between that man whom she knew as her father and that woman who was a stranger. Perhaps there *were* no words, but looks there were that no words could express. Looks that she caught on the downward and backward swing, the hell-bound way, but lost on the way to heaven. And all the time trembling, knowing that those looks were against the law. No words about that in the papers. Only about the children's last fling. Perhaps in that moment of descent, catching the glances between them, in that moment her childhood had ended. Perhaps, too, it had been the moment when, in all seven of her years, she had decided to opt for the desert, for its solitude and, yes, for its barrenness. For the world was too cruel for children. Nothing like that in the newspaper. Just the sun that shone brightly and blinkered a child's vision.

She took a new file from the cabinet and slipped the cutting inside. Upside down. So, in her own time, she would lay each drawer empty, one on top of another, ordering that part of her history that pain had rendered into chaos. She shut the drawer firmly, but took no care to lock it. It could hide itself no longer. Neither could it rule her. In time, she would empty it of all its sorrow.

Chapter Four

Without so much as an "Excuse me," or a knock on the door, He burst into her bedroom as the cock crew, or would have crowed, had there been any cocks in Surbiton. Veronica sat bolt upright in bed.

"What the hell d'you want?" she said.

"Make straight in the desert a highway for our Lord," He cried.

"Go and make it straight yourself. I'm not going back there. Why can't you leave me alone?" she said.

"You keep calling me. All the time."

"You're hearing things. I've been asleep."

"Honour thy father and thy . . ."

"Now look," she said, springing out of bed. "They're *my* father and *my* mother, and I'll do what I like with them. You're nothing," she screamed at Him. "You're not even *here*."

"If you don't believe in me," He said softly, "How can you hate me so?"

And He was gone, and the room throbbed with His whispering indignation. She sat on her bed and wondered what to do. If she'd had any doubts about returning to the desert, they were fully confirmed now. God had ordered her back and that was good enough reason for not going. But what was the alternative? Writing? But the completion of her book required at least one more Sahara expedition. Edward? Hardly a full-time occupation and a dead-end one, too, for her purpose. Whatever that purpose might be. She was unused to making choices. If one is obsessed with work, an alternative never presents itself, except in the particulars of the work itself. But the third drawer had overtaken that obsession and she now worked out that that was the only choice open to her. It would be a new vocation. The accommodation of her father. If people asked her what she was doing, she would say, "I am about my father's business." If God could plagiarize, so could she.

There was a picture of her father in her study. A portrait that his solicitors' firm had commissioned to hang in the dining-room of the board of directors. Her father had arrived. In professional terms, he could go no further. Did that explain the look of melancholy on his face as he stared beyond the camera lens into a settled predictable future? Or was that look born many years before, early in his marriage perhaps, when he was stunned by an equal predictability? For certain things about his wife would never change. He knew it when he married her, but he hardly believed it. For his wife already had a lover and would have for the rest of her days. A mountain. Any mountain. As long as it was worth her assault. That was for her to decide, for the mountain itself played no part in it. It was simply there, simply available. But, most of all, ready. A mountain is, by its nature, erect. It cannot cross its legs. You take it at your peril and your pleasure. On your own and with no co-operation.

Now a husband cannot fight a mountain. He cannot commit crime passionnel with a mass of rock. Veronica's father was hopelessly married to a woman who committed an adultery without collusion. How could he fight that? But Veronica did not recall her father as a melancholy man. He was jolly in their many games together when she was a child, just he and she alone, and it never occurred to her that there was anything strange about her upbringing. All women, she thought, climbed mountains or plumbed the depths of the earth. That was women's work. Men went to offices to earn their women's fares to those outlandish places. Children did for themselves until they, too, could earn fares or travel. That was the natural order of things, it seemed to her, and she clung to this notion with more and more tenacity as she grew aware of being less and less like other children. By all the laws of need and affection, she should have hated her mother. But when her mother left the mountain and returned to her father, when Veronica smelt and understood the resentment between them, even so, she took her mother's side. Especially after the swing lady, when her loyalty grew pugnacious.

Veronica went to the bedroom window and, peering into the gathering light, "Father, forgive me," she whispered. "Not you God," she added hastily, in case he thought she was calling on Him yet again. For there was no end to His megalomania.

She went to the bathroom and prepared the shower. She knew that she was ready, if not willing, for another dose of drawer. That in itself was an act of purification, so she would cleanse herself first in preparation. She lingered in the shower, anxious to postpone her next move. She had no idea what she would find as the next entry in the drawer, but whatever it was she had to face it and all those that came after it. Then she would never have to run away again. Then she could cease her desert atonement.

She oiled herself as if in preparation for a ritual. Then she covered herself with a black housecoat, the colour of expiation. She walked barefoot into the study and, with no hesitation, she opened the drawer. She took out the folded piece of paper on top of the file, with no attempt to peek at the tit-bit that followed. Once she had extracted the top paper, she closed the drawer and sat down at her desk. A single sheet, and, as she unfolded it, she saw the embossed address that shipped her right back into the children's cloakroom in the basement of her first school. She could even smell the rubber and sweat of the gym shoes hanging by their laces on each peg. She felt hot, too, as she had done at that time, feverish and nauseous, holding her head between her knees and, in her line of vision, the headmistress's terribly sensible shoes. "She'd better go home," she heard Miss Braithwaite say, and that advice Miss Braithwaite had expressed in her letter.

"Dear Mr Smiles," Veronica read. " I am sending Veronica

home in the care of Miss Wade. She has a temperature and I think she is sickening for something. Perhaps it would be well to call in a doctor. Yours sincerely, Celia Braithwaite."

There was nothing strange about the letter. It was straight-forward enough with nothing to read between the lines. But what was undeniably odd was the fact that the letter was in the file at all. And moreover that her father had placed it there and in its exact chronological order. It was relevant enough to his story, but that relevance was only known in retrospect and her father had not been allowed time for hindsight. Perhaps he had possessed an insight and an imagination for which she had never given him credit. She had always respected him well enough, not knowing why, and now she was glad to be given a reason. She remembered that by the time Dr Bruton had called, the fever had abated and he pronounced her well and ready to return to school. He'd asked her why she kept crying. She didn't know herself, or only partly knew, and the telling of that part was not for the doctor, or her father, or anybody in the world, except perhaps for God who already knew. Her father had come into the bedroom then, when her nightie was buttoned and she was fit to view, and she remembered how he avoided her eye. And she only seven years old, yet burdened, as he must have known, with an unfairly aging secret.

"Buy her a dress or a doll or something," Dr Bruton had said, "Something to dry her tears."

"We'll go out tomorrow," her father said.

With that remembrance, Veronica now folded the Braith-waite letter and put it into her own file, there to join the newspaper cutting as yet another item that had been dealt with. But Veronica knew that she had cheated on the Braithwaite letter. She had put a stop on her recall, which rendered the letter only half accommodated. For she balked at recalling that shopping expedition with her father. Fighting it, she clenched her fist but, despite that barrier, her father's hand slipped into hers as he led her across Surbiton High Street. And as she sat there in her study, oiled and in her black, in all her thirty-seven years, she could not help but follow him into the big department store, to notice the spring in his gait and the excitement in his eye. He knew exactly where he was going and what he was going to buy. She held on to him on the moving stairway, happy that they ignored the dress department on the first floor. On the turn of the second landing, they ignored sheets, towels and household, and on the third, electricals were given short shrift. As they climbed to the fourth, Veronica knew they could go no further, except to the sky, where, even in those young days, she knew there was nothing for sale. And there at the top of the escalator, they paused for breath, though little had been used in the automated climb.

"Is this the floor you'd like?" her father asked, then, without waiting for a reply, he dragged her through the teddy bears, the dolls, the train sets, the meccano. Even on this floor, having already narrowed his choice, he still seemed to be exactly sure of where he was going. There was to *be* no choice, Veronica realized. She would have what her father had decided. But that did not worry her. He knew her tastes and he loved her well enough to please her. Then suddenly he stopped and looking around, Veronica saw an assortment of skates. She tried to hide her disappointment and, most of all, her fear. For she hated speed and roller skates were gone before you could pronounce them. She couldn't understand her father's choice. He had taken her often enough to the fair and had known how she refused the figure eights and switchbacks, and was happy to sit on an up-and-down carousel horse and take her leisured, harmonium time. She wondered whether her father was punishing her. And why.

There were two available salesgirls, but her father did not approach them. He was waiting and Veronica hoped that he was changing his mind. But then a third saleswoman appeared and looked surprised to see her father. But smiled too and with much pleasure.

"Sir?" she asked mockingly.

Veronica stared at her, knowing her face, but then quickly looked away, giddied by the memory of the swing.

She remembered that her father sat her down and her foot was in the woman's hands as she fitted it with a skate. Then Veronica was sick and very neatly, over the woman's hair, as she bent her head to fasten the strap. The woman looked up horrified as the vomit dripped down each cheek. Her father had picked her up and carried her home. He damped her forehead as she lay abed, his face bewildered and melancholy. She shut her eyes, feigning sleep and heard him steal from the room. Did he then go to his study and open the file of what would be his legacy and insert Miss Braithwaite's letter? And if he had understood the dark connection so early on in the affair, why then did he pursue it to his own destruction?

She took Miss Braithwaite's letter and read it once more and was satisfied that it had been accommodated. She knew that the drawer dosage would become more and more painful; indeed she might even come to prefer the disease to the cure.

She put the file away and went to change her clothes, as she would do when she came home from church with her father. "Looking your best for God," he would say as he inspected her Sunday silks for worship. And when, on their return home, he'd told her to change her clothes, she surmised that God wasn't looking any more. Perhaps that was the reason why, ever since, she had never entered a place of worship, knowing that she would be safe from God's eye. Well, her chickens had come home properly to roost. Now she could go nowhere without running into Him. He was like measles, all over the place and catching, and there was no place where she could be sure He wasn't. She feared she was stuck with Him.

She heard the phone ring. She was afraid it might be God and she could do without talking to Him. She would disguise her voice, she thought, as that of a cleaning lady and declare that Miss Smiles was out and that she had no idea when she would return. She would affect a Scottish accent, one with which she was familiar.

"Hullo?" she asked the receiver,

"Veronica?"

It was Edward's voice.

She was relieved and, in her relief, she exaggerated her pleasure at hearing from him. "I'm so glad you called," she said.

Thus encouraged, he straightaway gave the reason for his call. "I have to go to Trier for a couple of days," he said. "Would you like to come with me?" He heard her hesitation at the end of the line.

"I . . . I have to think about it," she stammered, not least for the reason that she didn't know where Trier was. "Can I call you back?"

"Of course," he said. "But soon. I have to book the tickets. It's tomorrow. Ten am. We'll be back on Thursday."

"I'll ring you," she said, and put the phone down quickly, wondering what she ought to be feeling. Because she could not put a name to the quality of her response. It was not quite indifference but it was unnervingly close. Yet there was a small element of curiosity. Why had he asked her? Where would they stay and how many bedrooms would they have? These were questions she could not ask him. It would be like imposing conditions. She had never been to Germany, where she now discovered Trier lay. Indeed it was many years since she was anywhere in Europe. Very slowly her indifference began to wane. Moreover, it was more than possible, she thought, that she might even get away from God for a few days. It's true He said He was everywhere, but He probably gave Germany a wide berth, considering the Germans had been pretty unpleasant to His chosen people. The possibility of His absence was the biggest enticement of all. She searched in her bag for Edward's number.

He was surprised at her prompt reply and happy for it. Happier, too, that she agreed to come. He arranged to meet her at the Lufthansa desk at nine o'clock.

When she put the phone down, she began to consider the consequences of her acceptance. But when she tried, it was all too confusing. So she decided to regard it as just a holiday break and to enjoy it simply as that. Not easy. For Veronica was not by nature a carefree person. Most of her activities had to have some purpose of motivation.

"Fiddle-de-dee," she shouted aloud, uttering what she thought was the proper accompaniment to a carefree mood. But it sounded rehearsed and leaden. "Fiddle-de-dee," she tried again, but it only worsened with practice. She gave up and busied herself with packing a weekend case. Her months' long sojourns in the desert had necessitated a small rucksack of clothes. Now it seemed to her that for a mere few days she needed a portmanteau. For, lacking any idea of what was expected of her by way of appearance, she wanted to play safe and to take everything. Almost the whole day passed in crippling indecision, and towards evening she almost wished that God would come and pack for her. But she held her tongue on calling for Him. There was a price to be paid for His every visit. By nightfall, she had cobbled together a wardrobe that, at many stretches, would do for most occasions and she went to bed trying not to think of what she was letting herself in for.

At nine o'clock, Edward was waiting for her at the airport. He was clearly glad to see her and somewhat surprised, as if, in his poor want of self-esteem, he had not expected her.

"I have the tickets," he said.

"How much do I owe you?" It had not occurred to Veronica that she would not pay her own way.

Edward laughed. "Nothing," he said. "This is my invitation. I'm happy that you've come."

Veronica was uneasy. She would have preferred her independence and thus would have felt under less obligation. But obligation to what, she wondered. How could she be obliged to give him something that he was not able to receive? She was angry with herself for such an ungenerous thought. She tried not to pity him.

They flew to Luxembourg where Edward hired a car. Since she knew only little of the language, she could not tell whether Edward's German was fluent, but it tripped off his tongue with the ease and facility of a native. She felt comfortable with him and, though they talked little, she was unaware of the silences between them. They were going to visit one of his main Moselle suppliers, he told her, Herr Furstenbach, whose father had dealt with his father and their respective grandfathers as well. But Herr Furstenbach had been in ailing health for some time, and having only daughters – "not a woman's trade" Edward said – was obliged to sell out his holding. Today there would be a party to celebrate his retirement and Edward, one of his favoured clients, was invited to celebrate with him.

They drove along the Moselle. The vines were heavily laden.

"It promises to be a good year," Edward said.

"Why can't women enter the wine trade?" Veronica asked.

"There's nothing to stop them. But it's a question of tradition. One could break it I suppose. It's happening already, but it's still vaguely frowned upon."

"What about you?" she said. "*After* you, I mean."

"My brother Jonathan has sons," he said. "The business will stay in the family."

He was silent then and Veronica scratched in her mind for words to fill the space between them, if only for her own sake, for now the silence only served to feed her growing melancholy. Any talk of continuity, of inheritance, of lineage, always had the same depressing effect on her. She looked out of the window, but the lushness of the landscape only served to heighten her dejection. The silence seemed weighted between them.

At lunchtime, they stopped at a wayside inn. It was off the beaten track, at the top of a winding mountain road. Edward was clearly well acquainted with it and the proprietor gave him a warm welcome. Veronica was introduced but stood aside as the men exchanged pleasantries and items of news. Veronica rarely found herself in a sideline position and she wondered whether that was a wife's continuous role. For a moment, she considered herself as Lady Boniface and found the prospect more than pleasing. But then she remembered Edward's mumps and she saw the sheer pointlessness of such a union. Once again, she counted her years, a risk, she knew, for such a thought almost invariably preceded a God-appearance. Had she been alone, she would have shut her eyes or hidden, as vain a concealment, she knew, as that of Cain. But Cain had sinned and sinned mightily, and he hid from God's wrath. But she was innocent. Her only sin was that of aging. Yet there was more. God lurked in the corners of her mind for reasons other than the wrinkles on her skin. Reasons not so very far from those of Cain. She shivered. I must never open that third drawer again, she decided. Never. Never.

The proprietor led them to a table on the terrace which overlooked the rolling vineyards below. As she sat down, Veronica peered over the terrace rail and saw a shadow flitting in and out of the vines. She was drearily unsurprised.

After all, what happier hunting ground could He find to besport himself in than a vineyard? Every man under his vine and under his fig tree, she thought, that daft done-to-death lyric that no doubt, at this very moment, He was humming to Himself, and she leaned over to get a better sight of Him. She could hardly believe what she saw. The Almighty was actually rolling, lurching from vine to vine in a drunken stupor. He was fallible after all and, for the first time since the beginning of their acquaintenceship, she felt kindly disposed towards Him.

"Beautiful landscape, isn't it?" she heard Edward say. He presumed she was leaning over the terrace for a better angle of view.

"Lovely," she said, trying to suppress a smile, for in Edward's professional eye the view was serious in the extreme.

"I've ordered a Moselle," he was saying. "It's from this region."

"Those vineyards?" Veronica asked.

"It's a possibility," he said. "A good wine anyway."

With body in it, she thought, or at least a Holy Spirit. Oh, if it were only as easy to get rid of God simply by drinking Him.

"Why are you smiling?" he asked.

"I'm happy," she said, and felt a fraud for he might misread it.

"I'm glad of it," he said, misconstruing it exactly. He put his hand on hers. Veronica looked over the rail again to check that God was looking, but He was sprawled beneath a vine, too drunk to notice. She hoped He'd spend at least a few days sleeping it off. It was too much to hope that He'd die of drink. He was immortal, they said, and she wondered who before Him had granted Him the gift of eternal life. Did God have a father and a grandfather too? Or did He spring from matter mythically unsired? Like His Son and the whole kinky Holy Family. She looked at His sleeping face. But His look of innocence did not fool her. That was just sleep. Cain carried the same look in his slumbers. Soon God would be up and about, and revert to His usual self, the pain in the arse that He always was.

The waiter brought the hors d'oeuvre, a pink melon on ice.

She realized then that Edward had not consulted her about the menu. He had probably organized everything, no doubt choosing from the best. He had assumed a proprietory air, which was protective rather than colonizing. And that sense of propriety included herself. But Veronica didn't mind. Whatever Edward coveted, she had something that, for good or ill, belonged to her inalienably. That capital Something in the vineyard. As Edward glanced over the terrace, he didn't even note the Bacchus sprawled beneath the vine. Possibly he thought Him a tramp and not worth a mention. And in many ways, Edward would have been right. God *was* a tramp. He had no fixed abode. He turned up anywhere. And all the time he begged. Panhandling for love. For, though arrogant, He had no pride. He'd prostrate himself for a soupçon of affection. If she were nearer to Him, Veronica thought she would hear Him snore and, in token of that, the vine leaves over His face were fluttering. She wondered if He were dreaming. And of what. Of the Devil, she hoped. He'd wake up with more understanding. At the thought of the Devil she crossed her arms over her chest and hugged herself, and Edward took it as a sign of her pleasure with him. She was startled at the ease with which she could deceive him, or perhaps it was simply that he was gullible. She wondered if women often deceived men, either voluntarily, or despite themselves, whether many troths were pledged on the basis of such deception. And perhaps men did likewise with women and many an ultimate union was a collusion of güile and gullery. What did she know about Edward, after all? Or would ever know? His profession, yes. His status, too. And finally, his adult mumps. This last he had given out as his core. Whatever was more to him, he would hold within himself, as she would hold her untellable secrets. He could safely know about her deserts, her mother's mountains, her granny's potholes, but never would he enter the third drawer. And thus they might come together, as most couples were wont to do, their trappings shared, but each to the other, unknown.

He had ordered fresh salmon as a main course, with a green mayonnaise, a speciality of the house. And with it, a wine of the region.

"We shall taste more of these this afternoon," he said. "The Furstenbachs have a great cellar."

"Are you sure I won't be out of place?" she said.

"No. He's expecting you. I told him I was bringing a friend. He'll be glad. The more people the better. It'll be a sad day for him. The end of the line."

Veronica wished he wouldn't harp on it so. The subject was too close to the bone. For Edward, as well as for herself. She had been told by women friends that the maternal instinct was a man-made myth. Perhaps they were trying to console her. They could afford such theories after all, with their own children clinging to their skirts. Besides, she was not clear in herself how much she wanted a child. Really wanted. Or whether it was simply a matter of principle. Whatever the reason, her barrenness disturbed her and she looked across at Edward, who at that moment was sampling the wine, and she pitied him profoundly. For willing as he might be for heirs, he simply wasn't able. She looked over the terrace once more and into the vineyard, and she was relieved to notice that God was still sleeping it off.

They dallied over lunch, talking little, and by the time they left the restaurant the sultry air had cooled and Veronica's spirits were restored. They drove slowly along the winding narrow roads that led to the Furstenbach holdings, giving way to a number of drivers on their way back from paying their respects to the departing owner. There were few cars in the driveway when they arrived and Veronica was glad of it, for she was always nervous in a crowd. Edward was protective enough, holding her arm all the while. Herr Furstenbach spoke fluent English and welcomed her profusely, though he seemed to eye their partnership with some doubt. And as if to give that doubt some explanation, he mourned his lack of sons and Veronica's spirits plummetted once more. "One hundred and fifty years of Furstenbachs, Edward," he said. "I didn't know I would regret it so much. But come," he brightened. "Meet my successor. Herr Wodenfeld has five sons, no less, two already married with one son apiece."

Herr Wodenfeld hovered on the sidelines exhibiting that cunning deference due to one who had been deposed. Alongside of him were ranged his five sons and their male progeny, a line-up of fearful fecundity. Edward was introduced to them in turn and Veronica hung back sensing that this was a strictly business encounter. After the introductions, Edward seemed anxious to withdraw, as if it would appear an act of disloyalty to the old firm should he so quickly fraternize with the new. He seemed polite but cool, wishing to give the impression that, as far as he was concerned, the sundry Wodenfelds, no matter how fertile, were on probation. He joined Veronica and introduced her to a number of vintners of the area. Few spoke English and, though she felt an outsider, she was not discomforted. But suddenly she found herself alone. She watched Edward being shepherded along between two burly vintners who propelled him towards a table set out with wines and glasses. She watched as they urged him to taste. It seemed as if they were testing him. One of them slammed a wad of notes on the table. And then another did the same. They were placing bets on Edward's connoisseurship. She turned away, not wanting to see the outcome. A man stood in front of her, some feet away in fact, though his protruding belly almost touched her waist.

"Hullo," he roared.

She smiled politely.

"London?" he enquired.

"Yes." She did not elaborate. She had an inkling that Surbiton would have been beyond him. "D'you live near here?" she asked, without the slightest interest in the location of his dwelling.

He smiled blandly. He clearly didn't understand a word.

"London?" he tried again.

She nodded wondering how long this dreary exchange could continue.

"Chelsea."

Since it was not a question, she did not feel called upon to deny it.

"Arsenal," he said. "Manchester United."

Then with little difficulty, she cottoned on.

"Everton," he continued, and she shuddered at the thought of the four league tables and maybe even Scotland if he were so inclined. She would be there for ever.

"Wolverhampton Wanderers," he crowed, and she could

not help then but laugh, for that was pretty much of a mouthful for a foreigner and she was unsurprised when "Sheffield Wednesday" tumbled off his awkward tongue.

"Sehr gut," she said, the sum total of all the German she knew, but he took it as a sure sign that she equally shared his mother tongue and immediately plunged into a long recital of his football addiction. At the end of it, she gave no response and he turned and left her, seeking another ear for his bluster.

She was relieved to be alone once more. She looked at the tasting table and saw that the money had been removed and, by the smile on Edward's face, she knew that he had stood their test. He turned towards her and stretched out his hand. It seemed a public display of togetherness and Veronica wondered with some trepidation about his arrangements for their sleeping quarters that night. She had not thought much about it before. She had simply assumed that they would enjoy separate rooms. But that public gesture of hand holding did not in any way confirm that assumption and she wished herself back in Surbiton, safely alone in her bed and, with luck, with the Devil for company.

But, as it turned out, her fears were groundless. Towards evening, they had taken their leave of Herr Furstenbach and had driven into Trier to check into a hotel. She hovered at the reception desk while Edward spoke with the porter. Presumably he was confirming their booking and she was deeply relieved when the porter handed over two keys. Neither of them was hungry and Edward suggested a nightcap. He was tired, he said, and wished to make an early night. But, of course, she must do as she wished. It was the first time in the trip that he'd given her some small independence and she was grateful for its timing. "I'll make an early night, too," she said. "I may read a little."

Once in bed, she tried reading but had difficulty in concentrating. She knew that she was waiting for Edward to knock on her door. As the hours passed, she dozed fitfully, waking with a start at every creak. The sun was filtering through the window shutters when she finally turned off her light. No one had knocked on her door, not even God, and she fell asleep with the sour taste of universal rejection.

Edward had business to attend to most of the day, but he promised a very special dinner that evening. He told her what places of interest were worth a visit in Trier: Karl Marx's birthplace, the amphitheatre. But he was not pressing. Veronica told him she was happy to walk the day away in a strange city, since it was an entirely new experience for her. They arranged to meet in the hotel in the early evening.

Veronica made her way down the strange streets. Though almost languageless and at anyone's mercy, she had a sense of wellbeing. But the euphoria did not last. At the first turning of the street, she ran into God.

"I'll walk with you," He said. No "May I?" or "May I have the pleasure?" Just the simple assumption that she needed someone at her side. And not just someone. But the Only One, the Holy One, the ubiquitous leech Himself.

"You were drunk yesterday," she said.

"Who planteth a vineyard and eateth not the fruit thereof?"

"No excuse for being drunk," she scolded.

"Germany is not my favourite country," He said.

She quickened her footsteps, wishing to be rid of Him. But no such luck. Despite His age, whatever that was, He was nimble as a child.

"That Edward," He said after a while. "You covet him."

She turned and laughed in His face.

"You do," He insisted.

"You're jealous," she said. "You say so yourself. All the time. You're a jealous God. Go on, deny it."

Then it was His turn to laugh. "Who would covet *you*?" He whispered.

"Cruel," she said to Him, and turned her face away to hide the tears. She wanted to strike Him. Indeed she even raised her hand, but it fell through thin air, for He was gone.

She sat down on a bench near by and wished herself back in Surbiton. But more than that. She wished herself in Surbiton earth, close to her father, that only real, solid body that the family could muster. Dead, that's what she wanted to be. Good and dead, and the third drawer left unscoured behind her. *Who would covet you?* That holy whisper stung her ear. She would never forgive Him.

She began to walk but with little appetite and less direction. Perhaps, after that parting arrow of His, He would leave her alone for a whole. It was the first time that He had accosted her in broad daylight and in public view. But he was cunning. He knew that she spoke hardly any German and could call no one's attention to His presence. Neither could she stop a passing polizei and lodge a complaint of harassment. Let Him accost her one day in a souk in the desert where she was known and the pedlars were all on her side. Or even in the Promised Land, which she knew not but which He knew well, for there they would hardly recognize Him. Indeed it was highly unlikely that He would show up there at all on the basis that no man was a prophet in his own country. In any case, He might be ashamed to show His face there, beset with grave doubts that He had chosen the right people.

She found herself in a narrow alley. At the end of it was a very serious-looking church. She felt sure it was on Edward's list of "musts", but a church was the very last place she wished to visit if only in fear that God might have sought shelter there. Yet she felt somewhat accountable to Edward. He was paying for the whole of the trip and she felt in duty bound to give him his money's worth. She found herself entering the church. Not the church itself; she was wary of that, but the graveyard that surrounded it. The tombs were very old and laced with verdigris. From the dates that she could decipher, they had stood in memory and protection for over a hundred years. Occasionally from her scant knowledge of German she could make out the deceased's profession and sometimes she could pick out the ages of the dead. In their seventies mostly, a good innings for those days. And then the age of eighteen months slashed her eye and she fled into the deeper hell of the church. Inside she sat on a bench and then automatically knelt. Had her mother, head-in-air, seen her, her bones would have melted her avalanche shroud with their simmering wrath and granny underground would have died twice over. Only her father, resting in his improper Surbiton grave, would have turned over with pleasure and uttered a benign sigh. She wondered why she was kneeling. She had no prayer to offer. Or rather, she had no one to offer one to. Prayers she had in plenty. But no matter how often she ran into God, she simply did not believe in Him. Or at least, not in His divine power. He was just another person and she'd entered His house simply to rest herself. Quickly she got up from her knees and her eye caught the Christ at the far end of the church. She felt an indecent stirring in her loins, a stirring that had nothing to do with faith. It was not unlike those illegal titillations that had quivered her that night in Soho at the newsagent's window. She rushed with unseemly speed to the altar and gazed in shameless awe at the crucifixion. For a long time she stood there, her body raging with lust and bewilderment. "Jesus," she muttered to herself, "Christ is a veritable turn-on." She wondered what God would make of that and, lest He rush out of His hiding, she walked quickly from the church. Once outside, she ran down the alley and again into the main street and its company. She regretted not checking the name of the church so that she could report favourably to Edward. But she could not risk going back. Instead she went ahead briskly, hoping to find some object of tourist interest that would redeem her as a good pupil. She would look for castles or towers or statues, those landmarks that punctuate guidebooks. But she would avoid all churches. One dose of Christ was enough for one day, to say nothing of his Dad's shadow which no doubt at this very moment was stalking her. She dared to look round, but there was no sight of Him.

She walked for a long time, keeping to the main streets where most cities maintain their attractions. Once she sat down at an open-air café and ordered a cold beer, for she was sweating, both inside and out. And though, after a long draught, her body cooled, she still trembled with the after-math of the Christ seduction. She gave a wistful thought to her pre-God-infested days. Those months of sojourn in the desert, unhampered by doubt, unaware even that one doubted at all, for there was nothing to disbelieve or to question that one could not finally fathom by scientific enquiry. Until *He* had shown up and made a mess of everything.

She paid for her beer and plodded on. A church loomed threateningly before her and, in case it had not come to her attention, it brought her to its notice with twelve o'clock chimes. She did not even gaze up at the clock, but hurried on, and it was well behind her before the last chime echoed over the canal bridge that humped itself before her. She crossed it and found herself in a square, clearly a tourist attraction, for it was thronged with groups circling their leader. She assumed she had arrived at the amphitheatre that Edward had mentioned and greedily she sought out the nearest group in the hope of picking up their leader's waffle. But on close inspection they were Japanese and their courier, unsurprisingly, likewise. She moved to a second group but she had no clue either to its language or nationality. A further group was Danish and the last a straggling collection of German school children who clearly found their guide and teacher faintly resistible. Veronica moved on. She had begun to hate this city for reasons that had nothing to do with Trier. She was passing a newsagent and noticed a tourist city-guide on the outside rack. It was in English and she took it into the shop and paid for it, then hailed a passing taxi and gave the name of the hotel. She would give Trier a miss, she decided, apart from a scant perusal of its guidebook, on the basis of which information she could report back to Edward.

But as it turned out, he asked no questions. On his return, he rang her room and woke her, for she had slept the afternoon away, bored by the goodies that Trier had to offer. His ringing startled her, and it was some time before she realized where she was and who it might be. She cleared the sleep from her throat.

"I've just got back," she lied. "I was lying down for a bit."

"Did you enjoy your day?" he asked.

"Very much." She scrambled for the guidebook that had fallen across the floor. Quickly she turned to its contents page, at the ready to reel off with authenticating hesitancy and omissions, the headings down the page. But he asked no questions. His rights over her, it seemed, were limited and stretched only to protection.

"D'you want to rest a bit longer?" he said. "It's only seven. I've booked a table for eight-thirty."

"That'll be fine," she said.

"Then I'll see you in the foyer at eight."

She was grateful for his lack of interrogation. But she was not confident that she was entirely off the hook. So she picked up the book again and started to do some homework. But she could evince no interest in a second-hand acquaintance with the city, which, third-hand in its retelling, could only be thuddingly dreary. Yet should he ask her about her day, the thought crossed her mind to tell him of her God-encounter and to make it clear that it was by no means the first time. What would dear old strait-laced, impotent, sterile Edward make of all that? Perhaps he would flee in terror and leave her stranded in Trier, a fate that even Death would be hard put to better. No, she would keep her mouth firmly shut on God and translate him, for Edward's sake, into some tramp who had accosted her. From that beginning she could weave a story that Edward might even find entertaining. She could, if called upon, spin out the whole evening with the tramp's persistence, and thus she could avoid a grilling on what tedium Trier had to offer. She decided to dress attractively for him. It was the least that she could do since she had no fear of his seduction. She spent longer than was usual on her toilette and, when it was done, she was pleased with her efforts. And they delighted Edward too, for he remarked on her sparkle as she came out of the lift to find him waiting in the foyer.

They took a taxi to the restaurant. On their way, they passed the God-corner and skirted the church where Christ had turned her on. She refrained then from looking out of the window in case they should pass all those landmarks which she had not bothered to find, all those dreary monuments which the Japanese would commit to their cameras, at which the Americans would gawp with the awe of history, which the French would bypass in the sure knowledge that their monuments and churches were older and certainly much better and which would cause aging Englishmen, with memories of dive-bombing, to wonder how on earth they had managed to give them the miss. But Edward who, from his sundry visits to the city, must have had more than a tourist's knowledge, did not comment on the passing scenery, but simply took her hand in his, with a lustless and pressureless touch which neither surprised nor disappointed her.

Shortly the taxi pulled up at the restaurant. The doorman

greeted Edward by name. He was clearly a known customer. The same respectful greeting came inside from the maître d', and they were shown to what was obviously Edward's regular table. Veronica felt protected, valued and, above all, secure. So she was clobbered to catch sight of God, in the shameless disguise of a waiter, approaching their table. She trembled, terrified of what malediction or platitude He would hurl at her. As He touched their table, He veered sharply and went off in the direction of the kitchens but, in that split second pause of His turning, He actually had the consummate nerve to wink at her. It was not a wink of flirtation, or anything so harmless. It said that He was on to her and that, even with His one unwinking eye, she was constantly within His sights. She shivered.

"Are you cold?" Edward asked.

"No, I think I'm a little hungry, that's all," she said, though the sight of God had entirely blunted her appetite. But she was trembling not so much at the mere sight of Him; it was His disguise that so unnerved her. Hitherto, she had not particularly noticed what He wore. He was simply dressed and thus blended cunningly and comfortably into the background. Now He was taking that manoeuvre further. With disguise, he could pass as anybody and anywhere. She felt all avenues of escape closing around her and, like a rabbit trapped in the ever-increasing stubble, she trembled.

"Whatever one thinks about Germans," Edward was saying, "they certainly don't underfeed you. I've ordered a special dinner," he said.

She could have wept for his solicitude and resolved that, even at the cost of throwing up, she would do her best to merit his concern. It turned out to be a marathon.

German cuisine is atonement. In manic reverse. It shoves up two fingers and to hell with the consequences. They started with a "schinken-suppe", undisguised pig in broth. With croutons for superfluous solidity. It would have sickened the least sensitive palate. Even Edward could manage only half and Veronica was glad of it for it sanctioned her own half-eaten portion. She was glad she wasn't Jewish, or God would have had yet another axe to grind. She dreaded the next assault. When it came, the mere sight of it turned her already fragile stomach. The waiter introduced it by its name, with the awe and respect that a major domo would have endowed the arrival of majesty.

"Sauerbraten und Kartoffelklöse," he announced, laying each plate with reverence on the table.

Edward translated, but its interpretation in no way diminished the portion. The beef, he explained, had been marinated in vinegar and spices, and the accompanying dumplings, though there seemed absolutely no need for escort, were of potato stuffed with croutons. Wrapping up the whole package was the sour sauce. It was the speciality of the house, Edward said, and had to be ordered in advance. Veronica felt guilty even before picking up her knife and fork. If only God would show up, she thought, and like any decent-minded waiter, clear the plates away. But He was never there when you wanted Him and certainly never to do you a favour. She picked up her tools, shut her eyes and started on the impossible. She squinted over at Edward, who seemed undaunted. He went about it with determination if not appetite, as if to neglect it would be an offence to the establishment. But it was just for that reason that Veronica wished to forgo it. She was beginning to hate this country and it unnerved her a little to realize that she had something in common with God. What did *He* eat in Germany, she wondered. Or did He not have to eat? Did He simply cruise from one country's vineyards to another? That would rule out a good deal of the earth's surface. To say nothing of her own green and pleasant land where the vine was scarce on the ground. When next she met Him in Surbiton, she would invite Him home for dinner. But then she thought better of it. One did not get familiar with one's familiars. She dug into the kartoffelklöse expecting no resistance, but her fork came up against a solid crouton wall and the force of the collision cleft the dumpling in two, bathing it in the brine. Now it looked as if she had three dumplings to accommodate in order not to offend the establishment and it was a distinctly discouraging vision. She cast a glance at Edward's plate. One dumpling down, one more to go. She realized that it had been some time since he had spoken. He was clearly devoting all his energies to avoiding giving offence. He looked up at her and smiled.

"It's good, isn't it," he said, though without relish. She

agreed with his judgment and to prove it, she started into the house speciality with a brutal vengeance that she hoped would aid its digestion. She persevered with masochistic devotion until her plate was practically clean. No decent German could have outshone her. Moreover, she beat Edward to it and, relishing a respite, she downed a little wine in the hope of getting the ungodly mess well and truly down. Edward abdicated less than half way through, shovelling the remains to the side of his plate with a fork, so that what he had eaten looked more and what he had left seemed less. Still he did not speak, as if his mastication had consumed all his energies. She was not surprised and greatly relieved when he excused himself from the table. She watched him into the Gentlemen's cloakroom, then, as if given licence, she followed him, but veered off to the left and into the Ladies' and to the nearest toilet bowl. The relief of expectoration was sublime and she relished it for a while, hanging her head and breathing deeply with eyes closed. For she dared not look at what she had had the barbarity to consume. "Thank God for that," she said and, as she turned, the fake waiter's wing-collar brushed her eye.

"What are you doing here?" she fairly spat at Him.

"Acknowledging your thanks," He said.

"But this is the Ladies room," she said. "Have you no shame?"

"I am innocent," He said. "I still dwell in Eden."

"You've got an answer for everything," she said. "When are you going to leave me alone?"

"When you stop thinking about me," he said.

"But millions of people think about you. Why don't you go and pester them?"

"They are not *disturbed* by the thought of me," He said.

There was no answer to that one. And even less need. For He was gone, having made the point that He would haunt her without end. His message was clear. Either she began to trust Him and find ease in that trust, or she denied Him and found in that denial an equal comfort. Her father had believed, yet her pagan mother and granny had found more ease in their separate departures than had her poor Christian father in his last moments of life. "Poppycock," she said into the mirror, as she rinsed her face in cold water. Now apart from a sour God-taste, she began to feel well again and she returned to the table to find Edward already there, looking cool and well at ease with himself. He rose and held the back of her chair as she sat down, yet he made no reference to their separate absences. Edward had class.

"Would you like a dessert?" he said, and then he could not help but laugh at his preposterous suggestion.

"I'd like some coffee," she said.

"A little brandy too," he added.

After a while he said, "I'll make up for it in London."

She was glad that he envisaged a future for them even though it would probably be confined to restaurant tables. "Or if you like, I could make it up in Bordeaux. Difficult to go wrong there." The nature of his limit was the same, though he might vary it geographically.

"I've never been to Bordeaux," she said. Thus she accepted, because it was easier than hesitation. She had no doubt that God had a beat in Bordeaux as well, if only because of its superior vineyards. She wanted to ask Edward how he had spent his day, but she feared his retaliating questions and by now all memory of the tourist guide to Trier had been thrown up along with its kartoffelklöse.

But he volunteered on his own account to tell her. He had visited with three vintners along the Moselle, but he had ordered little. At this time of the year it would mean buying "on the stalk", cheaper but risky, and Edward was not a gambling man. He had called in again on the Furstenbach estate and the overwelcome of the fruitful Wodenfelds had unnerved him a little. He also added that he was tired from so much driving and would she mind if he asked for the bill?

In the taxi, as he took her hand, she wondered about him. She had now spent some time with him, but as yet he had made no positive impression. He was totally unaccusable, to the point even of being dull. Yet she enjoyed his company and she surmised that it was because it threatened her with no obligation.

In the hotel foyer, he said that he would see her for an early breakfast, since their plane left at eleven. Their parting was formal and Veronica wondered what the porters were making of their relationship. She would have liked to have asked them, for she herself had no idea at all.

She was not in the least bit tired, so she settled into bed to read. She heard midnight chime and gave a passing thought to the witching hour. So that a knock on the door on the last chime seemed to her to be right and proper. It was an obvious time for God to pay a visit. What was surprising was that He had taken the trouble to knock. Perhaps she had taught Him some manners.

"Come in," she called, not bothering to cover her nakedness. After all these years, He must be used to that sort of thing.

Edward stood there, he who had so lately pleaded fatigue and an early-morning rendezvous. He was menacingly pyjama'd. She looked at his presence in utter astonishment. She had no idea why he had come. She raised her eyebrows at him, lost for words.

"I'm only sterile," he said.

Only she thought. How could anything so terrible, so irreversible, be *only*? What in the whole world was left, after such an *only*?

He lifted the duvet and slipped on to the sheet beside her. His manner and his behaviour were, above all, that of a gentleman. Had he worn gloves, that would have been in keeping, too. He might well have been taking his seat in his club, so relaxed and so self-confident he seemed. There was no arrogance in his move, no sense of asserting his rights, so it did not occur to her to resist him. It suddenly seemed to her to be natural that he should be there at her side.

"D'you want to go on reading?" he asked.

What a strange unfathomable creature he was, she thought, and wondered whether all men in such circumstances were similar. She had no standard to compare him with and, as she laid her book aside, she switched off the bedside light, for if he was going to speak to her in bed, and she to him, she preferred not to see what either of them was saying.

It was only when Edward was settled by her side that she wondered what in God's name she was doing. For in truth she was a novice in such affairs. In certain spheres, Veronica was

73

a practised expert. There was little she did not know about deserts and even less in certain fields of geology, botany and zoology. But in the area of the bed, she was green. So green indeed, that she didn't know how green she was. She had lain with men in rough encampments. Certain events had occurred but she could not name them because she didn't know their terminology. Theoretically she was versed in virginity as well as in its loss, but she didn't know for which condition she was candidate. She decided to allow her body to respond as it itself dictated, but her mind kept getting in the way. Not with censure or disapproval, but simply with thoughts that seemed to her at the time to be highly irrelevant, for her mind was clogged with Jesus and the Soho Devil battling with each other for dominion. She felt his arm around her waist and she turned towards him. She was struck by his quiet gentleness, so deeply at odds with her sparring thoughts. And the more he caressed her, the more bloody their battle and, as he mounted her, they cried havoc. And when, after a while, she climaxed, it was with a sacrilegious splendour.

She remembered falling asleep, her body throbbing but her mind at peace. In the morning she woke, but did not open her eyes, wishing to savour for a little longer the aftertaste of her night's longings. She stretched out her arm to touch Edward and was surprised at the texture of rough tweed that greeted her fingertips. Quickly she withdrew her hand. Then opened her eyes. She quivered with horror. She was in bed with God.

"How long have you been here?" she practically screamed at Him, uncertain now with whom she had shared her bed, for of Edward there was no sign.

"I am always here," He said.

She wanted to shake Him. "Last night I mean," she shouted.

He seemed not to have heard her. "I view the wonders I have made," He said, ignoring her presence. "And I view them with joy. The way of an eagle in the air; the way of a serpent upon a rock; the way of a ship in the midst of a sea. And the way of a man with a maid."

"What makes you think I'm a maid?"

"You were," He said. "But not now. Not now."

She laughed. "I know you know everything," she said, "but even you have made mistakes. What about Mary then? After all that promotional hype you put out about her, it seems you have a pretty quaint idea of virginity."

She sprang out of bed and He turned away from her nakedness.

"But you *were* a maid," He insisted. "You were."

"Piss off," she said to Him. Veronica had come to bad language late in life and she was still wary of using it. She voiced it only on occasion, reserving it for the most shockable targets. But He was gone, possibly without even having heard it. In her rage, she threw the bedclothes on to the floor and the sight of the sheet stunned her. In the middle was a small blotch of blood.

She peered into the stain, sniffing at it like a dog. And suddenly she was overcome with a desolate sense of loss. She covered the sheet quickly, ashamed. She heard a clock chime and, counting the peals, reached nine. In panic she dressed, packed and hurried to the foyer. Edward was waiting there. Smiling. But it was his usual smile and he greeted her with his usual courtesy. He even asked, as he had before, if she had slept well. There was no sign from him that anything had changed, that their affair had terminated or that it had reached a point of no return. She ached to ask him if he had touched her. The blotched sheet still stained her retina and she could not rinse His words from her ear. She was not surprised to see God steal across the foyer.

She looked after Him and then at Edward and wondered which one of them had deflowered her.

Chapter Five

It was over a week since their return from Trier and still she
had not heard from Edward. As the silent days passed, she
assumed that it was indeed Edward who had lain with her that
night and that the act had signalled the end of their affair.
And in that assumption there was enormous relief. Not for his
lack of contact. That, she regretted. But as a signal to her own
sanity. Indeed, so relieved was she, that she began to dread
that he *would* call her and thus put God firmly back in the
running. God hadn't shown up either, but she had no hope of
His continuing absence. Nothing would put *Him* off. He
would come back if only for her insults, for His masochistic
appetite was sublime. Yet she was sorry that she had been
offensive. She had been angry that He had been proved right.
The next time He showed up, she decided she would
apologize.

She had tried to get back to her writing, but that self-
discipline. that she had always relied on, seemed to have
deserted her. At her desk, she found herself unfamiliar with
her notes, a stranger to all her expertise, and she would gaze
out of the window and wonder why her two escorts had
deserted her.

In the middle of the second week, she rose and showered,
as was her habit. But then she noticed how she was oiling
herself and how, afterwards, she donned her black house-

coat. It seemed that the ritual compelled her and that the inevitable move was now towards the third drawer. She did not fight it, but went with meek obedience to her study. At the chest she knelt before pulling out the drawer and then extracted the top insertion in the file. She closed the drawer and took the paper to her desk.

The missive was typed yet with a jumble of type faces. The letters seemed to have been cut out of a newspaper, each stuck together to form words. Her first impression was that it was an anonymous poison-pen letter. And her heart went out to her poor father who, on top of all his sorrow, had to suffer that, too. But on second glance, she saw that this letter was signed. And its signature did not surprise her. Her old and steady faithful. God. She read His message. *Fornication and all uncleanliness; let it not be named among you*. She smiled. Those were the words of an envious peeping Tom and they confirmed Edward as her lover. She folded the sheet and put it in her file. She was content. For the first time, it seemed, God had done her a favour. He had set her mind at rest. She felt strong enough now to risk further investigation. She returned to the drawer and extracted the next item in the file.

Her eyelids fluttered as she recognized her mother's handwriting and, for the first time since her drawer explorations, she felt like an invader. Hitherto, the contents of the file, the newspaper clipping, even the headmistress's letter, each could be regarded as public domain. As for the letter from God, that was her business and hers alone, and only she had read it. But her mother's letter to her father was private and never meant for her eye, and the fact that they were both now dead did not render prying less unpardonable. Quickly she refolded the letter. She was glad to have an excuse not to read it, especially an excuse that was based on morality. That somehow made it foolproof. Yet she knew that she was using ethics for her purpose, as the Devil might cite the scriptures. There was no escape from the drawer, even in the name of virtue. She opened the letter once more.

"Dearest Father," she read.

Since she could remember, that was how her mother had addressed her father, though he, in his turn, had always called her Priscilla. It was probable that, before she was born, her father was known to her mother as Oliver. In her eyes, parenthood had changed his name as well as his status. But he had never called Priscilla "Mother", for the obvious reasons that since birthing, she had ceased to fulfil that function. The subtitle of her appellation "Father" was, "Get on with our parenting," and the "Dearest" was to offset the severity of that injunction.

"Thank you for your letter," Veronica read. "I note Dr Bruton's remarks and his suggestion that Veronica is sickly because of my absence. I do not see this as an adequate reason for my return. Of course Veronica 'pines for her mother', as Dr Bruton suggests, but that is natural in any child whose mother is absent for a length of time. I pined for my own mother while she was potholing. I was sickly too, but in hindsight, I see it all as good training. Veronica will grow up to explore and to discover, in the way of her forebears. And above all, like them, to take risks. The latter is not possible without a certain hardening of the heart. I shall return, as scheduled, in time for Christmas. I look forward to that and wish you both well. Priscilla."

Veronica stared at the words, stunned by their cold formality. This was not the mother she knew as a child. That mother who had seemed to love her, whom she had loved beyond measure and whose frequent departures had twisted her little heart. This was not the mother on whose behalf she had committed the most heinous . . . No, no. She must not think of that. There would be a time for that. A ripe time. She must, above all, respect chronology. A deference to chronology would dilute the pain. Yet those cold words had come from her mother's pen and presumably from her heart, that heart that opened so rarely and with such fear. But now, in all her thirty-seven years, that same age at which Priscilla had died, Veronica saw her mother lying in her childhood cot fearing for her own mother underground. The heat of her pining had, over the years, cooled and finally turned to ice. Now Veronica began to understand herself a little, her withdrawal from human contact, and she disliked her mother a little for her frigid legacy.

One day, when she couldn't go to school, sick, crying and feverish, with Dr Bruton yet again at her bedside, she remembered how he had whispered to her father who stood anxiously at the foot of the bed.

"She misses her mother, you know. Could she not come home?"

"No, no," she remembered crying out. Screaming even, her fever at boiling point. For if her mother returned, she would find out about the swing-lady, and then everything would crumble around her.

"I'll write to her," she heard her father say, and she wondered why he colluded with the doctor's suggestion and why he wasn't even more fearful than herself of her mother's return.

"I don't want to see her," Veronica had wept. "Please, please, don't make her come home."

She remembered how Dr Bruton had looked at her father and had shaken his head, and she didn't know whether it was in disagreement of her mother's return or of her own pleading request. But she had been too exhausted to enquire. For the next week, she remembered, she had lived in terror of her mother's return, and when the days passed without event, she began to hope that her mother would never come back. She would willingly orphan herself in order to save her mother pain.

She returned to school after a week of fearful agitation. She counted the weeks until Christmas. Six of them. She reckoned on her fingers to forty-two days. Enough time, she considered, for the swing-lady to die, or at least to disappear from the park and the shops and everywhere else where the living gathered. She was happy then. Forty-two days was an eternity and by Christmas the three of them would be together again and they could go to the park without fear.

It was shortly after her return to school that her father had to go to Scotland to see a client.

"Will you be seeing Aunt Cissy?" she asked. "And Grandmother?"

"Granny" was reserved for the potholing one, because, as she herself would joke with Veronica, it rhymed with cranny, in which, somewhere in the earth, she could usually be found. But the name had died with her and, in her loved memory, it was not transferable.

"Yes," her father said. "I'll go there on Sunday."

"Can I come with you?" she asked. Grandmother was not a bit like Granny. She was fat, loving and comfortable. But, above all, she was always there.

"Of course not," her father said, and she wondered at the speed of his response. "You have to go to school. Mrs Dale will look after you. I'm giving her money to take you both to the pictures on Saturday. You'll like that, won't you?" he said. He ruffled her hair, but she shrank from him. She did not know the word "hush money", but she acutely felt its meaning in her seven-year-old bones.

Mrs Dale, their housekeeper, was usually fun to be with but, that week, it seemed to Veronica that she was very much on edge. Every night her father telephoned, and Mrs Dale was over-eager to pass the telephone to Veronica, without so much as an enquiry after his wellbeing. All week, she carried about her a look of disgust, which intensified itself as she over-pampered her charge, as if the poor child were be-reaved. In the cinema, she stuffed her with chocolates and each night let her go late to bed, reading her fairy tales in a tone of utter contempt.

When her father returned on Monday after school, Mrs Dale withdrew to her sitting room, her tutting lips chapped with disdain. That night her father put her to bed and as he bent to kiss her goodnight, she turned her face to the wall. Thereafter he cossetted her, even picking her up at school. One evening he drove her into London to see the Christmas lights and on another, he took her to a pantomime. But Veronica saw it all as compensation, though she didn't know that word either.

"When is mother coming home?" she asked him one day, making sure that she avoided his face in order not to see his reply.

"Christmas," he said.

"Yes I know," she insisted, "But when? What day?"

"I don't know," he said. "But you know your mother," he laughed. "She'll just turn up. But we'll all be together for Christmas. I promise you."

He seemed cheerful enough and Veronica began to have hopes that he no longer had anything to hide. Yet when, on the following Sunday, he suggested they go to the park, she was wary and refused. Her father was angry then and again her fears returned.

"It's a lovely day," he almost shouted at her. "Fresh air will do you good."

"I don't want to go," she insisted.

"But *I* do," he said.

"You're too big for the swings," she whispered and ran from the room, fearful of the innuendo of what she had said. Innuendo was yet another word whose meaning was beyond her and which, with all the others in her adult years, would add up to a glossary of pain-triggers, each one of which would ship her back to her childhood and the ghosts which haunted the third drawer.

A few days before Christmas, her father came home early from the office and together they dressed the tree. While he was dangling the tinsel from one branch to another, he casually informed Mrs Dale over Veronica's head that he would be going out that evening to the annual Christmas dinner given by his firm.

"Can I come?" Veronica asked.

"Only if you're one of the wives," he laughed. "Priscilla came with me last year," he reminisced. "And she actually enjoyed it. I thought it was a bit stuffy myself."

He tangled the tinsel as he spoke. His hands were sweating, Veronica noticed, and his fingers were sticking to the pine needles.

"I must go and change," he said quickly, and he went from the room leaving a trail of tinsel in his wake.

Veronica would not look at Mrs Dale for she sensed that that old look of disgust had returned. So, without looks or words between them, they continued to decorate the tree. During the course of it, Mrs Dale silently passed a chocolate bar to Veronica through the branches and, equally silently, Veronica accepted it. She had just finished the last chunk when her father reappeared. He looked like a penguin, she thought, with his white stiff front and black back tail. She stifled a giggle, lest he take it as a sign of her pleasure and approval.

"How do I look?" he asked.

"Fine and dandy," Mrs Dale said without looking.

"Will there be dancing?" Veronica asked nervously.

"They have a band every year," he said

"Who will you dance with?"

"I shall have to make do with the Chairman's wife," he said. "He'll be grateful," her father added. "He can't dance."

He kissed her on the top of her head and darted through the door like a hunted blackbird.

"Let's have some ice cream," Mrs Dale said, as soon as the front door slammed. She ladled it out of the refrigerator, clucking like a conspirator, but neither of them ate with much appetite.

"Would you like a lovely long story tonight?" she asked. She was almost weeping.

Veronica nodded, close to tears herself, and Mrs Dale gathered her in her arms and carried her to bed, tut-tutting all the while like a noisy clock. She tucked her in gently and took down the book of fairy tales.

"What shall it be?" she said and, without waiting for a reply, she started into Cinderella which she considered appropriate for the occasion. But barely had the first sentence escaped her when they heard the rattling of keys in the front door. She looked at Veronica, both hoping that her father had changed his mind and returned home. They heard the door open and waited, trembling, for his call.

"Hullo?" they heard. It was not his voice, but another's, a voice half-feared and half-forgotten, which echoed from the safety of mountains but which now was horribly non-resonant at the front-door.

"Your mother," Mrs Dale whispered and, like a thief caught in the act, or rather in someone else's act, she looked around as if seeking a way of escape.

"Your mother," she whispered again, enlisting Veronica as a co-conspirator. One of them had to do something, but Veronica seemed latched to the bed.

"Mrs Smiles?" Mrs Dale squeaked, then went to the door, because somebody had to take the responsibility for welcome. "Get up," she almost hissed at Veronica, but Veronica could not move. She felt the fever again and, even when her mother came into the room, she covered herself with a blanket, hoping that her positive non-welcome would send her mother back to the mountain. But Priscilla took the hiding as a tease and she stripped off the blanket and Veronica was bound then to effect some pleasure at her homecoming. She flung her arms round her mother's neck and as she hugged her she caught Mrs Dale's eyes. And they lifted themselves to the ceiling in a gesture of utter helplessness.

"Where's Father?" Priscilla said, disentangling herself.

"He's gone to the office dinner," Mrs Dale said quietly. "Only half an hour ago." Her tone was chatty, craving conversation and thus delay.

"Have you seen the tree?" Veronica jumped out of bed. "Have you brought me a present? What mountain did you climb? Was there a lot of snow? When are you going back?" Question after quick-fired question offering her endless topics of chitchat that would hold her in the house and delay any questions on her mother's part as to what news there had been during her absence.

"I think I'll surprise your father," her mother said. "I went last Christmas." She turned to tell Mrs Dale whose eyes had returned from the ceiling and were now tightly shut in horror. "I had a lovely time. Oh your father will have such a surprise." This to Veronica who was now shivering with fever.

"Don't go, Mother," she said. "Please don't go."

"You're cold, darling," Priscilla said. "Now get back into bed. We'll all be together for Christmas and if you like you can have me all to yourself. But won't it be a great surprise for your father?" she said. "You wouldn't want him to miss that, would you?"

"Aren't you tired, Mrs Smiles?" Mrs Dale made a vain attempt to dissuade her.

"Not a bit," Priscilla said. "I slept most of the way in the train. I'll have a quick shower and I'll be fine."

She was soon gone and they heard the gush of water from the bathroom. Her running footsteps, too, and even a snatch of distant song. But although all evidence pointed to her being elsewhere, her presence still throbbed in Veronica's room.

Mrs Dale tucked her charge into bed. "Shall I go on with the story?" she asked.

Veronica shook her head. "Why does she have to go?" she asked.

"It will be a surprise for your daddy," Mrs Dale said, though she did not care to elaborate on the nature of the surprise that would, in all probability, stun them both.

Shortly afterwards, Priscilla returned. She wore the long grey dress that Veronica dimly recalled from the year before. And now, as then, she looked beautiful. There was some small relief in that, at least for Veronica, in whose eyes her mother's beauty would win hands down.

Mrs Dale complimented her. "You look lovely, Mrs Smiles," she said. But lovely looks would not help her. Nor sudden surprises. A bird in the hand was worth two up a mountain, no matter how fair or foul its plumage.

"Thank you, Mrs Dale," Priscilla said. She crossed to Veronica's bed. "I've got a special present for you," she said. "I'll give it you in the morning."

Conscience money, Veronica felt, through another word that she didn't understand. But she did understand the difference in the term as it applied to her father and her mother. Her mother's gifts were by way of consolation; her father's sheer blackmail.

They heard her cheery "Goodbye," from the hall, and then the front door slammed.

Mrs Dale held Veronica in her arms.

"Shall I sleep beside you?" she whispered.

Then they cuddled close to each other, each finding refuge in the other's warmth and both waiting for the clap of thunder.

Veronica shut her eyes tightly and followed her mother to the ball. Even as the taxi drew up at the ballroom, she could hear the music of the waltz and she glided back easily into the interrupted Cinderella story. The best part, when Cinderella arrives at the ball. Her mother floated up the grand staircase and there were whispers all around her. Sighs of wonderment at her beauty. And as she entered through the golden arch of the ballroom, the Prince was stunned by her loveliness, and he ceased dancing and stood still. With respect to his Highness, the band stopped playing. The Chairman's fat wife hung on the Prince's arm. He tried to leave her and make his way towards the golden arch. But she clung to him, swinging him around, faster and faster, as she grew thinner and thinner and wasn't the Chairman's wife at all. Then the band started again and they waltzed away, the Prince and the swing-lady, while the clock struck twelve and Cinderella flew down the stairs as her silks shrivelled into rags.

Veronica felt Mrs Dale's hand reach across her chest to still her fluttering heart.

"There, there," she said. "Sh, sh," she quietened her, shouting it almost, hoping to drown the rumble of the key in the front door. The thunder was upon them and they held each other close, knowing that now was its time. They heard no call from the hall but each one was counting footsteps. Between them they could muster only one pair and, by the lightness of the tread, a woman's. Now they needed no clap of thunder to confirm their fears. Priscilla Smiles' swift return from the ball was evidence enough of her discovery. Mrs Dale knew it and so did Veronica, though each kept their fears from the other. They heard her weary tread on the stairway, their eyes glued to the doorknob as they watched its slow turn. She framed only half herself in the door, as if fearful to enter. Mrs Dale took her cue and her leave, and Veronica felt naked with responsibility. It's not my fault, she wanted to tell her mother, I never did anything. Except be sick on her hair.

She watched her mother approach the bed and slip out of her gold shoes. The straps were lowered from the dress and the stockings rolled off onto the floor. Then, in her long silk white petticoat, she slipped between the sheets and held Veronica in her arms. Her daughter did not know whether her gesture was a plea for her love or for her protection. By instinct, she felt the latter. But it did not matter to her. It was the first time in her life that she could remember her mother's embrace and, whatever its motive, she succumbed to it with overwhelming gratitude. And a modicum of greed too. For she heard herself saying, "D'you *have* to go back to the mountain?"

"Not any more. I'm staying with you."

Veronica dared not believe it. Dared not believe in the fearless awakenings, the feverless days to come. A whole future of freedom in the parks, in the streets, in the shops, yes, even the freedom, if she so wished, to buy skates. Her mother was staying at home, so the swing-lady must have died.

"I'll do anything for you, Mummy," she said. "Anything. Anything in the whole wide world." And she meant it. If there were ever another swing-lady, she would cut her down, step on her, squash her into a slimy pulp like that dead frog she had once stepped on, on a stone by the pond. She stamped on her, over and over again, as she squeezed her mother tightly and tried not to remember why she had come home from the ball alone.

The next morning, apart from Mrs Dale, who never broke with her seven o'clock waking routine, there was some hesitation as to who should arise first. Veronica woke and wondered for a moment in whose arms she lay. Then rising on her elbow, she wished to kiss her mother awake, but recalled her tear-stained face of the night before and thought she might prefer to go on sleeping. Though her mother had promised to stay at home, Veronica's recent sense of safety was now laced with confusion. She wondered where her father was. She crept out of the bed, careful not to disturb her mother and tip-toed downstairs to the kitchen. It was a relief to see Mrs Dale there, going about her duties as if nothing untoward had happened.

"Where's Daddy?" she said.

"Still in bed, I suppose. Why don't you take him up his cup of tea?"

That was normal procedure on a weekend when there was no school and Veronica always looked forward to it. But today she was wary, wary of being used as a scout, sent to sniff out the scent and readiness of the enemy. That would be Mrs Dale's purpose. But her father, too, might use her as an innocent informer. He, too, needed a spy in the enemy camp. She would be unarmed and freely available to all her father's questionings, and she didn't know how much or how little she was supposed to know and even less about what was the subject of her ignorance or knowledge. But Mrs Dale had already put the cup in her hand. She took it carefully up the stairs. The trick was not to look at it and then it wouldn't spill. She held it in both hands, but both hands were trembling. Outside his door she paused, to pour the tea from the saucer back into the cup, then put it on the floor to open the door. Her father was sitting up in bed, staring at the wall. Not a position she'd seen him in before. Usually she had to shake him awake and he'd turn over and growl and pretend to be angry. He didn't even look at her as she brought his tea towards the bed. She held it out to him.

"Mummy's home," she said. It was like giving away the enemy's position. But she felt that she had to say something, to pretend that she knew nothing about anything, whatever that anything was.

"I know," he said. "I saw her luggage in the hall." He took his tea. "Did she sleep with you?"

"Yes," she said, ashamed. "But it was my fault. I asked her to. I *made* her," she protested. "I absolutely made her."

Her father could not help but smile at her articulate insistence. "Of course," he said, "and I don't mind at all. Now perhaps it's my turn." He opened up the sheet for her and she was glad to climb in beside him, because, somehow, that made everything equal.

"And how is Mummy?" he said.

She wondered why he didn't go and see for himself. And then, to give him some excuse, she said, "She's still sleeping. She had a long journey."

She heard her own bedroom door open and her mother's footsteps on the landing. She couldn't understand why her father didn't rise from his bed.

"She's up," she had to say.

He made to get out of bed and Veronica tried to hold him. She knew that if he went, there would be more thunder. He tucked her under the chin.

"It's time I was up anyway," he said. "But you stay if you like," he added.

She knew he was trying to protect her. But she needed to know what was happening and it was a need beyond childish curiosity. For in some way she knew that her whole future depended on the greeting her parents would give each other outside the bedroom door. She snuggled under the sheets, watching with one eye while her father put on his gown. She waited for him to leave the room and listened to his slippered tread on the landing. Then she heard his voice. "Priscilla?" he called, and she wondered why he sounded so frightened. She tip-toed out of bed and peeped out of the door. He was not on the landing so she guessed he must have gone into her room. But as she turned the corner of the landing, she was witness to the encounter. The bathroom was at the end of the corridor and the door was open. She watched her father peck her mother on the cheek. So far, she thought, so bearable. She dared now to eavesdrop.

"Did you have a good trip?" her father said.

"Yes." Her mother's voice was calm, but for some reason it was not reassuring. She saw her turn towards the sink and she knew that she was going to speak to her father without looking at him. She was afraid of what she might hear yet, having come this far, she could not turn away. Then the words came out of her mother's back.

"I see Veronica is no worse for my absence," her back said quietly. "Perhaps it was something else that upset her."

I must move from here, Veronica thought, and wished that Mrs Dale would come and fetch her away from the fire. But she was rooted there, the hot tears coursing her cheeks. She prayed that her father wouldn't let on about the swing-lady. Then she saw her mother turn and the words were red and terrible, and visible from out of her mouth.

"I know about it," she said. "Don't lie to me, Oliver."

There was hope in that name. It was less distant than "Father". In Veronica's young but sorely exhausted heart, it betokened a kind of loving. She watched as her father took her mother in his arms and she craned her ears to hear his voice.

"It's not too late," he said.

Veronica darted back to her room and dressed in a shiver of joy.

When she joined them at breakfast, it seemed to her that everything was in order. The occasional conversational exchange, the excessive politeness and, above all, the many silences, all were part of the behavioural pattern when her mother was at home.

It was well into the new year, long after the time that her mother would normally have left on an expedition. They were sitting having tea around the fire.

"What a pity you have to go away again, Priscilla," her father said. "I like us as a family."

Her father had stopped buttering his toast and was eyeing her mother as if waiting for an answer. Veronica was puzzled, since it was no question he had asked. He had simply stated what was in his heart. She heard her mother's reply, but she could not take her eyes off her father's face, for it seemed to her to be covered in lies.

"I'm not," she heard her mother say. "I'm staying home for a while. Perhaps I'll find something to do in Surbiton."

She watched her father's face fall. That was the only way she could describe it. A lump rose in her throat, damming all the words she wanted to pour out between them. Above all that they must love each other. Just each other, with no one else allowed. But her voice refused. Instead she reached out and held her mother's hand. She felt it squeezed in its turn and though, as so often, she knew the feeling but not the word, she felt that she was being enlisted into woman's complicity.

"Shall we go to the park tomorrow?" her father said. "If the weather's fine?"

"Why not?" her mother said, who knew nothing of parks. "Veronica would like that."

But on the following day it rained without let-up and there was no reason to go out anywhere at all.

At the end of January, again over a Sunday tea, her mother announced that she was going back to the mountain.

Veronica kept her eyes on her father's face. She saw him put on a mask of disappointment. She knew it hadn't come from inside his face but was carried as separately from himself as a handkerchief.

"When will you come back?" Veronica asked, and heard her voice squeaking.

"At Easter," her mother said. "That's only three weeks away."

There was a small satisfaction in that.

"Perhaps we'll all go to Scotland for Easter," she heard her father say.

But after his mask, she didn't believe him any more.

It was a fine Sunday morning in early February, when they took her mother to the station to see her on to the train. On the platform, Veronica held her father's hand, while with the other she waved as the train pulled out. Her father was waving too, both of them standing there well after the train had left the platform. Then he picked her up in his arms, laughing. His gaiety, so soon after her mother's departure, made her tremble, and the beginnings of a fever chilled her bones. She wanted to scream after the train for her mother to return.

"It's a lovely day," her father said. "Let's go to the park."

Chapter Six

In time Edward phoned her.

"Have you been away?" she asked, giving him an excuse for his lack of communication. But he declined her offer.

"No," he said. "I've been in London."

"Then why . . . ?" she started, then regretted what must seem to him like a grilling.

"I wasn't sure that you wanted me to phone you again," he said.

"Why ever not?" she asked, then regretted that too, because she would not be able to manage his reply.

"It doesn't matter," he said. Then quickly, "Would you like to go to a concert? The Philharmonia are playing on Friday. All Brahms."

"Yes," she said. "I'd love to."

"I'll see you at seven-thirty at the Festival Hall bar," he said and he put the phone down as if he feared she might change her mind.

She was happy that he had called her at last. Happy, too, that he seemed to be widening the scope of their companionship. Suddenly she wanted to get back to her writing. All that day she worked on her book. She noticed that, as she worked, she left gaps that could only be filled as the result of a further expedition and she knew then that she had decided to go back to the desert. The sour taste of her last drawer discovery still lingered on her tongue. Her mother had returned to the mountain because, finally, it was only work that mattered and the discovery that grew out of that work. As her grandmother had done. But they had borne children. Both of them. That was the rub. To whom could she bequeath the legacy that work was more important than loving, when there was no concrete proof that she'd ever given loving a chance? And again she counted her years and, though she refrained from calling on God, she would have wished to see Him.

The Festival bar was buzzing when she arrived. She looked around for Edward wondering whether she would recognize him. For, in truth, she had entirely forgotten what he looked like. She tried to visualize the sundry restaurant tables where they had dined, so that the setting might suggest his features. In her own house, at her party, in the vineyards. Even in her bed his face was as blank as her memory. She heard her name and was glad, because it would be Edward who was calling attention to himself and thus save her the embarrassment of non-recognition. She turned quickly but could see no one with hand raised and with the aftershape of her name on his lips. She looked at her watch. She had arrived early and it was only just seven-thirty.

"I bought you a Martini," she heard, and turned again to find Edward behind her.

She looked at him and wondered how she could have forgotten his features. For his was a fine distinctive face and she felt she should ask his forgiveness.

"Did you just call out my name?" she asked.

"Of course not," he said.

Then she heard her name again and, turning, once more found no clue as to its provenance. But Edward seemed not to have heard. Then she knew for certain that it was God who had called her and that Edward's deafness confirmed her decidedly unbalanced state of mind. She did not look forward to the concert with His clear presence in the Festival Hall. She hoped He'd have the good manners not to interrupt the music.

Veronica urged Edward into the hall. She liked to take her seat early and watch the entry of the musicians and the small chat between them. Above all she loved the cacophony of tuning-up, the occasional brass-blowing and the tympani-tests. The front desk strings always seemed the first to arrive, as if to set a good example. The brass were always latecomers, as if they'd been gathering breath in the wings. But last stragglers of all were the back desk rank-and-file strings. Veronica watched them stroll on with that nonchalant sense of power that small cogs possess. One by one they filtered into their seats and tested their already finely-tuned strings. The back seat of the last player of all, the lowest rank-and-filer, was still empty and most of the players had settled before he wandered on. Rank-and-filer he might be and in the rearmost seat of all, but he assumed his place with pride, as if he was the king-cog, on which all those others hinged. And indeed he was. As Veronica knew. Her old and faithful follower. God on the fiddle. First a waiter, now a rank-and-filer. The meek would surely inherit the earth, as He was about to prove.

The concert started with the Academic Festival Overture. Veronica kept her eye on Him while He kept His evenly divided between the conductor and the music on the stand. He was uneasy with the work, Veronica noticed, and His bowing was occasionally at odds with the others in His section. In all the symmetry and perfection of the playing, His rogue presence was a refreshing eyesore and Veronica began to warm towards Him. She wondered whether she should go backstage after the concert and ask Him for His autograph. And she wondered too how He would sign it. With His love, of course, and His jealousy, too, as a by-product of that love and, as a rider, probably some homily that pointed to the error of her ways. Since her meeting with the Devil, the notion of sin had presented exciting possibilities. And indeed she must have sinned mightily to merit no less than the Arch-Inspector on her tail. She took Edward's hand in her excitement and held it till the end of the overture.

During the course of the clapping, Edward whispered in her ear.

"I've arranged a little supper at my place after the concert. Is that all right?"

She nodded with enthusiasm, then looked quickly at God who at that moment, having possibly overheard their exchange, was carrying Himself and His fiddle off the platform.

No doubt He would beat them to it and next appear to butler-open the door in Eaton Square. There was some relief in the knowledge that Edward couldn't see Him. That way, God could carry no tales. But that blindness of Edward's was also disturbing and once again she wondered whether she oughtn't to have herself seen to.

The violin concerto preceded the interval with a soloist from Korea. The orchestra seemed to manage very well without God. Indeed they seemed to benefit from His absence. As one would expect, Veronica thought, since His presence only prompted nervousness. She found herself unable to concentrate on the music. She could not help but surmize on the post-concert arrangements and all their possibilities. For some reason she was convinced that Edward would use his no doubt candlelit dinner as an appropriate setting for a proposal of marriage. She felt it in the air. She was convinced too that he had prepared a small speech as an introduction to his intentions. It was therefore incumbent on her to prepare some kind of response. She was in a quandary. She did not wish to commit herself to a positive acceptance, neither did she wish irrevocably to refuse his offer. She didn't know why she felt the need to prevaricate. She had neither the wish nor the intention to marry Edward. It would serve no purpose for, in the very real sense, it promised no future. No son, no daughter would come of it, to whom she could bequeath that dilemma of love and work that her mother had left her, inherited in her turn, from granny-underground. No. Marriage with Edward was, in all senses, fruitless. Yet if she refused him, would that mean the end of their affair? She was not sure that she wouldn't miss him. In some way she felt bonded to him. He had, after all, deflowered her. In time to come she might well forget what he looked like; she might even forget his name; but his body-print would cling to her for the rest of her days.

The sudden silence in the hall, during the short interval between the first and second movements of the concerto, shunted her back into the present. She sensed Edward looking at her. She returned his glance, but in the aftermath of her thoughts, he was already a stranger. Even so she smiled at him.

"Are you liking it?" he whispered.

She nodded her head, ashamed. She had not listened to a single note.

She settled in with good intent to listen to the adagio. But soon enough, despite the compelling melody, she returned to thoughts that centred around the dinner table in Eaton Square. But she no longer thought about his possible proposal. Now she began to wonder where she would spend the night or, more appropriately, where God would spend it, since her presence, wherever it might be, would surely be shadowed by His. Now she considered her answer to Edward's possible invitation to share his bed. At the thought of it she trembled and with a certain amount of pleasure, but not on account of her sleeping partner, or of God who would no doubt be somewhere present, but of Satan himself who would itch between the sheets. But once again the short interval before the final movement of the concerto held the Devil at bay. But not for long. For the fiendish tempo of the last movement was an apt accompaniment to his return and, by the time the movement came to an end, she was in a fever of excitement and was glad to join in the audience applause and thus use it as an aid to help disentangle herself from his diabolic coil.

In the second part of the concert, she managed to concentrate on the symphony, wary now of allowing her mind to wander and it was not until the final applause that she thought again of the post-concert rendezvous that was now so imminent that speculation was almost pointless.

He took her arm as they crossed to the car park. His car was sleek, long and shiny black, and whispered money. Veronica made no comment. Wealth neither bothered nor attracted her. But she could not help but be impressed by his establishment at Eaton Square. Though Edward lived there alone, the apartment was furnished as if multi-inhabited. It was as if it had served the Boniface family for many generations and had, in its time, echoed with children's voices, for the legacy of family was evidenced in every corner. A cabinet of silver dominated the living room and, beside it, an open, oak chest compendium of children's games. An embroidery frame was attached to one of the chairs. In it, a circle of half-finished gros point, with threads hanging. The lid of the grand piano was open and on its stand, sundry sheets of music, an open metronome, a sign of recent practising. The room was elegant yet untidy, with signs of such recent activity that Veronica wondered if and how the bedrooms were inhabited, or whether the family simply decamped when Edward took over.

He poured her a drink. "Welcome to my home," he said.

"Was this the family house?" she had to ask, then regretted it for such a question could lead to all manner of speculation.

"It was," Edward said. "Not just this flat, but the whole house. I was born here. So were my brothers. I've lived here all my life. I haven't changed it very much, as you can see. It's too big for me of course, but I'm so attached to it. It really needs a large family."

She refrained from looking at him.

"One could always adopt, I suppose," she heard him say, and she dreaded the expected corollary. Then it came.

"But for that, one would have to be married."

She said nothing, neither did she move. Her reaction must be neutral and passive. Though she ached to change the subject, that would have been construed as a positive reply, yet her silence now was so prolonged that that, too, was a token of some response.

"Could I have a little more ice?" she said. They were words to fill the gap. No more.

"Of course." He took her glass and into it dropped two small cubes.

"Are you happy?" he said.

She was relieved. They were back on familiar ground.

"Yes," she said. "Can I help at all?"

He took her hand. "Everything is ready," he said. Then to her astonishment, he pulled a bell tassel at the side of the hearth. She expected God to appear, valet-suited, to announce that dinner was served. She turned her back to the door, then shortly heard a woman's voice.

"You rang, Master Edward?"

She turned. A middle-aged woman stood there. Veronica stared at her, marvelling at God's inexhaustible talent for surprise. She wanted to touch her, to pummel her plump

96

comely body, to expose the sham of her large breasts and sturdy thighs.

"How is the dinner, Margaret?" Edward was saying.

"Everything is ready," she said. "Shall I light the candles?"

"If you would."

Veronica was utterly confused. Edward had seen God and was actually talking to Him. Now she craved simply to touch the woman to prove that Edward at least was sane. It was imperative. She felt herself driven to the door almost blocking Margaret's way.

"What a pretty cardigan," she said, and she touched the very ordinary and plain brown woolly that was draped over the woman's shoulders. As she did so, she clutched at her collarbone, kneading the flesh to seek out the muscle below. Then she smoothed her hand down the cardigan front, scaling the mound of breast and, en route, with her fingers, she tested its elasticity. Once over the knoll, she felt the body's heartbeat and was startled by its speed. Then she knew once and for all that God was not inside that woman. It was His very heartlessness that guaranteed His everlasting life. In His body was no organ, and thus nothing could deteriorate and cease to function. Only that lack accounted for His immortality. For there was simply nothing He could die of. Veronica stepped back, satisfied.

Margaret stared at her, bewildered, wondering whether to take offence or simply to overlook such unaccountable behaviour. She withdrew from the room, trembling.

Edward had observed every second of the encounter. It had been an extraordinary display.

"Shall we go into dinner?" he said. He took her glass, and then her arm, and led her into the dining room.

The furnishings of this room too were long-serving and the long oak refectory table would happily have sat an extended family. Edward's place had been set at the head of the table and Veronica's beside him. Between them were two small silver candlesticks. As they entered, Margaret was lighting the candles and, as Veronica took her seat, she sidled away, as if in fear of further contact.

"You have a lovely home," Veronica said, feeling that she should embark on some trivial topic of conversation that would tide them over until Margaret had served the first course, for Veronica sensed Edward's need for privacy, for secrecy almost, and Margaret would have to be well out of earshot before Edward put whatever cards he had on the table. For she was convinced that this was what he was about to do.

"I'm glad you like it," he said. "That helps a great deal." Veronica was not sure what he meant, but she knew that it was loaded, so she was careful not to take him up on it. Margaret's entry with the soup-tureen was well-timed, for it obviated the need for further conversation.

"Oh it smells so good," Veronica said, as Margaret ladled her portion. She sensed the woman's coldness and was anxious to compensate for any embarrassment she might have caused her. But Margaret did not even thank her. After serving Edward she withdrew to the kitchen, muttering unintelligibly, but audibly enough to make known her displeasure.

"I think your housekeeper is a little put out," Veronica said.

"Margaret is always uneasy when I have a woman guest. She fears she's going to lose her little boy. She used to be my Nanny, you see, and she still sees herself in that role."

"D'you have many women guests?"

"From time to time. Margaret serves impeccably of course, but without too much grace. On the other hand she adores a business dinner when there are only men. Then she's as proud as a peacock. But I adore her."

"You must have been her favourite," Veronica said.

"I'm the oldest, so she had me first. No one can ever usurp that position. But she's very frightened that I shall get married."

"This soup's lovely," Veronica said, grasping after terra firma.

"It's Margaret's speciality," he said. "In fact, it's the same soup we had in the nursery. Lentil, but now she calls it pulse soup and adds a little tabasco in deference to the undeniable fact that I've grown up."

They drank it in silence. Veronica was glad of the respite, but she feared that it would not last very long. She was still

98

convinced that Edward would propose to her and she had rehearsed no response.

"I enjoyed the symphony best," Edward said. "It's so stirring, the fourth. It's the first symphony I ever heard."

"Unusual," Veronica said. "One tends to start with Beethoven and often it's the fifth."

"D'you listen to music often?" he asked.

She noticed that he'd put down his soup spoon and his hand was straying towards hers. Now it comes, she thought, and I haven't even finished my soup. If now she were to say "No," there were two more courses at least and coffee and liqueurs to endure in an atmosphere of alternate pleading and rejection. For she had no doubt that he would not be easily denied. She let him take her left hand whilst she gamely got on with her soup. She felt his hesitation and knew with total certainty that she was about to be asked in marriage. And then the proposal came, as she raised the soup spoon to her mouth.

"Will you marry me, Veronica?" he said.

No preamble, no tarrying for the dimmed lights, the log fire in the drawing room, a little music perhaps and a liqueur. Edward was no metteur-en-scène. Mid-soup, with Margaret's sensible shoes squeaking at the door, Edward offered himself in marriage. Veronica willed Margaret to appear and, in clearing away the soup, give her a little breathing space. Margaret's entry was well-timed. She looked even more displeased than before. It's possible, Veronica thought, that she might have overheard Edward's proposal, for she took an inordinate time in clearing the soup course away.

"The soup was delicious."

"Thank you," Margaret said. She was too well-mannered to ignore a compliment a second time. Still she dawdled with the tray, even though Edward was on his way to the door to hold it open for her. Veronica noticed that, as she left the room, she did not cast a glance at Edward, positively ignoring him, as if they were back in the nursery and he had been a naughty boy. He shut the door after her and returned to the table. But instead of taking his seat, he stood behind her, his hand on her shoulder.

"Well, what do you think, Veronica?" he asked.

But Margaret was back, this time with a trolley and Veronica could barely stifle a giggle. The trolley was loaded and Edward was obliged to leave the table once more to hold the door yet again. Margaret was clearly determined to delay a response for as long as possible. But after this course she would have to give way, so she took her time over it. She waited for Edward to be seated before she started to serve. Then she lifted the silver cover of the platter and exposed a poached salmon. She looked to her Edward for his approval.

"It looks wonderful," he said.

She served him first, slicing a portion with a silver spatula, then did the same for Veronica. And as it slid onto her plate, so Veronica's response slid with the same inevitability off her tongue.

"I think that's a very good idea," she said.

If Edward was loath to make a production of his proposal, she would respond in the same vein. She didn't know why she had offered her agreement. It simply seemed a good way of temporizing. As long as one said "Yes," one could always later say "No." Meanwhile she would seek reasons for a negative. At least her temporary acceptance would see the evening out without embarrassment.

Margaret placed the vegetable tureens within Edward's serving distance.

"See that you eat the carrots," she said to him.

It sounded like a cry of despair, a last-ditch stand against the crumbling of her time-honoured status. He looked up and smiled at her, stroking the liver-pocked back of her hand. He knew she needed reassurance, but that was all he could give her. She left the room quickly and, no doubt, once outside, she let the tears fall.

"Margaret will stay with us," Edward said.

"Of course," Veronica agreed. "I hope she'll grow to like me a little." She had no idea of what she was saying. She had no more intention of marrying Edward than of marrying God, whose methods of proposal were less direct, but serious all the same. Yet she was behaving as if in preparation of her trousseau and she feared that it were possible that she could go through a marriage ceremony with Edward, knowing that it was folly and, still in a state of utter confusion and bewilderment, she would hear herself addressed as Lady Boniface. She must take a grip on herself, she thought, or else foolhardy events would overtake her.

"I'm overwhelmed with joy," Edward said.

"Are you surprised?" she asked.

"Yes and no," he said. "When I first met you on the train, I knew then that there was a rightness between us. Did you ever sense that?"

"In Trier," she said. "I suppose I needed a little more proof." She smiled at him to cover her confusion. She wondered where all her meaningless words were coming from, whether God prompted them from her lips. Or the Devil perhaps. But Edward would not be God's choice for her any more than he would be the Devil's. For in God's eyes, Edward had shown himself to be unclean and, in the Devil's, he was nowhere near unclean enough.

"I can hardly believe it," Edward was saying.

And neither could Veronica.

"Hadn't we better eat the salmon before it gets cold?" Veronica said. "And you your carrots?"

"I'm too excited to eat," he said.

"Well try," Veronica said, sounding like Margaret. "Or your Nanny will be cross with you."

Her phrasing seemed to excite him further. He rose and came round to the back of her chair, placing his hands over her breasts. "We could adopt a child you know," he said.

Now, it was all far beyond her, and too far for her to withdraw. Now, she could only compound her involvement with further fantasy. "Are you sure you can't . . . ?" She clasped Edward's hand.

"One chance in a million, according to the doctors," Edward said. "We'd need a miracle," he laughed.

And so, inside herself, did Veronica. She knew somebody in the miracle department and she could pull a string or two. He'd be glad to do her such a favour. Did he not adjure his children to go forth and multiply? Well, she was about to go forth. The rest was up to Him.

"We shall have to pray for a miracle," she said.

Edward took his seat again and started on his fish with appetite.

"Shall we live here?" Veronica asked.

"I'd like to," he said. "But that's your decision. But Margaret will be with us, wherever we go. Don't worry, she'll get used to you."

But would she get used to God, Veronica wondered, in all His sundry disguises, or would she, like Edward, be blind and deaf to His presence?

"Would I still be able to go to the desert?" she asked. She surprised herself with this sudden need for permission. She felt as if she were asking if she could go out to play.

"Of course," Edward said. "You must go on being yourself. I wouldn't want you any other way."

Now, as he sampled Margaret's poached fish, she saw herself returning from a safari, with Edward waiting on the Eaton Square doorstep, but with no small figure by his side, except perhaps for a shrunken Margaret, disgruntled at her return. For a moment then, she considered adoption, but her whole body trembled in veto of such a consideration. She wanted a baby out of her own self. Not so much desired that birth, as needed it, and needed it with the desperation of atonement. But for what did she crave to expiate? And to whom did she so desperately owe? To whom was she so hopelessly beholden? Her thoughts drifted to the third drawer and she shivered.

"I'm so excited, Edward," she said, forestalling his question as to why she was trembling. "When shall we get married?"

Again she wondered where the words were coming from. What was prompting her to set in motion an event in which she had no intention of participating? And how far would she manoeuvre to bring it about? She sensed that her person was split in two, the one part a stunned spectator of the machinations of the other.

"Soon, I hope," he said. "Very soon. I'd like you to meet my family, of course, and there are a number of things we shall have to arrange. The registrar, the reception, all that sort of thing. And the honeymoon, of course. Where would you like to go?"

"What about you?" she said.

"Why don't we just get a map of the world, shut our eyes and let our fingers land where we will go?"

"A lovely idea," she said, glad that he would take half the responsibility of a decision that would never be implemented.

"After dinner," Edward said, and both returned to their plates with renewed appetite.

As they finished, Margaret entered.

"Is there pudding?" Edward asked as she cleared the plates.

"Your favourite," she said, smiling, and back in the nursery.

"Treacle?" Edward's voice was suddenly unbroken.

She nodded.

"Margaret, you're a darling," he said.

She cheered up then, with a smile even for Veronica and promptly Veronica began to scheme how she would go about winning the woman's heart, though she knew that there would never be any necessity to do so.

"Would you like it in the drawing room?" Margaret said. "I've made up the fire."

"We'll have it in here," Edward said. "It's already set. There's no point in giving yourself extra work."

She wheeled the trolley from the room.

"Margaret makes the best treacle pudding in the world," Edward said.

"I think I ought to tell you, Edward," Veronica said, "that I'm not the greatest of cooks. I couldn't possibly compete with Margaret."

"You won't have to," Edward said. "She'll look after us both."

There were, without doubt, many bonuses in a marriage to Edward, and Veronica wished she had a suitable friend to introduce him to.

The dessert was eaten in silence and with pleasure and, for this course, Margaret stayed in the dining room hovering for her ward's approval. Not for any words that he would give her but for the relish that he showed.

"He always liked his treacle pudding," Margaret said to Veronica, as if in explanation of the second helping she was spooning on to Edward's plate.

"That's enough," Edward said. "I'll burst."

She stroked his hair. "I'll put the coffee in the drawing room," she said.

Once she was gone, Edward put his plate aside. "I can't eat any more," he laughed. He rose and took her arm. "Coffee and brandy by the fire," he said, and she went with him eagerly to continue the charade. She looked at her watch. The last train for Surbiton left in an hour. Edward had made no suggestion that she stay.

"My last train goes in an hour," she said.

"There's time for coffee, and after our atlas game, I'll drive you to the station," he said.

She smiled to herself. He was afraid of Margaret. Or else, now having secured her hand in marriage, he could afford to postpone that act of wooing. But she could not help but feel slightly disappointed. It's true that making love to Edward guaranteed the presence of God, but it also promised a tryst with the Devil and all the ecstasy that such a collision promised. It seemed to her now that Edward would only make love to her if she married him and she began to consider whether or not that price was too high for such a seductive joy.

Edward got down the atlas and placed it on the coffee table. He opened it to the world map and took Veronica's hand.

"Give me your first finger," he said. Then he clasped it and ordered her to shut her eyes.

"Yours as well," Veronica said, for he too must take the responsibility of not going to wherever her finger landed. She shut her eyes and he raised her hand in the air.

"We're about to land," he said, then he lowered her hand swiftly on to the map.

On opening her eyes, she was boundlessly relieved at the seeming ordinariness of their landing. They had nose-dived into Paris. Not too serious, not too committed, a place where they might travel anyway, without the excuse of honeymoon.

"Does that please you?" Edward asked nervously.

"Anywhere pleases me," she said.

"Let's drink to Paris then and afterwards I'll drive you to the station."

He kissed her fondly as he put her on the train. "It's been a wonderful evening," he said. "I shall make all arrangements. And as soon as we fix the date, I'll buy the tickets."

The train started to pull out.

"I'll ring you tomorrow," he called out after her.

She waved and quickly found a seat, wondering how on earth she could extricate herself from this monstrous labyrinth of her own making. She looked around and found that the carriage was empty. The train moved very slowly, shunting along, then came to an abrupt stop. She looked out of the window and saw a guard board the train and then it started moving again and picking up a little speed. The guard sauntered down her carriage and, though every seat was empty, he placed himself exactly opposite her and looked her steadily in the eye. At first his uniform fooled her, but only for a second, for His sudden appearances came as no surprise.

"How nice," she said. "I shall be glad of a little company. But I don't remember calling you."

"You call me all the time."

She decided to let that one pass. She didn't feel like arguing with Him. In any case perhaps He was right. In her heart she called Him, though she never knew why.

"I didn't know you played the violin," she said, then thought that stupid, since He obviously could play everything. "I mean," she added, "I didn't know you could play so well."

His face was stern. Flattery would not touch Him. Then she felt herself surrender a little. She leaned forward in her seat. "I have a problem, God," she said quite simply.

For the first time since they had met, she saw a flicker of a smile on His face. A smile without triumph or contempt, but one which hinted of simple pleasure. In the confidence she wished to share with Him, He probably saw the beginnings of her conversion, the first step in her salvation and the return to His bosom.

He put out his hand to touch her. But quickly she recoiled. She trembled, for she knew that she could not harbour all those feelings that would ensue. With God as their springboard, they embarrassed and irritated her. She simply couldn't trust Him. He smiled still, but now the smile was of something more than pleasure. It was of the sure patience of one who would overcome.

It was not lost on Veronica and she felt trapped. Now she would not dream of confiding in Him. She wished He would go away. He heard that wish too, as acutely as He heard her beckoning, and He rose and passed through the adjoining doors to the next carriage. The train began to shunt again and then stop completely. But only for a while. Soon it was on its way again to Surbiton. Veronica did not bother to look out of the window, but His retreating shadow crossed deftly over her mind's eye.

Chapter Seven

Lately God had taken to sleeping with her and each morning, on waking, she had a quaint and rather pleasureable sense of adultery. Each morning, too, she was surprised by His sundry disguises. Once he was wearing a white butcher's apron and its spotlessly clean condition made it faintly unnerving. On another morning He was arrayed in a frilly frock possibly thinking that, in that guise, Veronica could be better won over. Once He charged about the bed in all the accoutrements of Superman and then claimed that He was simply in His day-to-day working-clothes. Those nights she spent with God were dreamless and peaceful ones. He never laid a finger on her of course and, though relieved, it needled her that He didn't seem to fancy her. She would have much preferred to sleep with the Devil and, for that favour, would have forfeited her peaceful dreamless nights.

One morning He startled her out of her sleep. "Though your sins be of scarlet," He thundered, "They shall be white as snow."

"What in God's name are you talking about?" she said.

He didn't answer. He slipped out of bed and was gone.

"What d'you *mean*?" she cried after Him helplessly.

He popped His head back through the door.

"Be sure your sins will find you out," He warned.

"*What* sins?" she screamed at Him.

"Ask and it shall be given you. Seek and ye shall find. Knock and it shall be opened unto you."

This was His parting shot. He disappeared once more and Veronica stared into the space He'd left behind Him and it seemed to be streaked with blood.

"Leave me alone," she whimpered, and dragged herself from the bed. In mute helplessness, she showered and oiled her body and donned her black housecoat. God was sending her once more to the drawer.

Seek and ye shall find, He had said, and she had no alternative but to obey. She knelt before the chest and pulled gently on the handle. The drawer emerged oily-smooth, as innocent as a trousseau-drawer of blameless silks and finery. The top paper of the file was folded and, from the red imprint that showed through the sheet, it looked to be an official document of some kind and Veronica was fearful of touching it lest it be a warrant for her arrest. Gingerly, and with the tips of her fingers, she drew out the folded paper. In her mind there was a faint residual memory of what was written inside and an equally faint amnesia. But both memory and oblivion had left in their wake a sense of burden and pain. She took the sheet to her desk and unfolded it.

It was oblong in shape and straightaway recognizable as a birth certificate. The deed was divided into a number of columns. She covered them all with her hand. She would ration herself to whatever pain the document would inflict and, to this end, she uncovered only the first column. Its heading was "When and Where Born". Underneath was written, "3rd June, 1957. St Theresa's Hospital, Surbiton". The heading of the next column was "Sex", and instinctively she knew that it was a boy, a fact confirmed when she lowered her hand. As she uncovered the next title head, she felt feverish and inadvertently called on God to give her strength to tear the document, unread, into shreds. She waited for Him to come. Had He not said He would come when called upon? But He did not appear. His absence was a token of His refusal of her request. She was forced to read further. The offending column was headed, "Name of Father". "Oliver" was written in small letters, "SMILES" in large, underlying its sole relevance to paternity. That column was the very worst hurdle. Thereafter all information was sheer gossip. The mother was Millicent Wayne, formerly Harris. The father's profession was solicitor; the mother's address was a small crescent on the edge of Surbiton. Not very far from the park and the swings where Veronica had first discovered treachery. Smelt it, without knowing the word, swinging above and below it with prickly unease. On every visit to the park, they would make for the swings, strung there like gallows, and her father would push her in rhythm with the swing-lady who pushed her own. But one day the swing-lady wasn't there, nor on the next park visit. Months passed and the leaves shed and budded again, safe and welcome in the woman's absence. And then one day, one sunny blameless day, there at the swings, beside the swing-lady and her boy, there was a pram for company, standing between the two of them. With one hand, the woman, now known as Millicent, though neither that nor any other name would have absolved her, with one hand she held on to the pram, while with the other she pushed the boy's swing, thus establishing her ownership rights on both. And once, Veronica remembered, her father slipped his hand on to the pram-handle and she'd seen the two hands then, not touching and wide apart, yet a concrete declaration of shared ownership. Did she know that at the time, she wondered? She remembered the fever that came later that day and Dr Bruton again at her bedside. And again with his well-meant but mistaken diagnosis. He patted her head.

"Mother will be back soon," he said.

Her mother was in fact legally due to arrive within the week.

"You'll be all better then."

But because of her mother's imminent return, her fever simply soared, and Dr Bruton couldn't understand it. She couldn't tell him that it was the pram and perhaps she didn't even know of its connection. But the pram was all she ever thought about. Night and day.

Then her mother came home and announced that she was not going back to the mountain.

"Not *ever*?" Veronica was terrified. The pram could only grow smaller and what was inside it could only grow bigger, and there was no way that her mother could miss seeing it. Veronica knew where babies came from and how they were made. Her friend at school had told her because that friend had just had a baby sister.

Every morning after her mother's return, she dreaded the breakfast table, in case one of them simply wouldn't be there and Mrs Dale would have that look on her face again. But every morning, not only were they both there, but they were cheerful with it. Veronica could not bear their bonhomie, since in her terms there was very little to be cheerful about. Often it was on the tip of her tongue to talk airily about the swings in the park, just to drop a hint of sorts. Or sometimes she wanted to shout out "Pram," and run from the table. She was glad to go to school and be away from all the nothing that wasn't happening at home. Coming back from school was easier, for her father was never there at that time and she would often choose to go to bed early to avoid his return. Yet, lying in her bed, when she heard their laughter from below, her utter confusion sent her into hiding under the blanket and she began to wonder whether the pram was real or whether she had only dreamt it.

Then one morning at breakfast, her father announced that he was going to Cambridge for the weekend and probably for many weekends to come. Mrs Dale was at that moment pouring the coffee and Veronica knew that, wherever else she looked, she must not on any account look at Mrs Dale's face.

"Why Cambridge?" her mother had asked.

Then her father had spun a tale of such clear preparation, of such elaboration, and of such patent rehearsal that, even without knowing all those words, it seemed to Veronica that she was in a theatre, where once she had been to a pantomime and that she was looking at a performance. Now more than ever must she avoid Mrs Dale's face and she was unsurprised to see her back hastily leave the room.

He had a client in Cambridge, her father was saying, an old man in his ninetieth year. He was unable to travel up to London and, besides, he refused to part with any of his documents which had to be legally examined. The matter was about property and inheritance, her father said, two further words that Veronica did not understand, but even so, sensed

110

their irrelevance. It was going to be a long job, her father concluded.

"I'll be late for school," Veronica said, and rushed from the table, leaving the grown-ups to deal with the fairy tales.

There was some relief in her father's absence every weekend when she had her mother all to herself, but she always dreaded that one day her mother would suggest a visit to the park. And one sunny Saturday, her mother actually insisted upon it and there was nothing Veronica could do to dissuade her.

"I don't want to go on the swings," she said, as soon as they started out. "They make me feel sick."

"What about the slide?" her mother said.

"That makes me feel sick too."

She must at all costs avoid the playground and all the sick-making things that it held. But her mother chose an entrance to the park which actually passed through the swings and the slides and the roundabouts. While they did so, Veronica kept her eyes half shut, yet, even through the slits, she could see that the swing-lady wasn't there. Neither was the pram.

"I'll have a swing I think," she said, and darted across to them to savour the witnessless freedom. "Let's come to the park tomorrow," she said, as she swung upwards from her mother's push, with no fear of the downward drop. Then it was the slide and the roundabout, with not a tainted pram in sight.

Every weekend thereafter, Veronica and her mother went to the park while her father busied himself with the Cambridge inheritance. The swing-lady had swung with her pram into nowhere. It was not that Veronica was too young to make the connection, nor that she was simply too innocent. She was neither, nor ever had been. It was simply that she was by nature a survivor and part of the armoury of survival kit was a blind eye. Her father's weekend absences had by now become so numerous and regular, that Veronica assumed that they were permanent; both she and her mother accepted them as part of a pleasurable new norm. Though Veronica was ever-mindful of the ripe old age of her father's client and that, at ninety-one, nothing could ever be considered permanent, at night she found herself praying for his immortality.

It was her father's habit to return from the office early on a Friday evening, pack his weekend bag and, after taking tea with both of them, drive himself to Cambridge and his client. Lately on a Friday, Veronica noticed, her mother arrived a little late for tea and fresh from a short spell outdoors. Sometimes she claimed that she had been putting out the milk bottles, or that she had called in next door to give a message to a neighbour. Over the weeks, these short sorties of hers on a Friday night just before tea became part of the pattern of her father's absences and, as such, Veronica did not question them. But one Friday she herself was delayed. An injured bird had landed on her bedroom windowsill and in taking it inside into the warmth of her hand, she had noticed that her father's car door was open and her mother was seated inside, writing something in a notebook. She watched and waited, as her mother, seemingly satisfied, left the car and went back into the house. Veronica was puzzled but sensed that she must not question it. Nevertheless on the following Friday, she positioned herself at the same time by her window and was witness to the same spectacle. Still she held her tongue on questions.

On a Sunday after their park visit, Veronica would go to bed early, long before her father had returned from his client. But one Sunday, shortly after her Friday discoveries, she could not sleep and she lay awake long enough to hear his car pull up outside the house. She rushed to the window, hiding herself behind the curtain. She watched her father leave the car, brush himself down and walk up the path to the front door. She heard his key in the lock but something compelled her to stay by the window. And shortly she knew why. After a while, her mother came out on to the path and made straight for the car. Once again it was the same routine. Her mother sat in the driver's seat, the door left half-open to give her light, the notebook and pencil in her hand. Whatever she was doing did not take long and soon she was on her way back into the house. Veronica rushed into her bed. She didn't know why, but she sensed that this was the time for the thunder and she hid her head under the blankets. But all was silent downstairs and indeed for the whole of the following week, as if both her mother and her father were going about their separate businesses which had nothing to do the one with the other. Then on the following Friday, at tea time, her mother was not late. There was no outside sortie and she was actually there on time, by the fireside, pouring tea. Mrs Dale was putting an extra log on the fire as Priscilla was handing her husband his cup.

"How many miles is it to Cambridge, Oliver?" she said.

Her voice was gentle and innocent, and Veronica wondered why Mrs Dale dropped the log so hastily and left the room. But when her father hesitated in his reply, shuffling almost in his seat, his ears reddening like a boy's, Veronica saw the first flash of lightning. Her father opened his mouth to reply. His stammer was almost visible.

"About . . . er . . . six . . . sixty miles or so."

"How is it then," her mother said with sustained innocence and gentleness, "that every week when you go to Cambridge the car clocks up no more than six miles Veronica go to your room." And all of it in one calm, cool and gentle breath.

Veronica was grateful for the dismissal. She went quickly, not to her room, but into the kitchen, where Mrs Dale was sitting by the stove with that look on her face, that disgusted road-sign of hers to chaos.

"Come," she said, and she took Veronica in her arms and though the kitchen door was closed and a long corridor ran from it to the drawing room, it carried the peal of thunder like an echo chamber into the kitchen.

Shortly afterwards they heard her father's car drive away with what seemed angry and exaggerated acceleration. Then there was a silence in the house that neither Mrs Dale nor Veronica wished to break. For to break it would have opened the way to the truth which neither of them had the courage to face. Veronica imagined that her mother was crying, but the corridor did not echo that. Instead they heard her footsteps and the ringing ping of the phone in the hall. Veronica opened the kitchen door and blatantly eavesdropped and Mrs Dale, perhaps herself needing a clue, made no move to stop her.

"Is Dr Fisher there?" her mother was saying. Then a pause. And after a while, "This is Priscilla Smiles. Would you ask

him to phone me immediately on his return? It's very urgent."
Pause, then; "Yes, he knows my number." The phone clicked
again.

Veronica sat on the kitchen floor. "Who's Dr Fisher?" she
whispered.

"One of those men from the mountains," was all Mrs Dale
could supply.

But it was enough for Veronica, for it spelt out her mother's
departure.

They did not go to the park that weekend, and it was Mrs Dale
who took charge of Veronica and instructed her in the making
of jams to pass the time. And most of the while, her mother
was on the telephone. On the Sunday she announced that she
was going up to London on business and Veronica lay awake
waiting for her return. It came shortly after her father's, but
she heard nothing in the silence except for the opening of the
spare bedroom door. In the morning she had breakfast with
Mrs Dale. Her father had already left for work and her
mother was still sleeping.

"You'd better let her sleep," Mrs Dale said, handing
Veronica her satchel. "I'll tell her you said goodbye." She
wanted to let her charge off the hook and Veronica was
grateful.

But the day in school was torture. Though she was glad of
the silence at home, it was oppressive too, because it stifled
the truth that one day she must be told. And though she
dreaded that day, she yearned for it, too, for the limbo was
unbearable. When she got home she would precipitate it, she
thought. She would ask fairly and squarely to be put in the
picture. She thought that all out, without knowing the words.
In a week's time she would reach her eighth birthday,
chock-a-block full of unknown vocabulary, bursting with
feelings that she could not name, yet feeling them with
greater pain because she could not understand them. And all
could be translated and relieved in the simple questions,
"What the matter? What's happening amongst us?" But they
were unaskable, for there was no concrete evidence in the
house that anything was the matter at all. There were the
usual normal silences, the usual polite formality. Even her

114

mother's occupation of the spare room was nothing abnormal. She would often retire there if she was working late and didn't want to disturb her father. Yet something was most positively the matter and she ached to ask what it was. But propriety and lack of evidence stilled her tongue. Perhaps they would tell her on her birthday.

In Veronica's remembrance, her mother had been present only twice on her birthday, not counting that day when she was born, when her mother's presence was inevitable. Usually she would send a coloured greetings telegram from some mountain or another and occasionally she would telephone. But this year her mother had promised her what she called a proper birthday party, with balloons and games and presents and a candled cake and a new party frock. In the days before her party, Veronica would return from school to find yet more parcels of party aids. Streamers, hats and crackers stood piled up in their boxes on Mrs Dale's kitchen counter. The busied preparations unnerved her a little and she didn't know why. It was three long days to wait till Saturday, but often she wished it was all over. She wondered whether her father would put in an appearance, or whether Cambridge would call him to some stranger's inheritance. But the Friday night before the party there was no sign of his departure and Veronica did not know whether or not she was relieved.

On Saturday morning when she woke, she could hear the busy to-and-froing downstairs. They would be preparing her birthday table and she must wait until she was called. From some years of conscious practice, she knew the form. In time, Mrs Dale would knock on her door, sing "Happy Birthday" from outside, then she would rush in and kiss her, and Veronica would welcome it as the only unencumbered greeting of the day. But that morning it was not Mrs Dale at the door; there was not even a knock. The door simply opened and her mother and father stood there, and began to sing in uncertain unison, "Happy Birthday." They looked embarrassed both for themselves and for each other, and Veronica wanted to laugh either for sorrow or joy, but for whatever reason, she felt it would be rude. She waited politely until the end of the song and then, with some formality, they both approached the bed and kissed her in turn.

"Your birthday table is ready," her mother said, then left the room. Her father hovered for a second, then he too made his getaway. It was as if neither of them wanted to shoulder the responsibility of telling her quite simply what was the matter. Or give any hint of what was happening. And then suddenly Mrs Dale was there with her warm hugs and greetings. For a while Veronica felt safe, safe enough perhaps to ask the question, but then, fearful that she could not bear the answer, she held her tongue.

The birthday table was usually prepared in the kitchen, but this year it was on the dining table. With this unaccustomed ceremony that was attending her birthday, Veronica had the impression of finality, that this was to be the last such party, or the last appearance of one or other of the family. She wondered if she were going to die and if that was what the matter was, and why everybody was so kind and so respectful. She turned to Mrs Dale.

"Am I all right?" she whispered. "Am I very ill or something?" And then the whole cry of pain. "Is this going to be my last birthday?"

She saw her father cast her mother a look of intense hatred and somehow it filled her with relief, for it was a look of blame and no mother could be blamed for a daughter's death. So the site of the crisis had shifted and Veronica felt reprieved.

The birthday table, as well as its changed setting, was different too. Usually it was laden with so many packages that the wood beneath was invisible. For although she only had three sources of presents, her father, her mother and Mrs Dale, they managed between them to cover the table in small gift-wrapped parcels. But today there was even room for a large bowl of flowers in the centre. On either side of it lay one package. That accounted for two of her regular donors. But what of the third? Then she noticed something unusual in the room, a large object which stood by the sideboard, of indefinite shape and covered with a white blanket. Since no one was drawing attention to it, she decided to ignore it until called upon and she started to open one of the packets on the table. It was small. It was either a nothing, some trifle with

116

which to punish her, or a matter of some unwarranted expense as a form of compensation. All these thoughts passed through her mind, a mind which did not know the words to label them with. Her fingers stung with the sharp string and she knew that whatever the parcel contained, it would not please her.

"That's from me," she heard her father say. "Shall I help you?" He put his hand on the string, but she pulled it away. "I can do it," she said huffily.

Her father withdrew with a sigh. She knew he was hurt but she didn't care. She hated whatever was in the package for, whether cheap or dear, it was punishment. At last she tore the string away and ripped the oh so pretty wrapping. Inside was a small blue velvet box. Expensive. Even if the box had nothing in it. She unclipped the silver fastening. Inside, prone on the blue velvet, lay a gold watch. A ridiculous present, she thought, for a little girl. She managed to let out a sigh of wonderment, then one of appreciation, both of which she knew was expected of her.

"Just from you, Daddy?" she said, for it was a gift valuable enough to count for many birthdays and from all the family.

"Just from me," he said.

She should kiss him, she thought. But she did not want to look at him. His chest was on her eye level and she went towards it and clutched at him. He bent to kiss her and her heart was filled with sorrow for him that he had to make such great amends. And for something that it was too late to remedy. She hugged him less with gratitude than with pity.

That done, she went to the second parcel.

"That's from me," Mrs Dale said.

Veronica heard a small regret in her voice, as if the present she'd chosen had been in error. It was packed without string and Veronica eased her thumb under the sellotape, anxious not to tear the greetings paper that Mrs Dale had folded with such care. Once again the present was in a box, this one of black leather which in itself, and empty, would have accounted for one week of Mrs Dale's wages. She heard them all breathing heavily around her. She opened the box. Inside was a small battery radio.

"I thought you could keep it by your bed," Mrs Dale said quickly, as if in apology.

"Oh it's wonderful," Veronica said, and really meant it. It was grown up to have your own radio, but for a gold watch one could never be grown up enough. Even so, Veronica thought, as she ran into Mrs Dale's arms, it was an uncommonly over-generous gift for a mere eighth birthday and though Mrs Dale would never wish to punish her, she might be making vicarious amends.

"You can play it first thing when you get up in the morning," Mrs Dale said.

Veronica clung to her not wishing to face the clear absence of a present from her mother.

"You have to look for mine." She heard her mother's voice.

"But not very far," Mrs Dale said. "Go," and gently she pushed her away from her.

The hiding place of her mother's present was obvious.

"That?" she enquired, pointing to the white blanket by the sideboard.

"Why don't you look and see?" Mrs Dale said.

Veronica went to the blanket. It was draped with fullness, so that it camouflaged any giveaway shape beneath. She touched it. It was hard and cold and she guessed that it was metal. Her heart leapt at the thought that it might be the fulfilment of her wildest dreams. A bicycle. Yet she dreaded it, too, for there was no earthly reason in her eight-year-old mind, that mind which housed so many feelings and so few labels, there could be absolutely no reason for such monstrous and manic reparation. She pulled the blanket away and thus confirmed her joy and terror. No word could accept it, no marvel, no gratitude, not even a sigh, so overwhelmed was she by its sheer and shiny chrome ineptitude. But at least it represented a means of escape.

"Can I try it now?" she asked. "Oh Mummy," she said, giving way only to her joy and she ran to her full of love and she didn't know why she was crying. They would put it down to excitement, but it was more than that, she knew, but whatever was extra did not bear investigation.

"Just ride on the pavement," her father said. "We'll watch from the window."

118

She didn't mind as long as they didn't come with her and once outside and secure in the saddle, she no longer gave a thought to the questions that had plagued her indoors. She rode up and down the street, singing in time with her pedalling, until she was called inside for breakfast.

Indoors the questions did not return. There was too much to do to allow time to think about them. She helped her father blow up the balloons and she saw his face redden with the strain. Then they packed little presents for the games. Mrs Dale was cooking and most of the morning her mother spent in the spare room. Veronica supposed that she was working. But she came downstairs when the bell rang with the first guests.

And in the ways of Surbiton, they were all on time. Hilary, May, Wendy, Pat and, bringing up the rear, Gemma and Emily and Carol, all flushing in their pre-'n' days. And each of them carrying her carefully wrapped present. Veronica took them, one by one, knowing that they were safe, reasonably priced and apt. From donors unencumbered and with not one atom of atonement between them.

Only girls at the party. Veronica's non-male days started early and in many ways had never finished. But at eight-years-old it would have been considered natural that party and boys were antithetical. Within a year or so, most of the guests would have mocked that premise, in the slow peeling of their innocence, but at that memorable eighth birthday party, all apple blossom skin was intact. Since all the guests had arrived at the same time, the party got under way immediately. Veronica's father seemed to have taken over the organization of games. This role was usually filled by Mrs Dale and her father would pop in occasionally as a benign onlooker. But that eighth birthday departed in all respects from the norm and the atoning presents were the least of it. Now she watched her father as he lined up the girls to stick the tail on the donkey, blindfolding each one in turn. And when her own turn came, he seemed extra gentle, smoothing her hair under the bandage, as if the act of blindfolding was in itself a violation. Her mother now took the spectator's role, but at least, unlike most of Veronica's birthdays, she was there and the solidity of her presence indicated that she was there to stay. Until Veronica remembered the presents and the man from the mountain on the other end of the telephone.

"Why don't you play, Mummy?" Veronica asked, as if placing her in the donkey line would seal her presence for ever.

"I must help Mrs Dale with the tea," she said, and went quickly into the kitchen.

Because of her father's presence, the range of party games was broadened. Since he was passably competent at the piano, they were able to play pass the parcel and musical chairs. At her last birthday party, with mother on the mountain and father in the office, they had tried musical chairs with Mrs Dale singing, but her voice was so thin and so scarcely audible, it was difficult to be sure of when she had stopped. Now with her father strumming the piano, there was no question of the sudden silences, though he kept his eye on Veronica, ensuring she had a seat before he lifted his hands from the keys. Afterwards, from the piano, he scored pass the parcel and seemed to Veronica to be enjoying himself as much as the guests. And for some reason that she couldn't understand, she felt deeply sorry for him. Her mother reappeared at tea time but even then her father didn't stop organizing. He poured the lemonade, passed the cakes and sandwiches, and even sat down himself between Gemma and Emily, her two best friends and teased them like a favourite uncle. Then her mother sat down too, but at the other end of the table, laughing and joking with her friends and Veronica thought that, though everything was without doubt very right, there was something indefinable that was equally very wrong. Suddenly she couldn't bear the noise of the laughter, or the sight of happy faces and she left the table quickly, excusing herself for the bathroom. She wanted very much to be on her own. She ran upstairs and passed the open door of the spare room. Then she stopped and slowly, her knees trembling, she turned back to confirm what she thought she had seen on the bed. She stood at the door and stared at it, the bulging rucksack and the boots that hung from the strap. Beside it, a smaller bag, the zip half open. Sticking out were her mother's notebooks with their familiar yellow covers and the bunched towelling of her sponge bag, which item sealed her imminent departure. And suddenly all the presents were explained and all the party organization and bonhomie. She leaned on the door but she would not cry. It was unlucky, they said, to cry on your birthday and she wondered how much unluckier in her life she could ever be.

She heard them calling her from downstairs. It was time to cut the cake. She clenched her teeth and her fists. She would go downstairs, and cut the cake and blow out the candles. She would do everything that was expected of her. Everything that is, except cry. She would never cry again. Not even when her mother would leave, not even when she would wave goodbye at the station. Not even, dared she think it, when her mother died. Never, never again would she cry, because she knew it was expected of her. Her dry eyes would be her simple, straightforward and self-destructive revenge. She put on a smile and went downstairs.

Her father was drawing the curtains, darkening the room for the entry of the cake. More production. Her mother had once again disappeared. The guests were ranged around the table and ordered to stand.

"Are we ready, Priscilla?" her father shouted in the direction of the kitchen.

"We're coming," said Mrs Dale, her mother's spokesman. The room was now in silent darkness. Her father felt for the piano keys and gave a solemn chorded introduction to "Happy Birthday". It was a cue for their voices and the entry of the cake. Veronica found herself singing alongside them. In spite of the presents, the games, the paper hats, the streamers, the balloons, the cake, she did not feel that it was a celebration on her behalf. It was in aid of something quite outside herself. It celebrated the packed rucksack on the bed, it did honour to the fruition of a phone call, it toasted her mother's silence and the truth that her father had finally revealed. And all this had nothing to do with herself, with Veronica, except in hindsight, when she knew that that eighth birthday had celebrated the end of her ragged childhood.

Her mother and Mrs Dale carried the cake between them and it was placed in the centre of the table. Knowing her cue, Veronica moved towards it, her face lucent in the candle light. Though only eight gentle flames, their light seemed to blind her as if a hundred candles flickered there, marking an age of resignation and one beyond tears. She took a deep breath and blew, but even with all her conjured strength, she managed to extinguish only two.

"We must try again," her father said, relighting them. "It's bad luck not to blow them all out at once."

But what did she care about luck, since that, which was her life's portion, seemed to have already run its course? Once again she blew out her cheeks and felt the tears gather on her lids. She hoped they would ascribe them to her exertions. This time she managed it, extinguishing all her eight years in one tearless gasp. She heard their cheering and her father was back at the piano again with "For she's a jolly good fellow" and she wished with all her young heart that everyone would go home. But more had been organized. There were games to be played, fun to be had at all costs and it seemed that the only one who was paying the price was herself. She manoeuvred herself through the rest of the entertainment, a fixed smile on her face, with the tears having returned to where they came from.

Soon it was mercifully all over. Outside it was growing dark and her father had at last run out of games. The first mother arrived to pick up her child and then the rest in quick succession. Soon the house was silent again, with her parents in their separate hiding places and Mrs Dale separating the streamers from the half-eaten sandwiches.

"That was a lovely party," she said. "Did you enjoy it?" Then she took Veronica in her arms, because she, too, knew of the rucksack on the spare bed. Now would have been the time to cry, to shed tears in confidence, for Mrs Dale would tell nobody that she was still a child. Even if she still believed it, though she, too, like Veronica, sensed that those days were now over.

That evening they all took supper together. Veronica was allowed to stay up late. She assumed that that was yet another birthday treat of her father's organizing. It was a silent meal, the lull before the storm. Mrs Dale flitted in with each course and as quickly flitted out, wary of being caught in that flash of lightning that preceded the clap of thunder. It was just after she'd served the dessert that it came and her skirts slashed the edge of the dining room door in its wake.

"I'm going away tomorrow, Veronica," her mother said.

Why was this parting so different from all the others? Why the ceremony that surrounded the announcement? Why the secrecy of packing, when hitherto, Veronica had been called upon to help gather materials for her mother's journey? She wondered whether she was going to the mountain, or whether the nature of her destination had changed too.

"Where are you going?" she asked.

"Somewhere different this time," her mother said.

"Not Switzerland?"

"What's the highest mountain in the world?" her mother asked teasingly.

Veronica shrugged. "I don't know," she said. Neither did she care. Away was away, no matter how high. And why didn't her father say anything? He surely knew the highest mountain. But he sat there silently, knowing it well, but unwilling to collude in his wife's journey.

"It's Mount Everest," she heard her mother say and she saw the snow-capped peak of the poster that greeted her every morning in the school hall.

"We've got a picture of that in school," she said. It was by way of making conversation. As long as they could chat about it, she thought, Everest would remain where it was and her mother would stay at home and be satisfied simply with the talk of it.

"I'll show you on the map," her mother said. "I'll go and get the atlas."

She left the table then and Veronica was alone with her father who was shifting in his seat, as if anxious to make a getaway.

"I don't want her to go," he said suddenly.

"Why don't you tell her to stay then?" The tears threatened again.

"You know your mother. She will have her way. But I want her to stay. I do," he pleaded. "It's not my fault."

It seemed he was talking to himself, or *for* himself, for this was no conversation to have with an eight-year-old.

"I'm only eight," she had to remind him.

But he twisted it. "You're too young to be left all the time."

But that wasn't what she had meant at all.

He smiled with relief when her mother returned. She cleared a part of the table and opened the atlas to a double-spread of India and Nepal.

"I shall be flying to Delhi," she said, ringing the place with her finger. "And from there to Kathmandu."

Its name was magic to Veronica as if cousin to Abracadabra and this could only exist in one's imagination. But there it was, in letters on the page, proof of its being, beyond the magic wand.

"This is Everest," her mother was saying. Then she opened a coloured centrespread of another book which showed the mountain itself in every detail.

"We shall be climbing on this face," she said. She looked up at her husband to gather his interest. Her fingers were lovingly caressing the northern slope of the mountain as if she had yearned for it for a long time. "Here," she said, "along here," stroking it back and forth. "Remember this place," she said, and she circled it with her finger, scratching it with anger almost and the purr of her finger sounded like the toll of a passing bell. Then, leaving the open book on the table, she left the room.

Once again Veronica was alone with her father, but this time he had no patience or peace to stay with her and, muttering about some papers he had to attend to, he left the room. Veronica stared at the picture, then, with her finger, she traced the climbing route over the ice and snow. Up and down she went, on each journey pressing harder with her fingers. Then in her rage, she took a red crayon and pressed the track deep into the page, back and forth, up and down, until it was obliterated in a vertical fissure. Let her mother mend it and all those breaches she had made with her journeys. She wondered whether her mother had hated potholes as much as she herself hated mountains.

She decided to go to bed. On her way she paused at the spare room door. It was still unashamedly open, with her mother inside writing at the desk. She stood there without entering.

"Why are you going?" she asked. "You said you were never going back."

Her mother turned. "Come here," she said.

124

As Veronica approached the desk, she noticed that her mother quickly covered the paper on which she was writing. Veronica hated secrets.

"What's that?" she said.

"A letter. It's . . . er . . . nothing important. Come, I'll tell you why I'm going."

Veronica kept her distance, not wishing to be touched.

"My work is the most important thing for me," she said.

"More than me?"

That question framed all that had eaten at her heart since that first departure to the mountain.

"Of course not," her mother said quietly. "But you're different."

Veronica went to bed and left her door open. She wondered why she couldn't fall asleep. Children were supposed to put their heads on pillows and open their eyes to the morning light. It was only adults who lay awake. She stared at the ceiling for a long time and wondered if she had suddenly grown up. She heard her father's tread on the stairs and listened until it ceased at the spare room. She crept out of bed and peered in the crack of the door. Her father was standing in what she considered was her own special place, in the doorway.

"I wish you wouldn't go," he said.

She could not see her mother, but she heard her voice.

"I have to," she said. "It's all too late now. You know it."

What was "late", Veronica wondered. Trains were late, but there would be others. You could be late for school but in the end it wouldn't matter all that much. What else could be late? The late Mrs Kempsey, she suddenly remembered, recalling how Mrs Dale had once spoken of her granny-underground. Now she knew what "late" was. "Late" was dead and dead was too late for anything.

The next morning they took her to the station. Mrs Dale, for some reason, came as well, which was not the usual procedure. Other things were different, too. Her mother, though going much further afield this time, was taking far less luggage. And her father was more than usually silent. There were dark shadows on his chin and cheeks, instead of the clean-shaven look he presented each morning. She thought that, if he spoke, his words would cry. The leave-taking, too, was different. Her mother actually lifted her in her arms and, without saying a word, smothered her in kisses. She wanted to ask her when she was coming back, but by some God-given gift, she knew that it was a question permitted to nobody. Her mother put her down gently, then shook Mrs Dale's hand. Veronica did not wish to see the farewell to her father, but she knew that she had to witness it if only to add to her own confusion. There was little to see. They stared at each other for a while, then her mother touched the back of her father's hand with the tips of her fingers, brushing it slightly, backwards and forth. Veronica watched the movement minutely, and saw how the black hairs stood and fell at her brushing. And though the gesture was so infinitesimal, almost to the point of being no gesture at all, it told her quite clearly that her mother loved her father despite everything.

She waved from the train. On each side of Veronica Mrs Dale and her father squeezed her hand. She looked at them both. Each of them knew something that she didn't know, yet in her heart, without words, labels or understanding, she knew it too.

Thereafter, whenever she entered school, she shut her eyes and groped blindly past the Everest poster in the hall.

Chapter Eight

On the eve of her wedding, Veronica dreamt that God was lying by her side dressed in a grey morning coat and topper with a white carnation in His lapel. But that night God chose not to sleep with Veronica and, instead of His mundane homily that normally woke her each morning, she heard the alarming sound of dripping water. She leapt out of bed and into the bathroom. The floor was flooded from a sink overflow. The cold tap was running but the sink was unplugged. There was clearly a blockage in the drain. She looked at her watch. Seven-thirty. The car was due to pick her up at eleven. She lifted the phone and dialled an emergency plumber. He promised to come right away. While waiting, she mopped the floor, made her bed and laid out her wedding dress and accessories. Despite all laws and regulations, either of morality or taste, she had decided on white. Perhaps it was an act of defiance. She had taken it from the shop rail and looked around for an assistant. There seemed nobody about and, carrying the dress on its hanger, she had wandered around the showroom looking for some form of service.

"Madam?" A voice half-familiar addressed her back.

She turned round. "Oh no," she muttered. "Not you again."

"A whited sepulchre?" He enquired politely.

She walked swiftly past Him and took the dress to the cash

counter. She prayed that it would fit. Once home, she was afraid of trying it on, lest He had shrunk it with His curses and she spread it out now, on the bed, its fitting still unproved. At each side of it she laid a white glove and below the scalloped hem a pair of gold shoes. Around its neck she set down the gold and emerald necklace that Edward had given her. Then she took a pace back and viewed the ensemble.

In its untenanted layout it seemed to her to reach perfection. Just to possess it, the ensemble of it, was marriage enough. The wearing of it, the attendance at some form of ceremony seemed to her now to be superfluous, and she thought she might buy a dressmaker's dummy and clothe it in the entire rigout. This she would keep in her study and on each safari return she would view it as confirmation that she had not been left on the shelf. A museum piece, but unbequeathable.

She heard the doorbell ring. Quickly she wrapped her dressing gown over her nightdress and went to answer the door. A young man stood there, his rough beard early as the morning, his plumber's bag swinging at his side. In his lapel, he sported a wilting paper poppy, some faded relic of armistice. His pale blue eyes were half closed, offended by his interrupted sleep. Her heart fluttered and she didn't know why, or knew, but was ashamed. As she led him to the bathroom, she quickly shut her bedroom-door so that her intended folly could not be viewed.

"I hope it won't take long," she said. "I have to go out at eleven." She refrained from telling him she was getting married. For some reason she didn't want him to feel rejected.

He knelt down at the sink and opened his plumber's bag. He scanned the pipes for a while, then turned, still kneeling, and asked her where in the house was the main water tap. To Veronica, he looked like a supplicant kneeling there and his filthy hands and stubbled chin, his pleading half-shut eyes, were all tokens of some great sin that merited pardon. It occurred to her that she was the object of his prayer and, in answer, she considered that she should open her dressing gown.

"The main tap," he pleaded again, wondering at her silence.

128

"I'll show you," she said.

Still she hovered, unnerved by the feelings that assailed her. And something more. He'd asked for the main tap and her hesitation was partly due to its location. For it was in the cupboard, behind the chair, behind the desk and all of that in the spare room, that room that she rarely entered now, unwilling to face its hovering ghosts.

"I'll show you," she whispered.

She led him along the corridor. The door to the spare room was shut, that door against which, as a child, she had leaned so often and longed for her mother's return. She opened it now, letting him enter first, so that any ghosts within would fade in his unfamiliar presence. She followed him and slid past the bed, that site of so many packings. Now the two empty rucksacks leaned against the headboard, like a tombstone.

"It's in the cupboard, behind that chair," she said. "You'll have to move the desk."

She would not help him move it. It was seared with her mother's letters of farewell, those letters she had guiltily hidden on Veronica's eighth birthday. No, she would not touch it. To touch any part or parcel of her mother would have destroyed her. So she hovered at the door, watching him.

"I have to turn it off at the mains," he said, "while I disconnect the pipe. It won't take long."

She watched him move the desk and crouch by the cupboard. He found the tap and turned it, but remained crouching. From the back of him it seemed he was cogitating. But of what, she thought. She hoped he knew his job. She saw him shrug which could have been a sign equally of his doubt or his confidence. Then he leisurely unfolded himself to his feet and turned to face her, and she saw that it was the latter, not only of the job in hand, but in the spin-offs that it would entail. He gave her an almost imperceptible smile, closing his already half-shut eyes, and he strolled past her out of the room. She watched the back of him down the corridor. He swaggered like a confident matador, who turns his back on the erstwhile raging bull, knowing that it is time for the kill. But first he had to unplug the drain.

She followed him into the bathroom, watching him all the time. He hummed a little while he worked, occasionally looking back at her to make sure of her vulnerability. She sneezed and the devil entered her flesh. She noticed that the belt of her dressing gown was hanging loose. She didn't recall untying it, but she made no move to knot it again. He was plunging a long rod down the drain with equal strength and rhythm. The latter she heard in his song; the former was visible in the muscle of his upper arm. She stood at the door and watched him with infinite pleasure. All thought of her morning appointment had gone from her mind. Eventually the job was done. He stood upright at the sink. The kneeling was over.

"It's all right now," he said. "It won't give you any more trouble. I'll turn the mains on again."

He knew the way to the spare room, so she need not lead him. Nevertheless, she followed him. He was positively strutting now, like a peacock. She leaned against the door as he approached the cupboard. Then watched him finish off the job.

"That's done," he said after a while. He picked up his bag. "£20 to you, Madam," he said.

She took off her dressing gown. Whether it was in response to his bill, or whether in any case she would have offered herself, she might one day wonder, but would never care.

"I need the money," he said.

She noted that he did not say that he *preferred* the money and for that, in her half-naked state, she was grateful.

"You can have the money in any case," she said. Though it saddened her. She would have preferred to pay him in kind. It was the Devil's work she was about and payment in kind was Devil's currency.

He came towards her and lowered his plumbers' bag to the floor. Then, holding her roughly by the shoulders, he pushed her on to the bed, that packing bed, that tombstone. She had not expected gentleness. Indeed any caress would have amounted to a social gaffe. In any case, his roughness only served to excite her. He was not a man of foreplay or any preliminary. Such manoeuvres were tokens of relationship and neither of them was interested in anything more than

130

simple connection. As he hoiked up her nightdress she realized with pleasure that she didn't even know his name. After a short unbuttoning delay, she lowered her weakened but willing head and with his gleaming sword he plunged inside her. She cried to the Devil with joy and he, too, with great obscenities in the Devil's tongue. When it was over, she rose and went to her study. From her purse she extracted £20. She handed it over.

"Thank you," she said without looking at him.

"My pleasure," he said, and he was gone. Soon she would have forgotten what he looked like.

She heard the church clock strike nine. She vaguely recalled that she had some appointment that morning, a meeting of some import, but where and why she could not remember. She went to her desk and consulted her diary, but the day was blank. More than anything, she wanted to go back to bed and lie within herself and savour in recall the Devil's business she had been about. On entering the bedroom she saw the nuptial layout on the counterpane. Only then did she remember her appointment. "Jesus," she whispered to herself with some annoyance, "I promised to go and get married." Now she viewed the rig-out as part and parcel of all the paraphernalia that had overtaken her. While her back had been turned, a marriage had been arranged, a honeymoon to Paris had been organized, an honourable family had accepted her into their circle. Her rooms had been made ready at Eaton Square. And now, that morning, she had to go and countersign all their arrangements. It was totally beyond her. She felt like a mechanical puppet, wound up to the full and now she must perform all those turns for which she had been programmed. She would shower and anoint herself; she would paint her face; she would line her body with nuptial silks; and finally she would pour her splendidly damaged goods into the virgin white dress. The figure of Edward as a groom was a shadow, indefinable. But she would go and have herself married and *somebody* would be there to take her hand. Somebody would guide the knife to cut the cake and that same somebody would take her to Paris.

She went to the bathroom and turned on the shower. But as she undressed she decided that she didn't want to cleanse

131

herself. That the plumber's tainted print was part and parcel of her wedding attire. And of the trousseau, too. She turned off the shower and powdered and oiled her body, for no cosmetic purpose but to act as a seal to hold the stain. As a small concession she washed her hands and face and then proceeded to assume the fancy dress. When it was done, she looked at herself in the mirror·and laughed, for her reflection was the punch line of the joke that Edward had initiated and that she herself had fed. She went downstairs and waited for the car to fetch her.

The elder of Edward's two brothers, Jonathan, was to be the best man and it was he who came to fetch her. He complimented her on her appearance but with forced politeness and little enthusiasm. Veronica had met him only once before and had found him cool and distant. Edward had assured her that that was Jonathan's manner and had nothing to do with her own person. But it seemed that that manner ran in the family, with Edward as its outsider. All of them knew of Edward's unmentionable deficiency and they couldn't understand why any woman would wish to sentence herself to barrenness. So they assumed that she must be after his title and wealth, but assumed it in solitary secret, for their class would not allow tittle-tattle. Veronica, for her part, was not concerned that they should not accept her. She could hardly expect otherwise, since her own feelings towards their heir were highly ambivalent.

As Jonathan helped her into the wedding car, she caught sight of her face in the driving mirror.

"I'm crazy," she said to herself.

Jonathan shifted uneasily by her side. Of all the family, he was the least happy with his brother's marriage, for it threatened his son's title inheritance. Not that Edward could have children. His infertility was absolute. And in Jonathan's eyes, Veronica looked a bit long in the tooth for children. But with this marriage, there was now the possibility of adoption. Some male heir, of God knows what sire, might assume all the rights of the Boniface title. He comforted himself with the thought that if this future sister-in-law of his still insisted on her desert journeyings, she would have little time and less inclination to rear a child, whatever its provenance. And

Edward anyway was too involved in the business. All his life Jonathan had keenly suffered the deprivation of title and when Edward's incapacity was declared, he took it as a God-given compensation for his pain. A reward that he would pass to his son. But now that reward hung in the balance. He tried to put a brave face on it all, but he was not pleased.

Shortly they drew up outside the registry office. It was to be a quiet ceremony, followed by a modest reception at Claridges. Edward's family would be present; and, for Veronica's own comfort, Emily'n'Paul would attend. She had invited Mrs Dale – they had never ceased to be in touch. Some years ago that good lady had left Surbiton and gone to care for her widowed brother in his house in Worthing. But she had written to say that her brother was ill and that she could not leave him. Veronica was deeply disappointed. Mrs Dale's presence would have betokened family.

As she stepped out of the car, a flash of light temporarily blinded her. Then another, and another. Then there was a respite and she was able to discern a posse of photographers. She should not have been surprised. A titled groom merited some recording. But Veronica was disturbed. Such recording made the act less revocable. It made fact and truth of an event that she'd hoped to pass unnoticed, even by its participants. Tomorrow, in some newspaper, she would be framed as Lady Boniface, and whether she liked it or not, she would have to believe it.

Edward was waiting in the anteroom.

"You look beautiful," he said, even before she reached him. He made to put his arms about her, but she drew back, mindful of the plumber's print which in no way she wanted smudged. Edward assumed her withdrawal to be pre-nuptial modesty, and thus deception became official handmaid to their marriage. And ever more would be so.

But there was another handmaid too. In the corner, a large matronly figure, shamelessly beribboned and bedecked, was waiting to play her part, whatever part it was she had chosen to play. Veronica winked at her. Her ever-present companion. God in drag. Next to Him, innocently unaware of His presence, stood the loyal Emily'n'Paul hovering in the background waiting to play a part that, unlike God's, was well-defined and within the law. And she saw them all, Edward, Jonathan and even Emily, her closest friend, lined up against her as enemies, manoeuvring her into a role for which she had no talent and even less appetite. In that company she considered God as her only ally. She went towards Him.

"I like your get-up," she whispered. "Makes a change."

"There is no peace unto the wicked," He said.

"I know," she said, looking him squarely in the eye. "But it was so enjoyable."

The registrar entered and, though everyone was standing silent and in order, he called them all to attention. Then the ceremony, such as it was, was under way. And thus Veronica was promised, ringed, bespoke, kissed and it was as if it had all taken place in her absence, by the hand of some unelected and unknown proxy, while she herself was in the desert going about her right and proper business. As she sat in the car next to Edward on their way to Claridges, she realized that she would never regard their union as anything but a piece of fictionalized drama, suitably rehearsed and well-enough played, but make-believe withal.

In Claridges ballroom, she looked around for God. This should have been a happy hunting ground for Him, this temple of money changers and whores. But there was no sign of Him. She hoped that He'd gone somewhere to change. He'd looked pretty ridiculous in those frills and furbelows. He was probably packing for the honeymoon. She sought out her friends, weaving her way through the silks and titles and lingering long enough to overhear their seemingly universal judgement. "She's done rather well for herself." She was not offended. In their terms, she had certainly struck gold. A title and an apartment in Eaton Square, together with land and property, were assets not to be sneezed at, but they were never assets that she had ever sought. But the judgement of her friends was different. "Edward's a lucky man," they said, and indeed sincerely thought, for Veronica had published books to prove her worth and assets too, none of them unearned or inherited. In the amalgam of everyone's judgement, we should make a happy pair, Veronica thought, and wondered how soon she could decently get back to the desert.

But first she had to navigate the honeymoon. She thought fondly of her plumber and gave him thanks that he had provided her with sufficient erotic ammunition to cover all the Paris nights. And when that fantasy had worn thin from lack of refuelling, she would seek more in other places. The Devil, like God, was everywhere. At the thought of the plumber, her body trembled and she longed for him again, right here, in Claridges, on the marble floor underneath the chandelier, with all those who for different reasons thought she had done so well for herself, all those as witnesses, just to prove to them how much better she could have done.

Toasts were being made and, knowing her place, she went to Edward's side. A gentleman who claimed he was speaking for Edward's mother, though Edward's mother sat loud and clear by his side, welcomed the guests, and someone else who claimed he was speaking for the guests responded. Then the younger of Edward's brothers toasted the newly-weds and Edward, who claimed to be speaking for Veronica as well as for himself, gave brief and grammatical thanks. The formalities were over and now Edward took her arm and circled amongst the guests, introducing her here and there, and muttering that soon they could be off. It was so easy to get married, Veronica thought, and all so quickly over, as swift as a plumber's performance, though far less memorable. Now I am married, she told herself, and I must try to give a thought to my husband.

They had taken a room in Claridges where they could change before catching the evening plane to Paris. The reception would be over long before they left and there were to be no more goodbyes. Margaret was the last to see them off. Over the past weeks she had softened a little as she took note that Veronica made no attempt to break the partnership she had with her ward. She told Edward to wrap up warm. "And see that your wife does too," she added. It was a generous concession.

It was evening when they arrived in Paris. They were staying at L'Hôtel, that establishment that pays homage to its country's culture in key rings, furnishings and objects d'art. And for the purpose of outrageous profit. There was a time, in its poor and seedy days, when the establishment was indeed a place of sojourn for those who really wrote, really painted and sang. Now the rich artistic fringe idled there in the shade of Mistinguett and sniffed the fading fumes of Wilde's alcoholic, exiled breath. Sir Edward and Lady Boniface were not appropriate clients of L'Hôtel but neither of them noticed, or if they did, it did not disturb them. Edward, unlike Veronica, had been often to Paris, but usually the city was a mere stop-over for his business dealings in the Rhône valley. He had never been there simply as a tourist, and this, he told Veronica, he intended to remedy on their honeymoon. Veronica was happy to fall in with his plans. She had been to Paris only once, as a schoolgirl on a school journey and from that visit only recalled the top of the Eiffel Tower and the lower depths of Les Invalides.

"We'll go to Notre Dame in the morning," Edward announced.

Now for Veronica, churches were another matter. It was enough having God on her back, liable to show up anywhere and in sundry disguises. But to enter a church was voluntarily to hobnob with His whole family. Neither had she forgotten her experience in the church in Trier. God's Son was something else and gave her problems of a different nature, more pleasurable, but problematic just the same. Moreover she would have Edward as witness and it would be like undressing in public. She could hardly decline, but as they entered the church, she would walk a few steps behind him and dear Edward would take it for humility.

They set out early in the morning like any pair of tourists, she with her guidebook, he with his camera. They idled a while on the square outside Notre-Dame, a paddling ground before the serious plunge into the cathedral. Eventually they joined the line of chattering viewers who fell suddenly silent as they crossed the threshold. Huge, Veronica thought as she entered, and that sense of vast expanse was her abiding impression. And with it came an adjusted view of herself, of herself as a nothingness within its magnitude. Sometimes in the desert she had that same feeling, that she was less significant than a grain of sand which, in its minute entity, at least contributed to its extravagant sweep. In the desert she

136

accepted that diminishment of herself without question. But here in the church it was different. Harder. Here she was overcome by the banality of awe. And awe has the capacity to shrink those whom it touches. This she resented. For of what was she in awe? Certainly not of the stained glass, the candles, the intensely pious wood and marble. All those were beautiful and it was to their beauty that she responded. But of what was the awe made? In the desert it was made of threat and it made her tremble. But she had always accepted that the desert would defeat her, that to its uncertain moods she could fatefully and even willingly succumb. But of what was she afraid in this place? And for what reason? She very much wanted to leave. Edward was strolling down the centre aisle, stopping occasionally to marvel at the stone carvings. He was perilously near the Christ. She would not follow him. The Christ she would avoid, knowing what it did to her. So she kept safely to the little side chapels. She found herself at the grill of the Virgin's shrine. Pretty, was all she could think of. No more than that. No awe here. Perhaps it was only men that gave it off and women, relegated to the alcoves, were no threat to anybody. The Virgin's figure seemed to shudder in the flickering candlelight. She was clearly a favourite, by token of all the burning wax that had been invested in her. Candles big and small. Their prices ranged from one to fifteen francs. For one franc, your worship would endure no longer than an hour, a five franc investment would ensure half a day's idolatry, a ten franc candle would absolve you during your office hours and for a rich fifteen francs you need not worry about eternity as the odds on your entering heaven were lengthened. All that stuff about the camel and the eye of the needle was bullshit, as all those glowing fifteen franc candles proved.

"Veronica?"

She heard a voice behind her. She knew it was not God. He never called her by name. Perhaps He didn't even know it, though it was respectable enough, having been canonized in its time. She turned. Edward stood there watching her and looking as if he had been watching her for a long time.

"You look beautiful in the candlelight," he whispered. The sanctity of his surroundings dictated a low decibel level.

"Candlelight flatters anybody," Veronica said, with no attempt to lower her voice. In fact she shouted a little as if daring the edifice to crumble.

"I'd like to take a picture of you," he said. He placed her against the railing with the Virgin glowing in the background. She was ashamed of being photographed in such second-hand aura. She was sure that God was looking and taking a very dim view. She wished that Edward had a Polaroid. It was faster and left less time to consider how unworthy one was of one's backdrop.

That day they did the Madeleine, Sainte-Chapelle and Saint-Denis, and finally the Sacré-Coeur. But after Saint-Denis, Veronica cried off churches. After all, she could see God at any time and in the flesh too. She didn't have to surround herself with carvings and statues to make believe that she was in His presence. She told Edward that she would wait for him in a café on the Place du Tertre.

When she sat down at an empty table, she wondered why He was not already there. In her heart she had called on Him all day. Longed for Him even, for the flesh and blood of Him, after all those tatty representations. He would come, she was sure. She ordered a coffee and looked around the square.

There were many stalls selling souvenirs and in between some of them, a painter sat at his easel and sketched a willing tourist who needed proof of where he had been. A few tables away from her, a woman artist was drawing one of the diners. Those who had no easels were forced to the tables with crayons and charcoal, a quick if meagre turnover and possibly a glass of wine thrown in. Across the square a young artist was making his way towards her table. His stride was purposeful. Veronica was his target and no other. She felt vaguely flattered. He was dressed in the exact fashion of tourist expectation. His black silk trousers were held up by a red cummerband into which was tucked a white artist's smock. A black cape draped his shoulders and a bandana held in place a shock of unruly hair. He was by nature good looking, with that exact air of precious frailty acquired over many lean years in an airless attic. He was a tourist's gift and simply had to be a genius.

"May I draw you?" he said when he reached her table. He spoke in English with an Australian accent.

"If you like," she said.

He picked up his pad and rested it on his knee. Then he stared at her for a long time. For a while she stared back at him giving him ample chance for a likeness. Then she grew embarrassed. He seemed to be staring through and beyond her. She lowered her eyes.

"Would you like a coffee?" she asked. "Or a glass of wine?"

She saw him shake his head and lift a black crayon from the table. Then she relaxed a little and lifted her coffee cup. "May I?" she asked.

"Of course. Just relax. I know your face now," he said. Then he began to draw. She wondered how much she should offer him, or whether he had a fixed price. She tried to peek over the top of his pad but could see only a black half circle which she assumed was her hairline. She sat back and drank her coffee. She noticed that he did not look at her again. He'd memorized her face from that first long and studied eyeful. She was eager to see the result of his labours. For labours they were. He seemed to be shaking violently with his crayon, his face tense and almost angry. She grew anxious about the result. He did not look as if he were pencilling beauty. She finished her coffee and quickly ordered another to give herself something to do, for with all his concentrated vehemence he seemed to be taking his time. She hoped he'd finish before Edward arrived. Somehow it seemed to be a private transaction between them. She took her second coffee slowly, sneaking occasional glances at his face. His brow, which was essentially smooth, was furrowed now and the eyes, which once she had seen as clear, bright and blue, were almost shut as if in disgust at what he drew. She feared for the outcome.

At last he put his crayon down and, with it, gathered up the rest of his equipment and put it in his bag. Then he ripped the drawing off the pad and put it on the table. There, in front of her, she saw a large black circle, the results of his furrowed brow and violent shading. That was all. A large circle, not even symmetrical, and unevenly filled with jagged and jet rage. Even if she made allowances for his possible cubist/

139

kinetic/geometric leanings, there was no inkling of recognition.

"That doesn't look a bit like me," she said weakly.

He turned and stared at her, his blue eyes bright and clear again and his brow smooth.

"I've drawn your soul," he said. "The likeness is remarkable."

Then he rose and weaved his way through the tables and as she watched him, that proud back of his, she knew that it was He. She wanted to call after Him, but she was ashamed. Not because of what He had drawn but because, for the first time, He had managed to fool her. As a waiter, a fiddler, even as a woman, she had never been taken in by His disguise. But as an artist, He had hoodwinked her completely. For the first time since she had encountered God, she sensed that she was on the losing side and she dreaded to think that possibly it was the first step towards surrender.

She was relieved to see Edward crossing the square. Quickly she scrunched the drawing into a ball and stuffed it in her bag. At that moment she thought of her mother and how she had quickly covered the letter on her desk before her last departure to the mountain. But her mother had only temporarily hidden her secret. It would, in its time, be known to all. And she shuddered at the thought that, one day, her secret, too, would become public domain.

Edward sat down beside her. Spontaneously she reached out and hugged him. Her unaccustomed gesture surprised Edward as much as herself, but she saw him as a gentle haven and she clutched at him with gratitude. He disentangled himself, but not without pleasure.

"I think you are happy," he said. He called for a bottle of champagne.

"What are we celebrating?" she asked.

"Our happiness," he said.

When the wine was uncorked, he toasted her and then, before sipping, "Better than the desert," he said.

Not even a question. Just a simple statement. His considered judgement. Then she knew that she could not stay with him.

*

Edward too had had enough of churches, and the following days were devoted to museums and galleries. On the fifth day they took a boat down the Seine and afterwards they felt they had exhausted Paris as well as themselves. Edward suggested they drive south, and leisurely, to Aix-en-Provence. He had no pressing business that urged his return to London and he took it for granted that Veronica had no reason to return. For himself, a daily phone call to his office was enough to keep the wheels turning. In any case, they could stop over in Beaune where he could do some business.

The weather turned as they moved south and an early beautiful summer made them both undesirous of a return to London. So they dallied, avoiding the highways, dawdling through villages and hamlets and staying in country inns. Often Edward would wander off alone and Veronica was glad of it. Both of them, so accustomed to the single life, needed the occasional fix of solitude. At those times she came close to loving him and she knew that when she returned to the desert she would miss him profoundly. As her mother had probably missed her father on a mountain peak. Her granny too, in the caverns underground. A safe kind of loving, distant, un-encumbered, the only kind of loving those women could muster.

They stayed in the south for almost a month. Still they dawdled on their way back to Paris. In the many silences between them, they were close. Their frequent lovemaking, too, was without words. Neither wished to encumber the other with phrases that might in the future be deemed as commitment. At moments Veronica wondered whether she would be jealous if Edward took another woman. The swing-lady still swung from her childhood, that shadow that had driven her mother to her final despair. In such moments, Veronica would cling to Edward as to a life raft.

Eventually they reached Paris where they dined and spent the night. They had stretched their week's honeymoon to five.

"Margaret will be missing me," Edward said.

It seemed reason enough to return to London.

Margaret wasn't exactly waiting for them on the doorstep of

Eaton Square, but she was hovering in the hall listening for the sound of the taxi. She was too well-trained to open the door before they rang and in any case Edward had his key. As she heard them approach the front door, she went quickly into her sitting room. There she waited and from there she called, "Edward?" It was his response that allowed her to make an appearance and to moderate her joy at seeing him again.

He kissed her warmly. "We had a wonderful time, Margaret," he said. "Did you miss me?"

"It's good to have you back," she said. "It's almost six weeks."

Veronica hovered behind them. For Margaret some kind of greeting was unavoidable. She decided to make the best of it.

"You look wonderful, Miss Veronica," she said. For the weeks of their absence, Margaret had sat in her sitting-room considering how she would address the new mistress of Eaton Square. First she had tried "Madame". That appellation had only partially appealed to her. Given the right inflection it could convey a certain measure of contempt of one who played a part above her station. But Margaret was a woman without malice and after a little practice with the title, she decided against it. Then she tried "My Lady" which might have been flattering to Veronica, but it also served to diminish her own status in the household. So that title too was discarded. The Christian name kept suggesting itself, but Margaret baulked at it. It would put the wife on a par with her Edward, by which name, with no diminutives, she had called him since his birth. Thus she rehearsed, even at one point, trying "Mistress", but the name "Veronica" kept nudging her. To use it would spell out a total acceptance of her ward's new status and that she was not ready for. Finally she made a generous compromise, "Miss Veronica", and with it, she rehearsed a number of requests. After a few weeks, it slipped easily off her tongue and in the hallway, on its début, it sounded sincere enough.

She had prepared a cold supper in front of the log fire in the drawing room. She saw it as a prolongation of the honeymoon, in which she could play a small part. Veronica was glad to accept that manoeuvre for, once the honeymoon was officially declared over and done with, she would have to apply herself to

142

the roles of wife and mistress of the flat, for which roles she was about as unsuited as Margaret was for the desert.

In the morning, Edward went off to the office and left Margaret to show Veronica around the flat. It was not a task accomplished in one day. In fact it took the best part of a fortnight, during which time Veronica grew close to Margaret as she introduced her, through the furnishings and fittings of the flat, to each member of Edward's family and sundry stories of their lives together. Veronica found difficulty in accepting the role of wife. Short of sharing Edward's bed, it was Margaret who performed all those wifely duties and Veronica was happy to let it remain so. It allowed her time to get back to her book and to do all those things that Edward had claimed he wished her to continue. "I wouldn't want you any other way," he had said. Yet it was he who had asserted that Paris was better than the desert. That comment still rang in her ear and made it difficult for her to concentrate on her work. But it was not only that. She was feeling distinctly unwell. A malaise had overtaken her towards the end of the honeymoon. She had ascribed it to the sudden change of life style and climate. But her feelings of weariness persisted. Then one morning, when she went to the bathroom on rising, for no reason that she could think of, she was sick. And the following morning too. After a week of the same symptoms, she thought she ought to see a doctor. But she didn't know of one. Dr Bruton had long since gone, together with his misdiagnoses. She did not want to ask Edward, since sickness was a private matter. She knew that Harley Street was the area where doctors practised and the following day she made her way there and noted a number of names and addresses. She avoided those who had specific qualifications – gynae-cologist, orthopaedic practitioner, neurologist – for she did not know in which area she suffered. She returned home with a list of general practitioners and was able to make an appointment with a Dr Truelove on the following day. She was sick again that morning and, in her anxiety, began to fear for her life. She was convinced her illness was a punishment from God and the black soul that He had drawn for her was the first alarming symptom. And if that's how her soul appeared, God help the state of her body. For a moment she

143

thought she might not go to the doctor at all. He would only confirm the worst of her fears. But it was more than that. Since the time that God had so cleverly hoodwinked her on the Place du Tertre, she was wary now of holding a conversation with any stranger. Dr Truelove could well be God in disguise. God could be anyone and anyone could be God, and she had no way of proving otherwise. She considered asking Emily to go with her. Emily, who she was sure loved God with all her heart, could tell whether or not He was Truelove in disguise. But again she felt her condition a private one. She would go alone. She would take the chance. If Truelove turned out to be God in a white coat, He would not examine her. Though God had slept with her, he had never laid a finger on her. That would be some kind of proof of identity. This thought cheered her a little and she dressed carefully and went on her way.

She had to wait for a while in reception with two other patients and the receptionist for company. She examined them all very closely, suspecting each one of them of harbouring the divine spirit. When one of them, catching her eye, smiled at her, she was convinced that it was He. She turned her face away and pretended to read a magazine that lay on the table beside her. In time her name was called and a nurse showed her into Dr Truelove's consulting room. He got up as she entered and politely ushered her to a seat at his desk. But Veronica would not be fooled by his courtesy. God could be as gracious as you pleased if it so suited Him.

"Now what can I do for you?" Dr Truelove was saying.

Her tongue was tied for a moment. If this man were God, why was he asking questions to which he already knew the answer? Dr Truelove sensed her embarrassment.

"Then may I ask you some questions?" he said.

She nodded, on her guard.

"How old are you?" he said.

Well there was no doubt that God well knew the answer to that one. She had reminded Him often enough. The sum of her years was the rub between them, the hold He had on her that, as she aged, would grow forever firmer.

"Thirty-seven," she said. She was beginning to have a little more confidence.

"And what's troubling you?" he asked again, knowing already the area of her malaise.

So she told him, bewildered and tearful. He gave her a gown and asked her to undress. It was the final proof for her that he was not God. She almost hugged him in gratitude. She did not care whether he was a good or a bad doctor. It was enough for her that he was simply a human being.

She laid herself on his examining couch and he slipped on a pair of rubber gloves and went to work inside her. Now her fears of the Divine were replaced by others. She wondered whether she was the subject of professional rape. What had her morning sickness to do with his exploration of those regions that were the Devil's domain? She was tempted to scissor her legs closed and to trap his hand inside her, just to serve him right. But very shortly he was done. He took off the gloves and told her to get dressed. Her body tingled with a profound sense of let-down.

She went into the cubicle that adjoined his consulting room and dressed herself. She knew from his confident manner that his diagnosis, whatever it was, was sure and she braced herself for his verdict. She sat opposite him at his desk.

"It's good news, Lady Boniface," he said, though he did not smile, wondering how good she would find it. Veronica, for her part, didn't know what he was talking about and couldn't understand how the news of any disease, alarming or benign, could be deemed good. She looked at him quizzingly.

"You're pregnant," he said. "About seven weeks."

She didn't take it in at first. They were words presented to her. Single words with no ensemble. She heard the tap drip in the sink in the corner and she thought of her plumber, and then the totality of what Dr Truelove had said flooded her mind. Then something happened to her face. It creased, almost splitting itself in a smile and there was a leap in her heart, too, and she knew that never before and never again in her life would she know such joy.

"Are you sure?" she whispered.

"Absolutely. At your age," he said, "you're what we call an elderly first." He smiled at her. "We must monitor you carefully throughout your pregnancy. But don't worry. With care and caution, everything will be all right."

But Veronica was not listening to him. So overcrowding was her joy that she had no room for his words. She floated out of his consulting room taking the papers he pressed into her hand. In the street, she seemed to be flying. She gave no thought to the plumber and even less to how she would explain it all to the infertile Edward. She was pregnant. Soon she would be a mother. She walked down the street in her heaven-leagued boots and touched the sky.

Chapter Nine

She did not go back to Eaton Square. She went home. Home was Surbiton and the third drawer. When she married Edward, she insisted on keeping her family house. Not that Eaton Square was too small to house her belongings. It was large enough, with its bedrooms and drawing rooms and studies without number. But it was still too small to house the third drawer. And though silent and private, it was neither silent nor private enough. It echoed with the ghosts of others' wrongs, or others' neglect. Edward, if he so wished, could deal with all that. She had her own ghosts in Surbiton.

It was the first time she'd been back to the house since leaving it to get married. She went straight to the bathroom, the work site of her child's sire. She checked that the sink was still in working order. Although he would never be a father to her child, she hoped that at least he was a good plumber. That would be a skill worth inheriting. All was in order. Then she went to the spare room. It held no fears for her now. It had been the shrine of her mother's secrets, the rucksacks she had stealthily packed, the letters she had cunningly hidden. But now that same room held her own and terrible secret, and this shared conspiracy bound her to her mother with a sudden affection. She wished that she could talk to her again. But there was a way. There was a contact. She knew from some distant memory that her mother was surely the next item in the third drawer. And now she would go to it willingly. But first she showered and oiled herself and put on her black housecoat. Then she went to the study and, with no preamble, opened the drawer. In the beginning when, having found the key, she had first opened the drawer, she had noticed and had been alarmed by the thickness of the file and the density of the Furies that it held. Now it seemed to her slim and benign, and she withdrew the top document without fear. It was in fact, three papers clipped together, each clearly pertaining to the whole. She took them to the desk and unclipped the top sheet. It was a Xerox copy of a newspaper clipping. Central to the writing was her mother's picture, blackened by the ink of facsimile. It was barely recognizable. Veronica stared at it for a long time by way of postponing the matter of the copy. She had never seen that picture before. There was no discernible background that could have given her a clue as to location. It looked like a studio-posed portrait, but Veronica knew that her mother would never have submitted to that procedure. Certainly the look of sadness on her face was unstudied and unrehearsed, and the camera had recorded it with no apology. She began to read the accompanying text.

"The death was announced on Monday of Priscilla Kavanagh, the celebrated author and mountaineer."

Kavanagh. Her grandfather. That shadow in the doorway waiting for granny-underground's return. But Granny was no Kavanagh. Flora Kempsey, her obituary had read, after yet another shadowy figure in the doorway. Veronica's own obituary would read "Smiles" and thus her father would be commemorated. She read on.

"She was the author of six books, three of which were popular and best selling guides to climbing in the Swiss Alps. It was in this region that she learned and practised the art of mountaineering and there were few who knew the area more intimately. She died on the Northern slopes of the Himalayas, her first climbing attempt in this region. She was thirty-seven years old."

Veronica stopped short. She shivered with the brush of mortality. Within her own body there was life in its very beginnings. If the child were a girl, she would call it Priscilla. Children owe their parents nothing, any more than parents owe their children. What passes between them are gifts. No more, no less. Veronica would give her mother the gift of continuity.

There was one more paragraph to the obituary and Veronica read it slowly.

"Miss Kavanagh was a much loved and respected figure amongst the mountaineering fraternity. She will be greatly missed. She leaves a husband, Oliver Smiles, and an eight-year-old daughter, Veronica."

She shivered. "Leaves" was the exact word. Deserted. Her most painful rejection. And on opening the drawer, she had thought the remainder of the file benign. Now she knew that what was left inside would tear her heart in two. She read the obituary again and let the unaccustomed tears fall. There was something missing, she thought, and so patently omitted, that it seemed that there was something to hide. In all the words that were written, there was no indication of how her mother had died. Had she had a heart attack while climbing? Had she fallen? An unlikely possibility in one so experienced and expert as her mother. Or had she simply had enough? No. Not that. She must not think of that. She would rather never never know.

She folded the sheet and made to put it on her own file, adding to all that evidence that she had already so painfully culled from the drawer. But she paused. She wondered what her mother's obituary was doing in her father's file in the first place. Whose death was it after all? Did it not belong in her mother's file, that file in which she had found the key to uncover her death at all? To whom did her mother's death belong? Yet her father had coveted it, had taken it unto himself as his own. It was his, by right of his own complicity. It evidenced yet more of his guilt which littered his file. Poor mother, she thought, as she placed the obituary in her own file. But why in mine, she wondered. "I am not guilty," she whispered to herself. Yet she laid it there, knowing that it was its ultimate resting-place.

She looked at the second entry. It was a letter. The notepaper was headed and announced that it came from a Dr Fisher of Knightsbridge. The name rang a distant and painful bell. Then she remembered it. The voice at the end of the telephone when, as a child, she had eavesdropped through the kitchen door. She braced herself to read it.

"Dear Mr Smiles," the letter began. Clearly Dr Fisher was not intimate with her father. He had probably never even met him. "I write to tell you how devastated I am by Priscilla's sudden death, and to extend my sincere condolences to you and your family. I was with her shortly before she disappeared."

Veronica pulled herself up at the word. Her mother had not died. She had simply gone away and disappeared. Now she feared to read further, for her anger was brewing. Rage that her mother did not have to die, that Death had not come for her on the mountain, that she had volunteered herself into his reluctant arms. She forced herself to read on.

"It was an exquisite day. The sun had begun to set, and its rays had caught the shining surface of a rock just above our heads. Priscilla thought it beautiful and she told me she wanted to get closer, higher and closer to watch it finally disappear into the horizon. I did not accompany her. Sunset is a time when many mountaineers wish to be alone. She disappeared around the bend of the rock. I never saw her again. Her death was a mystery that will remain forever. Where she climbed, a matter of a few feet, presented no risk at all. I stood where I was until the sun went down and then I called her name. I heard no sound and after a while I followed her track. Her body lay some fifty feet below the rock ledge and for some reason that I cannot explain even to myself, it did not surprise me. We went to where she lay and we buried her where she fell. We were five of us there. Watson, Jones, Berry, White and myself. We were a broken, bewildered gathering. I think Priscilla would have liked her resting place. Her life and soul came from the mountains, and to those heights they were returned. I enclose a photograph of her grave and hope it will do a little to comfort you. My deepest condolences. Yours sincerely, Desmond Fisher."

But there **was** no photograph. She turned the sheet over, thinking that Dr Fisher might have Xeroxed it on the back. But it was blank. She was tempted to leaf through the rest of her father's file, but that would have been cheating and would have annulled the instalment principle that she had decided on when first opening the drawer. Perhaps her father had destroyed the photograph, finding it too painful a memento. It crossed her mind to seek out Dr Fisher, but she reckoned that after thirty years he might be dead and gone and his unexplained foresight along with him.

She turned to the last clipping of the entry, hoping that that would provide a clue. She presumed it was her mother's final letter to her father and she braced herself for the ordeal. She shut her eyes and unfolded the sheet and laid it on her desk. She kept her eyes shut. She was aware of prying, but she had pried before and, in the matter of the third drawer, it was too late for morals. She opened her eyes and saw that the letter was addressed to herself. There was small relief in that, for already she wondered why her mother had not written a farewell letter to her father, to whom it was most due. She did not feel privileged, rather she felt resentful and it was in this mood that she began her reading.

"My dearest Veronica," she read. "This will be a sad letter for you and I hope you will be grown-up before you read it. What I leave you, my dearest, is the most horrendous bequest a parent can leave to a child. I cannot ask you to understand me, since I don't understand myself, but if it is possible to forgive without understanding, that I earnestly hope you will be able to do. Do not blame your father. That would be too easy. Blame always is. It is but a temporary and unreliable source of comfort. But it is only when we cease to blame that we start to grow. Unlike myself, your father has a talent for loving. Be kind to him, for this will be sad for him too. Think kindly of me. I have no regrets except for the deep pain I bequeath you. Your loving mother."

She noticed how the letter trembled in her hand. Quickly, as if impelled, she went to the spare room and there leaned against the door, as she had leaned almost thirty years ago and seen her mother at her desk covering that same letter with her hand. She was dying, even then, and she had been caught red-handed.

Still at the doorpost, Veronica read the letter over, trying to imagine that she herself had written it, insinuating herself into her mother's despair. And as she did so she was overwhelmed with a love for her that was physically sore.

151

And anger too. A rage against her father whose philanderings had sent her mother to the mountain for the last time. And now she hated him. Now, in this moment, with she herself at her mother's death age, she hated him with that same fury when, all those years ago, he had pulled her by the hand, pigtailed and protesting, to her mother's memorial service at the Surbiton church. Then, at that time, she did not know the source of her anger. But she knew instinctively that her mother needn't have died. That her mother had fallen no more than Humpty Dumpty. It was simply that, like Humpty Dumpty, she had been pushed. And pushed by nobody on the spot. But by a pram, thousands of miles away in a Surbiton park. And by the woman who pushed it.

And then, to her horror, she actually saw her, sitting there in the church, brazen as brass in a back pew. Millicent Wayne, come to claim her due. Had her father invited her, Veronica wondered, then watched his face as they passed her down the aisle. She was relieved a little to find that it expressed astonishment and a hint of displeasure. Once past her, Veronica turned and poked out her tongue, and though the woman's eyes were closed, assuming mourning, Veronica felt relieved and certain that she had done it on behalf of her father. Mrs Dale shortly joined them, having stayed behind to put the finishing touches to a buffet lunch they were holding for a select gathering after the service. Veronica wondered whether the pram-lady would gatecrash that too. If she did, Veronica decided, if she were to take tea from her mother's cups, share conversation with her mother's friends, snoop in her mother's shadow, Veronica would simply kill her. Mrs Dale had a great cauldron in her kitchen, copper-bottomed, ornamental and hanging from the ceiling. Mrs Dale would without doubt, help her carry it, that tut-tutting look on her face, and together they would mash the pram-lady like an unseasoned potato. But better still, Veronica mused, they could together entice the pram-lady into the kitchen and stand her beneath her means of destruction, and then unhook it from the beam and thus save themselves a lot of trouble. She giggled at the thought and her father took it for uncontrollable grief. She looked around the church. On the other side of the aisle, in the front pew, the entire row was taken up by a group of men, all bearded, rough-hewn and solemn. They seemed to be a delegation of sorts.

Veronica nudged Mrs Dale and asked who they were.

"The mountain-men," she whispered, neutrally, with neither respect nor pleasure.

Behind her Veronica could see her father's business partners whom she knew by sight, having been taken to his office for treats. They, too, were bunched together in a row. The church was full of people whom Veronica didn't know and there was no point in asking Mrs Dale, who probably wouldn't have known either. In any case it would have been too noisy and Veronica suspected that this was an occasion for silent solemnity, and the music that suddenly came from nowhere confirmed that mood. When it was over, the priest mounted the pulpit.

"We are gathered here," he said, "to celebrate the brief but wonderful life of Priscilla Kavanagh, a woman of worth and virtue."

At this point Veronica heard sobbing and she turned with a child's forgivable curiosity to seek out its source. She was not surprised to find the pram-lady weeping into her hanky and she was outraged. What had her mother's death to do with that woman that she should weep for it? Except that she was the cause of it and was weeping now with remorse. But that was too kindly a thought. It was more probable that she was drawing attention to herself as a woman of more worth and virtue, worthy and virtuous enough to succeed. Such thoughts without words assailed her and she looked at Mrs Dale, who was crying with real and hot tears and without even a hanky to hide them. She thought she ought to cry too. But she did not feel sad. She thought she would not miss her mother, who had so rarely, in any case, been at home. But if anger could weep, then her tears would be a deluge. It's not fair, she wanted to scream, and to everybody, especially the pram-lady and the mountain men. But, above all, to her father. She looked at him. At least he wasn't crying. There was some refreshing honesty about his dry eye.

The priest droned on. "We weep for her," he said, "that she died in mortal sin."

Veronica didn't know what he was talking about and she

sensed, too, that her ignorance was a blessing. But she had her rights as her mother's child to know everything. She nudged Mrs Dale. "What's mortal sin?" she said angrily. She did not bother to whisper and her voice rang through the church. In response there was a sigh from the whole congregation. The priest heard the question, too, and hesitated, wondering whether he should offer an explanation. But they were, after all, in a house of God and since God gave life, it was only in His right to take it away.

"What *is* it?" The child's voice insisted again.

By now, it was asking everybody. The priest looked at the next sentence of his oration. "The Lord giveth and the Lord taketh away. *Only* the Lord." He decided to skip it.

"There are many here who wish to celebrate her," he went on, conscious of the non-sequitur. "Among them, her mountaineering companion Dr Desmond Fisher." Then he practically flew down the pulpit steps and made his get-away.

Veronica was nudging Mrs Dale again. "What is mortal sin?" she whispered, realizing by now that it was an un-answerable question.

"I'll tell you later," Mrs Dale said.

But Veronica wasn't satisfied. As Dr Fisher mounted the steps, she turned to her father and poked him cruelly in the side. Had she had a knife, she would have stabbed him.

"What did Mummy die of?" she whispered.

"A heart attack," he said. His wife's heart indeed had broken. It was undeniable.

"At the top of a mountain," Dr Fisher began, "we are very close to God. Our friend, Priscilla Kavanagh, facing death, would surely have chosen such a resting place. For many years we climbed together." Veronica's father took her hand, but Veronica snatched it away. She didn't want any interfer-ence of Dr Fisher's speech, for she too was hearing stories about her mother that she had never known. How she was as a teacher and how she had guided young hopefuls up the nursery slopes. How, too, she had established a fund for a mountaineering training school for the underprivileged. Veronica did not know the meaning of that word, but she sensed that it had to do with have-nots.

154

"Did you know that?" she whispered to Mrs Dale.

The woman shook her head, marvelling.

Veronica turned round to spot the have-nots, who too must have come in a delegation to honour her mother. But everyone was in their Sunday clothes, a leveller that made discernment difficult.

Dr Fisher was coming to the end of his speech. Veronica could tell because he had already closed his notebook and she noticed how another of the mountain men took some papers from his pocket and made ready to take Dr Fisher's place. She was getting very bored. And ashamed, too, that she was bored with her mother's memory. She wanted to go home and ride her bike. She wanted to have fun, not like all these miserable people in church. If she couldn't cry for her mother, why should they? There would come a time when she would cry. Round about Easter, when her mother was due home. It was only then, when she had concrete proof of her non-return, that she might shed a tear, but by then, time would have healed the wound that she'd barely felt inflicted.

The service dragged on, interrupted occasionally by the unseen choir. At last it ended and the assembly filtered down the aisle. Veronica kept her eye on the pram-lady. But she did not linger, as Veronica expected, but made her determined way out of the church. She hoped she would not be waiting outside. Her father took her hand once more and this time she clung to it, for she would hold on to him against all encroachers. She allowed him a few words of thanks to Dr Fisher and overheard that they would meet later at the house. Outside the church she looked around quickly, but there was no sign of the pram-lady. She was relieved when they got into the car and drove home. None of them spoke and they had almost reached the house when the silence was broken.

"What's mortal sin?" Veronica tried again.

Her father waited and hoped for Mrs Dale's reply, but Mrs Dale likewise of her father. Veronica took their silence for their ignorance.

"Don't you *know*?" she practically screamed at them. She had given them a let-out.

"No," her father said eagerly, and equally eagerly did Mrs Dale.

"Then I'll ask the priest," she said. "He said it. He must know."

"The priest isn't coming to the house," her father said with relief. "He's got another service."

"Someone else to remember?" Veronica said.

"That's right."

"Someone who died in mortal sin?"

"We don't know," Mrs Dale said, "because we don't know what it means." She was happy to stress their ignorance.

"Maybe it's something that they wear," Veronica suggested. "Like a nightie or something. Or pyjamas."

"Perhaps," her father said, allowing it to be anything on earth except that which it really was, and of his own terrible making.

Once home, Mrs Dale went straight to the kitchen and Veronica followed her.

"D'you think Dr Fisher would know about mortal sin?" Veronica asked.

"I don't know," Mrs Dale was nervous. "But if I were you, I wouldn't ask him. Just in case it's a nightie and that would embarrass him." She thought she'd acquitted herself rather well.

There were about twenty of them in all, but no sign of the pram-lady. Veronica was delegated to help hand around the drinks and sandwiches and she wondered how soon she could decently excuse herself and go out on her bike. She saw her father talking to Dr Fisher, and then he called her over and told her that Dr Fisher wished to see her mother's study.

"Would you show him, Veronica?" he asked.

For a moment she didn't know what he was talking about. Did her father mean the dining room perhaps, where her mother used to do her writing? Or did he mean the spare room? It had a desk in it certainly. But they'd never called it the study. It was the room where her mother packed and unpacked and occasionally slept. It was the site of Veronica's nightmares and had nothing to do with study. It was "spare", in all senses and could well, to everyone's profit, have been done without.

"All right," she said with reluctance. He must have meant the spare room, since they were standing in the dining room.

She started on the stairs, conscious of Dr Fisher's climbing tread echoing behind her. She opened the door, that leaning door of hers, and let him inside. She did not enter herself, but leaned against the door as was her wont. She thought it a dangerous room to enter. Even its threshold was a source of pain.

"Is this where your dear mother worked?" Dr Fisher said, fingering the top of the desk.

"Yes," she lied, wishing to make short work of it.

"She was a wonderful woman, your mother," Dr Fisher said.

"What's mortal sin?" she asked, throwing caution to the winds. If Dr Fisher thought her mother was wonderful, he wouldn't mind about nighties.

"There was nothing mortal about your mother," he said angrily. "And even less that was sinful. Priests should be forced to climb mountains," he said. "Then they would begin to understand God."

That settled it for Veronica. Whatever mortal sin meant, it certainly wasn't worth bothering about. She warmed towards Dr Fisher. She would have liked to ask him more about her mother, for she sensed that he probably knew her better than anybody. But that intimate knowledge, when questioned, could have led to all manner of disloyalty, so she held her tongue.

He looked at his watch. "It's time I went," he said suddenly. "I have to be somewhere."

He had nowhere to go, Veronica knew. He was anxious to get out of the room, away from her company, for he dreaded those very questions she had decided not to ask. She let him pass her through the door, but she stayed in the room, still leaning, fearful of entry.

As she was leaning now, thirty years later, with the rage against her father still seething. She looked at her watch. Four-thirty. For a moment she was disorientated, wondering what she was doing in this room and where she had come from. She wondered what she would do in the evening and why she wasn't in the desert. Then she realized with a shock that she was married and that she would have to go home, and that was in another place, a place to which the man she had married would shortly return from his office. Then the events of the morning crashed into her memory and for a moment her anger against her father abated. She recalled the doctor's diagnosis. She was to be a mother and, with new-found assertion, she left her leaning post, and entered the spare room. She sat at the desk, that site of decisions, and wondered for the first time what cock-and-bull story she could cook up for Edward. For there was no question of telling him the truth. It wasn't that she was afraid of losing him. She simply did not want to hurt him. The thought crossed her mind to pass the child as immaculate. Edward would believe anything. But God might take exception to that. He would consider it an act of poaching and, in her present state of fruitfulness, she did not want to risk offending Him. She would play it by ear, she decided, not knowing what, in the circumstances, that could result in. She was loath to leave her mother's desk. In fact she didn't really want to go home at all. Since she felt she was already in it. And in any case, she had business to attend to. There was more in the third drawer, information that might help to abate that father anger that was slowly creeping back on her. Eaton Square was a nuisance, and an explanation to Edward an interference in the serious business of her explorations. Still, she owed it to him at least to tell him the news and to invent some fairy tale that would entail his participation in the result. She took Dr Fisher's letter, together with her mother's and placed them in her own file. Then she turned on the central heating. The house needed warmth after its long vacancy. She was going back to the other place only for a little while. Shortly she would return and get on with her own affairs.

"I'll be back," she said, as she closed the front door.

She took a cab to Eaton Square. She tried to think of her baby as a means of off-setting her rage. The reading of her mother's letter and the recollection of the memorial had left her bitter in the extreme. Her mother had written that to blame was futile. But it was natural, too. She had to lay blame, if only for a while, before she could come to terms with her mother's painful bequest. She hated her father now with that same childish intensity that she had felt when he'd told her that her mother was never coming back from the mountain. She'd gone to God, he had said. She hated God too, and had done so ever since, for appropriating for Himself that which belonged to her. If only her father had told her that her mother had gone to the Devil, her subsequent life might have been smoother, for its absence of God-encounters. She fidgeted at the back of the cab. She ached to recapture her joy of that morning when she had left the doctor's rooms. But that she could only do once she had effected some armistice with her father, an interim truce during which she would cease to blame him.

The cab drew up at Eaton Square. She rang the doorbell. She could never bring herself to use the key. Such a gesture would have spelt ownership to which she did not feel entitled. Margaret would always answer the door quizzingly and then Veronica would have to explain that she couldn't find her key. It had become a colluding drama between them.

"Is Edward home?" she asked.

"Not yet," Margaret said. She avoided any appellation as often as she could. "But there's a fire in the drawing room. Shall I bring you some tea?"

"That would be lovely, Margaret," Veronica said, and meant it, for it would give her a soothing time to rehearse a poppycock story. But nothing occurred to her, except the thought that she would not tell him at all, and go away quietly to the desert and gently drop her baby in the sand. But how to leave innocent Edward? Perhaps she ought to be thinking of an explanation for that. She heard his key in the door and she trembled. He never called her name from the hall. He would seek her out and, then, face to face, greet her, as he did now, coming into the drawing room.

"I love getting home nowadays," he said, "knowing that you'll be here."

"I've news for you, Edward," she said, and then could have bitten her tongue on her lack of rehearsal.

"Good news?" he asked.

"*I* think so."

"Then I'll think so too."

"Would you like some tea?" she asked, stalling.

"Please."

She poured him a cup and settled down opposite him by the fire. It was undeniably her move.

"What would you like best in the world?" she asked, hearing how inane such a question was but hopefully temporizing still.

"Just for you to be happy," he said, Edward could temporize too.

"Well, my news makes me happy," she said, defeated.

He waited for her to tell him. There was nothing more he could contribute.

"I'm . . ." she started, then lyingly emended, "we're going to have a baby."

He was silent. She tried to read his face. She looked first for suspicion there, but found no trace. Then slowly she saw his wonder as his face creased into a smile. He was glad of the baby. That in itself was enough. Perhaps he didn't even care how it got there.

"Are you sure?" he said.

"The doctor confirmed it this morning. Seven weeks, he said. I worked it out. It must have been our last night in Paris. You remember. The night we dined at Maxime's."

She saw relief on his face then, as if he had been making a private reckoning, realizing that she had not really been out of his sight, day nor night, during the whole of that period.

"I can hardly believe it," he said.

She saw a tear spring to his eye. She crossed over to him and held his hands. "D'you remember when you told me about your mumps?" she said. "You said the doctors told you a baby would be one chance in a million. We've had that chance, my darling." She felt a heel.

"A miracle," he said, and he held her close and she thought of her plumber and, though she had entirely forgotten what he looked like, she hoped to God that her baby would not resemble him.

"We must tell Margaret," Edward said. "She'll be over the moon."

Veronica had not reckoned on Margaret. With her it would not be such an easy passage. But Edward had already left the room and, contrary to his habit, he was calling Margaret's name from the hall. She heard Margaret's shuffling tread.

"Come, my dear," she heard Edward's voice. "We've something to tell you."

There could be no stalling with Margaret, but Veronica knew that a lifetime of rehearsal would result in nothing that would convince Margaret that her Edward was father to a child. Veronica would do her best to avoid her eye.

Margaret entered nervously. She expected some intimate disclosure.

"You tell her, Veronica," Edward said.

"No. It's your news, darling. It really is your achievement."

"Can you guess, Margaret?" Edward was giggling with pleasure.

Margaret shook her head, bewildered.

"We must make a toast together," Edward said, and he went to the cabinet and poured three glasses of pale sherry from the decanter.

Veronica wished he wouldn't make such a fuss. All this paraphernalia seemed to compound the monstrous deceit. He handed the glasses round, then raised his own high.

"To our baby," he said. His voice broke in his excitement.

Margaret's glass trembled in her hand. She was staring into space, as if transported. Which indeed she was, right back into Edward's bedroom shortly after he had returned from hospital. She'd settled him with a sleeping pill and the doctor was just leaving. She'd followed him into the hall. "He'll be fine," Dr Wyndham had said. "A week in bed and he'll be as right as rain."

"Doctor . . ." She had touched his shoulder. "Will he . . . ? Will . . . ?" He'd known her question and sensed her embarrassment. "No," he had said. "It's highly unlikely. I would say it's totally impossible. But it's not the end of the world," he'd comforted her. "He could always adopt." And as she stood there in the drawing room, her glass trembling in her hand, she looked at Veronica and dared her to meet her eye.

"Seven weeks," Edward was saying. "A miracle."

But Margaret needed no pocket calculator and she didn't believe in miracles. She lifted her glass to her lips and sipped.

"That's wonderful news," she said, with a total absence of

enthusiasm and Edward ascribed her mood to a natural pique and he put his arms around her. She gulped at her sherry, then she disentangled herself from Edward's embrace and hurriedly left the room. Did she, once in her sitting room, give herself up to her sorrow that her Edward had been so grossly deceived? But Veronica knew that never, never would she utter a word.

"Once she gets used to it, she'll be very excited," Edward said. "It's a bit of a shock to her. Almost as much as it is to me. Tonight I shall take you to dinner," he said. "This is really worth a celebration."

Veronica had hoped to go back to Surbiton. Her urge to return to the third drawer was imperative. The thought of her baby had already become secondary. She was sure that the clue to all her dilemmas lay begging in the next entry in the drawer. A clue that would finally get God off her back and allow her to live in peace. But there was no getting out of Edward's need to celebrate. She would have to contain herself until morning.

"We'll say nothing to Mother," Edward said. "We'll wait a little, until it's noticeable."

She was grateful for that. Edward's mother would be a hurdle as insurmountable as Margaret.

It was a Friday, ladies' night at Edward's club, so they dined at the Savile. Edward had many friends there and all evening he kept his news manfully on the tip of his tongue. Over dinner, Veronica viewed him with a mixture of affection and pity. He had been totally duped into paternity. When they returned to Eaton Square, they found a thermos of cocoa on the drawing room table. It had been many years since Margaret had made that nightcap gesture. It was her vain attempt to ship her Edward back into the nursery, talcummed and fresh from his bath, the rocking horse in the corner, his voice unbroken, long, long before his mumps and this woman who had so traduced him. Veronica got the message. Margaret was not hoodwinked. One day she would have to tell her the truth.

"What shall we call our baby?" Edward said as they made for bed.

Again she deferred to him.

"I'd like Albert if it's a boy," he said. "After my father. Or James. That was his second name. I like Alastair too."

She let him ramble on. Her baby was going to be a girl. And she would call it Priscilla. In memory of her mother.

Chapter Ten

In the morning, shortly after Edward left for the office, Veronica took the train to Surbiton. It had not been difficult to avoid Margaret, for during breakfast Margaret had kept herself strictly out of the way. But her attitude was unnerving. Her incredulity was no surprise but it was depressing. Edward's ready acceptance, likewise. Veronica found them both unpalatable. On the train to Surbiton, her mood was one of despair. On top of everything else, she was no longer angry, a feeling that might have offset her depression. Overnight her anger had abated and now she looked forward to her Surbiton exploration only with fear of what she should discover. She was not comforted when she entered her study and found God waiting for her. She hadn't seen Him since the honeymoon when, on the Place du Tertre, passing as an artist, He had so brazenly taken her for a ride. On account of that last meeting, she did not feel well-disposed towards Him.

"Oh you again," she said coldly.

His look frightened her. It was one she'd not seen before. His face was creased with wrath and indignation.

"What do you want?" she whispered.

He opened His mouth and she knew there would be thunder.

"Where is Oliver thy brother?"

His breath was fire.

"How should I know?" She tried bravado. "Am I my half-brother's keeper?"

He turned from her and went to the door. "Nobody makes a mockery of my story," He said quietly, and He was gone.

She wanted to follow Him, not so much for His company, but to get out of that room, and out of the house and Surbiton and to put a million miles between herself and the third drawer. But she knew there was no escape. Not any more. Even the desert would offer her no shelter. God might as well have turned the key in her study door. Only her answer to His offended question could unlock it now.

She resigned herself and slowly opened the drawer.

A note was on top, unfiled. She swore she hadn't seen it the day before. It was probably from God. Wearily she pulled it out.

"If I were you," she read, "I wouldn't investigate further."

She examined the note closely. It was written undeniably in her own hand and not for the first time did she fear for her reason. Now more than ever it was imperative to get rid of God. Only an empty drawer would send Him back where He came from. She crumbled the note and pulled the drawer out to its full length. Her manner was of courage and fearlessness, but inside she was weeping like a baby. She withdrew the top paper in the file. A document of sorts. Folded, legal and black. She took it to her desk and opened it out. She heard and felt the loud beating of her heart, and she thought it might beat itself into smithereens by the time the document was absorbed. But she didn't care. She just prayed it would not injure her baby. She spread the document on her desk. A death certificate. Of one Oliver Smiles, aged eighteen months. Dated December 19th 1958. Veronica shivered with fear as she forced herself to confront that winter's day, thirty years ago, when, trembling with the cold, she had played snowballs in the park with her father. And as she re-entered her childhood, all her anger returned.

It was the first time they'd been alone together since her mother had died. Her father had used the snow to lure her to the park with the promise of a snowman that he would build for her and swoops down the slippery slides and rides on the swings.

"No, not the swings," she pleaded.

"All right, no swings," he said.

It was a bright day and, despite the thick snow on the ground, it was exhilarating. There were many people in the park and Veronica cast a frantic eye amongst them. But there was no sign of the swing-lady. Her father set about building the snowman. He chose a spot outside the swing area, underneath a bare oak tree. There were better sites to choose, she thought, places where snow had already drifted into piles, ready-made torsos and heads. But her father insisted on that spot, and kept looking round about him as if he were being watched. He built a castle of snow and asked her to go and find pebbles, matching pebbles, he insisted, both in size and colour, that would do for buttons on the snowman's coat.

"We shall have the best-dressed snowman in the park," he joked with her.

She went off, glad to be on her own. She didn't particularly want to go back to him, so she didn't take the pebble hunt seriously. As she wandered off, further into the park, she heard him calling. Her name rang through the trees with no foliage to mute its call. It sounded cruel and angry, and hurriedly she picked up a few pebbles, not caring about their shape and size. Then, with a random handful, she turned and walked sullenly back to where she had left him. From the distance she could see a large body of snow and her father was standing beside it. He was not working on it. He was looking about him. Not for Veronica whom he had already seen in the distance. He had actually waved to her, but nevertheless continued his search. After a while Veronica saw him raise his hand as if to signal to somebody. She hid behind a tree and waited. In her now restricted vision, she could see only her father but, even from her distance, she observed a wide grin spread over his face and, shortly, a pram came into her view and, behind it, the swing-lady. Her father took her hand and kissed her cheek, bold as brass in the middle of the crowded park, and barely a month after her mother had died. Now her hatred was fed, and not only for her father, but for the whole sordid trio of them. She wanted to go home. But he called her name again and she wished he wouldn't shout it so that

166

everyone in the park would know. Now she hated him for everything he was and did. His very being offended her. She wished that he was dead. She dragged her feet towards them.

"Come along," her father called. "The snowman's cold. He wants to button his coat."

The woman beside him laughed and so did he. Perhaps the baby was laughing, too. Veronica alone didn't find it funny. Then she saw her father bend over the pram and tickle whatever was inside. She wanted to be sick. There would be a fever soon and another visit from Dr Bruton, but no more promises of mother coming home. She wondered what anyone could now give her to make her better. In time she reached them.

"This is my friend Millie," her father said. "Say Hello nicely."

She said Hello nicely as she was bid.

"And this is little Oliver." He pointed to the pram.

Little Oliver? she thought. Were Olivers ever little? She looked at the pram. It was a smaller pram than the one she remembered, with a bigger thing inside it, filling it up almost, muffled in blankets and furs. Its face was framed in a woolly cap and it was asleep.

"Why don't you get him up, Millie?" her father said. "Let him run around a bit."

"I've just put him down," the woman said. "I'd like him to sleep for a while."

"Later on," her father said, "we'll go back to the house for tea and he can play with Veronica."

Whose house? Veronica wondered. Her mother's house? And Mrs Dale gone to see her brother.

"I'll tell Mrs Dale," she whispered. It was a vain enough threat and her father didn't hear her.

"Why don't you take Oliver for a walk around the park? Is that all right, Millie?" her father asked.

"Of course, if she'd like to," the woman said.

"I don't want to."

"You can pretend it's your own baby," her father said, "and by the time you get back, I'll have finished the snowman."

She threw her handful of pebbles at his feet. Then placed

her hands on the pram-handle. It was better to be away from them, even if she had to take the baby with her.

They put her steadily on the path. In doing so, the woman touched Veronica's hand. It felt like a snake and Veronica shuddered.

"Are you cold, dear?" the woman said.

She shook her head, not trusting her voice, and pushed the pram along the path.

"Keep to the path, dear."

That awful "dear" again. Veronica pushed. The baby was facing her. It looked a bit like a doll, with rosy cheeks and pursed mouth. She liked playing at being grown-up and here were all the tools to hand. But she took no pleasure in it. The game of Mothers and Fathers required at least three players, two parents and one offspring, but in this little drama, the role of father was unplayable. Another pram-pusher passed her on the path. She paused and looked at Veronica's load.

"Your sister, is it?" the woman said.

"Yes." It was easier to think of the doll as a girl.

"Pretty little thing," the woman said, and went on her way.

She pushed the pram to the end of the path, then turned. Her father and the swing-lady were building the snowman together, working on the head, the torso between them. They leaned either side of it, meeting at the top, like two sides of a triangle. Again she thought of her mother and, when her father looked up and waved to her, she did not respond. She couldn't bear to see him so happy. She turned the pram and took the path that lay at right angles. At the end of it was the deserted bandstand. In the summer, boys would gather there, and girls would wander in pairs around its circle and pretend not to notice them. But now only a few dogs played there, ignoring the occasional whistle from their owners. She walked on. She wanted to look round again, but she was afraid of what she might see. She would wait until she reached the end of the path, then turn. At a greater distance, whatever they were doing would be modified. She started to hum. The tune of *Miss Susie had a Baby*, came through her lips. But she didn't say the words. Because she was alone, they frightened her. She would sing them with Emily when they played Mothers and Fathers. The words were easy then because of the shared responsibility. Now she would just make do with the tune. It took two renderings before she reached the end of the path. Then she paused and dared to turn. At the side of the finished snowman, she saw two figures closely entwined and, from the red scarf round the neck, she knew that one of them was her father. She turned quickly, manoeuvred the pram off the path and crossed over the grass towards the bandstand. As she did so, still humming, the words filtered into the melody.

> "*Miss Susie had a baby,*
> *She called him Tiny Tim.*"

And then she started humming again, as the words refused. She was itching to turn round once more, but forced herself to reach the bandstand before she would do so. She hurried, pushing the pram. The baby murmured a little, then settled. At the bandstand steps, she turned. They were exactly in the same position, as if frozen. Then the words surfaced once more.

> "*Miss Susie had a baby,*
> *She called him Tiny Tim.*
> *She put him in the bath tub,*
> *To see if he could swim.*"

Then she hummed again, as the words refused once more. She pushed the pram round the back of the bandstand, from which point, even if she turned and stared, she would see no more of them. The baby whimpered again. She looked at it. It was shifting and seemed to be waking up. Once more she sang to it and the words volunteered.

> "*Miss Susie had a baby,*
> *She called him Tiny Tim.*
> *She put him in the bath tub,*
> *To see if he could swim.*
> *He drank up all the water,*
> *He swallowed up the soap,*
> *He died, poor little fellow,*
> *With a bubble in his throat.*"

She began to rock the pram, not wishing the baby to wake, and lapsed once again into humming. Soon it would be Christmas, she thought, and her mother would not come home from the mountain. And after that Easter, and still her mother wouldn't come home. Then her mouth was chock-a-block full of the words and she sang aloud.

> *"In came the doctor,*
> *In came the nurse,*
> *In came the lady*
> *With the alligator purse."*

Over and over again she sang it as she took the pillow from under the baby's head and placed it gently over his face. Then she pressed, singing all the while.

> *"Dead said the doctor,*
> *Dead said the nurse,*
> *Dead said the lady*
> *With the alligator purse."*

Then she sang it all through all over again, because her mouth was still full of the words and her mother would never come home from the mountain. If the baby whimpered she did not hear, but she kept the pillow there, pressing with all her strength. Then she heard them call her name. So lost was she in her song and its accompanying drama that for a moment she wondered who Veronica was. Then, remembering, she turned the pram and cornered the bandstand so that she would be in their view. Her father, unsoldered this time, waved to her and she waved back, pushing the pram meanwhile. She wondered why she felt so happy and what the pillow was doing on the baby's face. She stopped pushing for a moment and took the pillow away, tucking it under the baby's head. His little face was blue and his tongue was sticking out of his mouth. He must be very cold, she thought, so she tucked the blanket around him.

> *"Dead said the doctor,*
> *Dead said the nurse,*
> *Dead said the lady*
> *With the alligator purse."*

She sang it solemnly now, like an anthem, slowly and in marching rhythm, and she had just swallowed the last syllable when she reached her father and the swing-lady.

"He's gone a bit blue," she said. "He must be cold."

The swing-lady looked into the pram and screamed aloud. So loudly and with such terror, that the park stopped singing, snowballs froze midair and snowmen shivered, astonished.

Her father went to the pram then and gave a moaning sound that didn't seem grown-up at all. Then he laid his mouth over the baby and panted into his little body, his face rinsed in tears, sudden icicles from the eye. Veronica watched, fascinated. Then he raised his head. "Come quickly," he said, and taking the woman's arm, and pushing the pram, he almost carried her from the park. Veronica stood there. He did not call to her or include her in their cosy little party, but she followed because she had nowhere else to go. She had to run to keep up with them, the woman screaming all the while, her feet dragging beside the pram. People stared at them as they passed. Once they stopped and Veronica was able to catch up with them. The woman turned on her. "What have you done? You monster!" she screamed.

Her father clapped his hand over the woman's mouth.

"Don't say that," he said, his voice breaking. "Never, never say that."

"Dead said the doctor."

Veronica sang to herself. She knew she must not sing it aloud.

At last they reached the house. Once inside, her father went to the telephone and the woman picked up the baby from the pram. She could not look at its face but hid it against her breast, stroking its head the while. Then her father came from the telephone and enfolded the two of them in his arms, and together they wept, almost silently.

Veronica left them and went to her room. On her way she passed the open spare room door and leaned against it, her eye on her mother's desk, and she thought she saw her again, quickly covering a letter with her hand. She heard the doorbell, and crept towards the banister and peeped over. Dr Bruton was there, and her father and the swing-lady and the baby, still entwined. Dr Bruton looked between them and shook his head.

Veronica went to her room and lay on the bed.

"In came the doctor,"

she started to sing,

> *"In came the nurse,*
> *In came the lady*
> *With the alligator purse."*

And then aloud, for she didn't care who heard:
> *"Dead said the doctor,*
> *Dead said the Dad,*
> *And the silly swing-lady*
> *Was very very sad."*

She was pleased with herself. Perhaps, she wondered, when she grew up, she might be a poet. She fell asleep on such a thought, but soon woke, startled, as if from a nightmare, a nightmare that for thirty years had appalled her soul.

Veronica stared at the black certificate. Was it all over now, she wondered. Would God in all His mercy now go away and leave her alone? She folded the certificate and put it in her file. Before closing the drawer, she looked at what was left. Not much. A few papers, it seemed. But she could not explore further. That last discovery had wrung her dry. And after that, how could there be more? Why should her punishment be so relentless? How much longer would she have to atone? Then she heard a still small voice. He didn't even bother to put in an appearance.

"It's not over yet," He said. "Not yet. You know it."

She closed the drawer. She was tempted to lock it and throw away the key. But she knew that God would haunt her forever and that was no way to live. He would midwife her baby; He would shadow it to school; and one day, in a fit of pique, one of those to which He was so often prone, He might tell on her. She left the key in the lock and went quickly from the house. There was a small relief in leaving it all behind. I won't go back for a while, she decided. Maybe I'll wait until after the baby is born.

She took the train back to London. A cab would have been too easy. Too quick. And she needed time. Time to cushion that collision with her present reality. For that was the true and astonishing meaning of Eaton Square, and somehow or other, she would have to come to terms with it. She had just missed a train and was glad of it, for it meant a twenty minute wait at the station. But given the time, she did not know what to do with it. One did not need time to think since it was not an act that other activities could interfere with. Time was no help in clearing the mind nor in lending perspective to a dilemma.

She did not need time. She needed courage. The courage to tell Edward the truth. But even given that strength she knew how Edward would accept it. With equal courage and infuriating decency, he would offer to adopt as he'd already suggested before they were married. He would even rejoice that it was only a partial adoption. But would she feel any better for it? Was that really the truth she wished to tell him? Was it not rather the truth about herself and why, if she had a son, she would wish to call him Oliver? But it was too soon for all that. The third drawer was not yet empty. And, when it was, perhaps the only truth she could give Edward was simply to go away from him, leaving him no outlet for decency or reconciliation. That's what she would do, she decided, and she needed no more time, so she left the station and took a cab to Eaton Square. Having made the decision, she felt easier and now it was only a question of one last journey to the drawer. Then at least she would be clean and even God would find her unsullied enough to leave alone. She ached for her pre-God days, when no nudging thought disturbed the even tenor of her life, when to be motherless was simply to have lost a mother and when to be a spinster was simply not to be married. No innuendos, no subtitles. Just a simple orphaned unmarried lady scouring the desert. And the sooner she got back to that, she decided, the better. But for a desert return, she must wait for her baby to be born. And that was reality, too, the one happy reality with which she could come to terms.

When she got back to Eaton Square, she used her own key to let herself in. Not that she felt any more entitled to ownership, but she was nervous of having to face Margaret in the hall. She knew that Margaret had not been taken in by the baby story, that she knew that whatever Veronica was carrying was certainly no Boniface. In her eyes, it was simply a conception that had been perfectly timed. Veronica would have to brazen it out. And on her own. Edward would doubtless defend her, but that would be too painful. She tiptoed through the hall and went straight to the drawing room. She was surprised to find Margaret in there, making up the fire, and Jonathan, his back to her, taking tea. "Let me do

173

that, Margaret," he said, as she stretched for a log. And in doing so he turned, and caught sight of Veronica at the door.

"Veronica," he said. He seemed pleased to see her and for a moment she thought that perhaps she had misjudged the reason for his call. For when she had first seen him, the back of him, she sensed she was interrupting a conversation about herself and that Margaret had broken the news. He came towards her.

"Just in time for tea," he said. "I was in the area. Thought I'd pop in. Have a look at the old home."

It was then that Veronica knew that he was lying. Jonathan was not a "popping-in" man. He was strictly by appointment. His lie had been for Margaret's benefit. He had come to see Veronica privately and this clearly he was about to do as Margaret quickly left the room.

On her way out, she managed to whisper to Veronica, "I didn't tell him."

Jonathan poured her tea and waited for her to settle herself. Then, with small interval, he said, "Saw Dr Truelove last night at my club. He's an old friend of mine."

Her heart sank. What a piece of monstrous bad luck, she thought, that of all the carefully compiled list of doctors she should have chosen a friend of her brother-in-law.

"Oh yes?" she said, her voice steady.

"Congratulated me," he said, not taking his eyes off her. "Was surprised I didn't already know."

She looked at him straight in the eye. "I hope you're pleased, Jonathan," she said.

"Well, let me put it this way," he smiled. "I'm more puzzled than pleased."

She wished he would sit down. Towering over her, he clearly had an advantage.

"Puzzled?" she said.

"More than puzzled," he repeated. "Flabbergasted, to be exact. According to the doctor's reports, it is impossible for Edward to father a child."

"Not quite impossible," Veronica said. "The doctor said there was a chance in a million." As she said it, she thought what a silly phrase it was. Like the first line of a pop song and thus immediately unbelievable. "We've been given that

174

chance," she added, and that sounded lamely like the second line.

"I don't believe it," he said. Jonathan was not a man to mince words. "Think it only fair to warn you," he added, "I shall insist on a blood test."

"Of course. If you wish," she said. And then she realized how stupidly she was behaving. If she were indeed telling the truth, she would hardly take his insinuations so calmly. So with a simulated frisson of anger, she rose and faced him.

"I am seven weeks pregnant," she said. "I'm sure your friend gave you all the details. I have been married to Edward for just over seven weeks."

He walked towards the door. "A man cannot keep his eye on a woman every minute of the night and day," Jonathan said, and Veronica felt infinite pity for his poor wife.

"I assure you," he said when he reached the door, "that if I am proved in error, I shall be the first to apologize. I'll see myself out," he said, opening the door.

She heard Edward's key in the lock. It would be an untimely collision, but there was little that she could do about it.

"Jonathan," she heard Edward say. "Why are you running off?"

"Must rush, Edward," he said. "I've got an appointment. Just popped in to see the old home."

"Do stay," Edward said. "Have some tea."

"Already had it. With Veronica. See you."

Then she heard the front door close. She decided to say nothing to Edward. She could rely on Jonathan holding his tongue at least until a propitious moment. She was floundering in a sea of lies by omission and she wondered how long she could withstand it.

Edward kissed her and asked after her day. Had she been busy?

"I didn't do very much," she said. I just happened to kill my brother this morning was on the tip of her tongue. It had seemed to her very much like this morning. The pain of that death was still very raw. "I did a little work on my book," she lied. "And you?"

"The usual routine," he said. "I have to go to Bordeaux next week. Would you like to come?"

"Yes," she answered straightaway. She didn't want to be left alone in the house with Margaret and open to attack from Jonathan whenever he chose to pop in. Besides, she might be tempted back to Surbiton and the drawer and, though she knew she had to empty it before God would leave her, she was dimly aware of the high cost of its final clearance and she was not ready for that.

"That's lovely," Edward said. "We go on Tuesday and we can stay over the weekend. Mother phoned me today," he added without pause. "She's coming up on Friday. Wants to try a new hairdresser, Pierre's."

"Pierre's?" Even Veronica had heard of it. "But that's very trendy. Hardly for your mother."

"Perhaps she wants a change."

"It's more than a change. It's a drop-out."

Edward laughed. "Anyway, I asked her for dinner. Is that all right?"

"Of course," Veronica said. "It'll be lovely to see her." But thought quite otherwise. This sudden influx of Bonifaces pointed to a conspiracy of a kind.

"Shall we invite others?" she asked, by which she meant non-family whose presence would disallow any discussion relating to inheritance.

"I thought Jonathan might like to come. With Flora."

Flora was Jonathan's appendage on whom one's eye could not be kept every minute of the day and night. Married to Jonathan for fifteen years, with four sons, she was sufficiently entrenched in the Boniface clan to consider herself born into it. She would be no ally of Veronica's.

"If you like," she said limply. She could not deny Edward his family.

"Keep it a family dinner," he said.

"What about James and Helen?" she asked. James was the youngest Boniface and had nothing to lose in the inheritance stakes. He might even take her side.

"They're going to the country for the weekend," Edward said.

That left her alone and utterly defenceless, her only

armoury a brazen face and a brazen lie, and the indignant support of Edward that would only serve to disarm her. And certainly God would be there, in some form or another, and there was little doubt which side He'd be on. To say nothing of Margaret, that infinitely hovering, infinitely silent majority. She dreaded Friday and for a moment she thought she might retreat to Surbiton, or even flee to the desert to avoid the supper party.

On the Friday morning she ventured into the kitchen, in a vain bid, without words, to get Margaret on her side. She covered her visit by an offer to help, to cook some part of the meal perhaps, by way of asserting herself as hostess. Margaret was not pleased with her presence in her domain. Her infinite politeness verged on freezing point. But Veronica would not budge.

"May I watch you?" she asked. "I'm sure I could learn something."

"If you wish, Miss Veronica," Margaret said.

"I've never learned to cook. I've never really had to." Veronica thought she might try being chatty. "In the desert, it's mainly survival cooking. There's not much call for haute cuisine." She hoped that, with that introduction, Margaret might ask her about the desert, or at least what survival food was made of. But Margaret affected no reaction. She simply continued beating eggs in a bowl.

"My mother never cooked either," Veronica tried again.

Margaret beat the eggs as if they had offended her. It was like talking to a stone wall.

"Why don't you like me, Margaret?" Veronica played her last card.

And at last there was a reaction. No words. Just a small but highly visible frisson. But she gave the eggs no respite. "That's nonsense Miss Veronica," she said.

"I have that impression though."

"You are wrong," Margaret said, and set about attacking the eggs again.

Impasse. The conversation had closed itself. Veronica went to the door, defeated. "Has it got something to do with the baby?" she asked.

Margaret did not reply, but her silence was answer enough.

Veronica went back to her room. She would make no more overtures. She would simply have to weather the day. She started to work on her book, and by some God-given grace she was able to lose herself in it and to know that it was the only thing that mattered not only in her own life, but in everyone else's too. While writing she achieved that egotistical arrogance that is a writer's imperative. So much so, that when Edward returned in the early evening she was furious with his interruption and she had to recall that there was a further engagement that day which would keep her from her desk. Now it was the simple nuisance value of the dinner party that disturbed her. All thoughts of what the dinner might entail seemed peripheral and she began to regard the whole Boniface sense of exclusivity with contempt. But that feeling did not extend to Edward. She greeted him with genuine warmth. He was an ally after all, albeit a misguided one. But it was too late to tell him the truth. She had already abused him by lying to him in the first place. Margaret was right about her. She was a deceiver. She put her arms around him and kissed him lovingly. It was her only way of asking his forgiveness without him knowing what she craved.

"It smells good," Edward said. "What's Margaret cooking?"

"A secret I think," Veronica said. "I offered to help but I had a feeling I was not welcome in the kitchen."

"I don't wonder," he said. "It's her domain. Always has been."

"It suits me," Veronica said. "I spent the whole day on the book."

"Good," he said. "Can I see it sometime?"

"You wouldn't make much sense of it, I'm afraid."

"Well, I'm going to have a try. After all, our child may take after you. He may become a writer. I want to make sure he's got a good model."

He was punishing her with his decency. Alongside it, even Jonathan's priggishness was preferable. Edward was compounding the lie she so brazenly had given him, as if he were doing it on purpose. She wondered about that. Edward was decent enough for that too.

"Shall we change," he said. It was no question. It was his way of telling her that they must dress for dinner. And dress with the severest formality.

Veronica wore a long black silk that Edward had bought her in Paris. She looked very skinny in it, she thought, but Edward liked her that way. "You look like a young boy," he had told her, and with a certain ambivalent pleasure. She wondered how he would view her as her pregnancy progressed. But she would not stay long enough to find out, she reminded herself.

They had a while alone before their guests were due. Veronica felt she was playing a part in a drawing room play. She was standing on the set, with Edward, her leading man. Shortly the bit-players of the subplot would enter and the interval curtain would come down on crisis. And there was no way she could get out of the second act. She shivered as the doorbell rang.

She heard Margaret's steps in the hall and the whispered polite greetings at the door. There were several voices and she presumed that the Bonifaces had arrived en famille, a united front. Neither she nor Edward moved. It was not done to anticipate their welcome. Margaret opened the drawing room door and all but announced them. The way was cleared for the entry of Lady Boniface, the real one, she who had gone to the altar in divinely sanctioned white and of whose male progeny there was no sliver of doubt. Jonathan and Flora followed her, in Indian file at a strangers' distance. There seemed to be very little connection between any of them, as if they had never met before and, as they accepted their drinks, Veronica wondered whether she should introduce them to each other. Flora admired Veronica's dress and Veronica did the same for her. Edward complimented his mother on her hair and she on his general appearance.

"Marriage seems to suit you Edward," she said. It was her single acknowledgement of Veronica and Veronica wondered whether Jonathan had already tipped her off. The drinks were sipped and Veronica thought of approaching the night-and-day Flora, not in an attempt to win her to her side – there was little hope of that – but as a woman-to-woman gesture of friendship. But she seemed glued to Jonathan's side. Any contact with Flora would have to include he who was keeping an eye on her and Veronica preferred her own isolation.

Lady Boniface was asking Edward about his honeymoon, as if he'd been on it alone, and Edward launched into a recital of a journey which seemed utterly different from the one Veronica had shared with him. Perhaps this was the version for the family, with its culture stress on churches, museums and places of historical interest. It all sounded uncommonly dull. In the whole of his telling, there was not one moment of fun.

"You and Father went to Italy, if I remember, Mother," Edward concluded, wishing to give her the floor she always wanted. And of which she was to take full advantage.

"We started in Milan and ended in Naples," she began. Veronica was delighted with her itinerary, for the length of that journey would take them well into dinner and, perhaps with luck, with a detour or two, right through it, and the risk of mention of her little illegal surprise would be minimized. She looked at her mother-in-law and affected an air of profound interest. But to her dismay, in less than no time, they had reached Rome. So uneventful seemed that honeymoon, that there was little to report save the starting and stopping of trains at various stations. Or perhaps it had simply been unmemorable. With Sir Albert, she had just arrived at Naples station. Veronica heard what sounded like the finale of her recital unless she was going to itemize all the stations on the way home. Oh please, please, stick around Naples for a while, she inwardly begged her.

But Lady Boniface had suddenly paused in her itinerary. She looked around the small assembly and on her face was a smile of recollected joy. "I remember Naples most of all," she said. Veronica breathed with relief. It looked as if they might stay in the south for a while. But she was not prepared for what was to follow. Neither were the others.

"It was in Naples," she said, whispering, as if from another time and place, "it was in Naples that our marriage was consummated." And she'd only had one glass of sherry.

In the silence that followed Veronica noticed that everyone was very careful not to look at anybody else. The floor seemed to rivet their attention, all except Lady Boniface who had clearly turned her face towards Naples. Jonathan shivered with shame at so uncharacteristic an outburst from his mother. For a second he raised his eyes and gave Veronica a mean and contemptuous glance. There was no doubt in his mind that his mother was adjusting her tone to her company. Night-and-day Flora looked at her, too, and silently underwrote her husband's assessment.

Edward was less fazed. Surprised of course, but in no way disconcerted. He merely supposed that his mother's tone was due to her change of hairdresser and that her remarks were in the aftermath of the tone of the conversation she had overheard under the scissors. In fact, he was rather pleased with her. It was one of her rare admissions of womanhood. He decided to encourage her.

"Is it possible then that I was conceived in Naples?" he asked.

Jonathan looked as if he might throw up and poor Flora wilted by his side.

"It's more than possible," his mother said, smiling at him. Now they seemed to be in conspiracy against poor old Jonathan who had only managed to be conceived in the suburbs.

"That's probably why you're so fond of Italy," Lady Boniface said. "The Castle of Kings," she reminisced. "That's what the hotel was called. It had the most beautiful gardens. It was the most heavenly place in the world to start a family."

Jonathan gulped on his sherry and spluttered. Flora tapped him helplessly on his back. For both of them, things had got entirely out of hand.

But Veronica, too, wished the conversation to take a safer turn. It was already perilously close to her own little secret, now unhappily suspected by her brother-in-law. And then Margaret, with unintentional heaven-sent timing, sounded the dinner gong. Edward took his mother's arm and Veronica's on his other side. Jonathan and Flora brought up the rear.

Margaret was waiting in the dining room, keeping watch over the silver soup tureen on the trolley. Edward allotted places, giving his mother her old seat at the top of the table.

Jonathan sat on her right as had been his custom in his youth. Margaret beamed at the arrangement. Despite some absences, it reminded her of the old and happy days when there were guests but no strangers at the table and her eyes passed over Veronica's presence, since she would have disturbed the symmetry. She uncovered the soup tureen.

"I do believe it's my favourite sorrel, Margaret," Lady Boniface said.

Margaret grinned. "I made it specially for you," she said. She served her first and afterwards Edward. Jonathan and Flora were next on her list, and finally Veronica. Margaret had her own notions of hierarchy. Veronica was disturbed to see Margaret leave the room after the serving. As long as she was in the dining room, her presence would have silenced any intimate and familial conversation. Now, in her absence, anything could happen. She waited, hoping that comment on the soup would fill the sudden silence. She caught Edward's eye and he actually winked at her. She had never seen him wink before. It was completely out of character. Perhaps, now suspecting his Italian origins, he felt entitled to Italian manners. She would not be surprised if, before the evening was out, he had pinched her bottom.

"I wonder, does it influence a person's character?" Edward said. "I mean, the fact that they're conceived in a certain country."

"Not at all," Jonathan said with some contempt. "What forms a person's character is genetic. Good genes and bad." He stared undisguisedly at Veronica. "It has nothing to do with geography." Veronica stared back at him. How pompous he is, she thought, and it crossed her mind that a rogue strain of plumber's blood would do no harm to the Boniface circulation.

"I prefer to think otherwise," Edward was saying. "If a baby were conceived in Paris, for instance." He looked at Veronica and winked again.

Was the temptation to spill the beans too great for him, she wondered. Or was this his simple overture? And their soup barely finished.

"No difference at all," Jonathan said with authority.

"Well," Edward said slowly, "we shall see."

182

The guests put down their soup spoons. Jonathan allowed a pause. "And what exactly does that mean?" he said, knowing full well its meaning and delighted that the cards were now on the table, and satisfied too that he himself had not dealt them.

Edward looked questioningly at Veronica. She knew she had to nod her head, or simply shake it. But whatever she did was irrelevant. All at the table had guessed what misleading proof Edward was about to offer. He simply had to confirm it. So she shrugged her shoulders and prayed for Margaret's entry.

"We're having a baby," Edward said.

And then Margaret came in. It was a respite of sorts, but it had its drawbacks too. For it gave time for reflection, for a careful fashioning of reaction. Veronica looked around the table and suddenly all were diligently at their soup. Margaret had taken the soup tureen around and offered second helpings, which each one of them gladly took in order to give themselves something to toy with while deciding exactly how to receive Edward's bewildering news. But Margaret was delighted. Eventually she withdrew and privacy was theirs once more.

The silence was broken from a surprising quarter. Day-and-night Flora who, through her husband, was well-acquainted with the sorry state of Edward's fertility, nevertheless offered her congratulations. But all she got for her pains was a withering look from Jonathan. Thereafter she held her tongue.

"Thank you, Flora," Edward said, noticing the singleness of the reaction. "Well, and are you not pleased, Mother?"

Lady Boniface put down her soup spoon. "Of course I am, Edward," she said, but there was little pleasure in her voice or on her face. "As long as it pleases you."

"And you, Jonathan?"

"I feel the same as Mother," he said.

Veronica prayed for Margaret again. If she didn't come in pretty soon, somebody around the table, and most probably Edward, would chorus that old platitude of a chance in a million. She was sick of hearing it out of her own mouth, knowing the lie as well as the triteness of it. But Edward seemed to have given up and was drinking his soup without appetite. She felt deeply sorry for him. She caught his eye and winked. That seemed to cheer him a little.

"Well, that's my news. What's yours, Jonathan?"

Then Margaret made a tardy entrance and cleared away the soup. There would be time now for small talk while the second course was served. But then they would be private again and Veronica dreaded what turn the conversation would take.

But she needn't have worried. The subject of the new and questionable Boniface never arose again. Small talk of business and politics filled the rest of the courses and those Margaret-timed intervals between them. Coffee and liqueurs were served in the drawing room, and the trivia continued. There seemed no end to it. At last Lady Boniface expressed her fatigue.

"Will you take me home, Jonathan?" she asked.

"We're ready, Mother," Jonathan said.

She was staying the night with them and no doubt, Veronica thought, they would all give up on the trivia once in Flora's drawing room, armed with a night-cap.

Edward took his mother's arm as he showed them to the door.

"Get in the car, Jonathan," Lady Boniface said. "I'll be with you shortly."

Now would come the clap of thunder, Veronica knew, as Jonathan took Flora's arm and left the house. Lady Boniface waited for the door to close, and in the unbreakable silence and uninterruptible privacy of the hall, she said:

"You will acknowledge it as your own child, Edward. I want no scandal in the family."

"But it's mine," Edward spluttered.

Don't say it, Veronica silently pleaded, but it was out before her plea was over.

"It's a chance in a million."

"Nonsense, child," Lady Boniface said.

This to her son, a grown man of forty.

"I don't want to discuss it ever again," she said. She went towards the door, then turned to peck Edward on the cheek. She gave no word or gesture to Veronica who was stunned into silence. She watched as Edward opened the door and

184

took his mother to the car. Then she went back into the drawing room.

She was not surprised to find God at the cabinet, helping Himself to a drink. He turned to her and raised His glass.

"One for the road," He said.

"Are you leaving?"

"I'm going back to Surbiton. I'll wait for you there."

He downed his glass and was gone.

She was prepared for Edward's despondency on his return. But he practically skipped back into the drawing room.

"That was some evening," he said. He put his arm around her. "Don't worry about Mother," he said. "We can't really expect her to believe it. You wait," he joked, "the child's going to look exactly like me and then the whole family can eat their words."

At that moment, for the first time since her wedding day, Veronica recalled the face of her plumber. It was as clear as Edward's in front of her. But no more like Edward's than her own. The Bonifaces would never eat their words and, in time, would be offered visible proof never to do so. It was not over yet, God had told her, but it was up to her to finish it. Perhaps telling Edward the truth would bring it to an end and God would leave her for good. But He was waiting for her in Surbiton. That's where the finishing chapter would be written. She was glad of the reprieve. She held Edward's face in her hands.

"I don't care what the baby looks like," she said. "We don't have to prove anything to anybody."

Chapter Eleven

Veronica did not go back to Surbiton. Although she knew that it was the only way to get rid of God, the price for that release was too high. He had said that all was not over, with a clear hint that there was worse to come. She recalled her last Surbiton visit and could not imagine any more painful confrontation than that of her own fratricide. Whatever was left in the third drawer would have to bide its time, or rather hers, until enough courage would prompt her to discover it. Or self-destruction perhaps. But whichever it was, she had no appetite for either. So she bound herself to Eaton Square and its safe environs.

Over the next few months, she grew larger and avoided the kitchen. But Edward found her more and more delightful. She saw nothing of his family during this time. She did not consciously avoid them. It was simply that none of them made a move to contact her. As far as they were concerned, her condition was beyond discussion. In the light of his mother's resigned acceptance, poor Jonathan prayed for a miscarriage. When he met Dr Truelove at his club, he made oblique enquiries as to his sister-in-law's progress and he would hide his disappointment on hearing that all was in shipshape order. Veronica used the waiting time to renew old friendships that she had sadly neglected since her marriage. It was an uneventful time with no sign of God anywhere. But in her heart she knew He was waiting. And she knew where. But she could not bring herself to go to Him. Yet she feared He would grow impatient and return to heap curses upon her. It was the fear of the latter and their dreadful consequences that prompted her each morning to think of making the journey to Surbiton, but each morning she recoiled in fear of what she should discover. So she busied herself elsewhere, meeting her Surbiton friends in town and working on her book.

It would be two and a half months before she came to term. She wondered if she should postpone Surbiton until after the baby was born, but she knew that, no matter how He claimed to the contrary, patience was not God's forte.

One day, Edward had to make a sudden trip to Bordeaux. Veronica was too advanced in her pregnancy to risk flying. He didn't like leaving her, but promised to be back within the week. Veronica drove him to the airport and on the way home the baby started to kick more boisterously than was usual. And with greater frequency. She took it as a sign. With a small detour off the motorway, she could be on the road to Surbiton and whatever awaited her there. The baby kicked again and she turned off the highway. Thereafter the baby lay quietly. Its subsequent kicks were infrequent and gentle as if in approval of what she had done. It seemed that the baby had taken upon itself the onus of the decision. There was a small relief in that and Veronica drew up outside her house with less fear.

She went straight to her study and found God waiting for her. He smiled at her as she entered.

"I'm glad you've come," He said.

She was sure that He was about to forgive her and that the remaining contents of the drawer were not so terrible. She was even anxious now to get it over with. She turned to the chest. The drawer was open.

"You've already looked," she said accusingly.

"I know what's in the drawer. As well as you," He said. "It was you who left it open."

She was fearful again. "And after this, will it all be over?" she asked.

"Soon," He said. "Soon."

He went out of the door and she knew that she had not seen

the last of Him. The baby kicked again. She closed the drawer, wanting to start afresh. And then she waited a while, gathering her strength for what God had hinted would be the last onslaught. She knew she was not ready, but she knew too that nothing but the cleansing of the drawer could prepare her. She caressed her stomach as a talisman. Then opened the drawer for the last time.

There was very little left, but that was small comfort for she knew that even a single minute entry could wreak havoc. She made to extract the top sheet and as she did so, she sniffed. There was a sudden odour in the room as powerful and as evocative as taste. And it thrust her into a sudden awakening nearly thirty years ago when, sitting bolt upright in bed, she called out to Mrs Dale.

"There's something burning," she shouted.

It was breakfast time, later today than usual because it was Saturday, and it could have been something special that Mrs Dale was cooking. But it was not a food smell. Nothing so benign. She rushed to the landing, but smelt nothing. It was not in the house, the smell. It was outside and seeping through her bedroom window.

"Where's Daddy?" she shouted, not knowing what had prompted such a connection.

"He's gone to church."

"But it's Saturday."

"Churches are always open," Mrs Dale said.

Her heart fluttered. Why should anyone want to go to church on a Saturday?

"But God won't be there. He comes tomorrow."

"God is always there," Mrs Dale said. "Get dressed. Breakfast's ready."

Something was wrong and she knew it. Daddy had never been to church on a Saturday. Why should anyone want to go if no one else was there, with no incense, no bells or anything? Unless they had a terrible secret to tell to God that no one else should hear? She panicked.

"Are you sure he went to church?" she practically screamed down the stairs.

"Yes, my darling," Mrs Dale said. "He's probably back by now. I think I heard the car."

She didn't bother to dress or even wash. Just her dressing gown and slippers and she went downstairs.

"Can you smell anything?" she asked.

"No."

"What's that noise?"

"What noise? First it's a smell, then it's a noise. What's the matter with you this morning?"

There was nothing the matter with her. But there was something the matter with the morning. It was different. Not like a usual Saturday. Yet it wasn't the smell, the noise, or even her father's absence from the breakfast table. It was a special feeling and one she had known before. When, for the first time, she had seen the pram in the park. When her mother had last waved goodbye at the station. It was that heavy, heartbreaking feeling of loss. The pre-pram days, the pre-train-waving days, all were now over. All gone, beyond repair, beyond replacement.

She started to cry.

"It's too late," she said. "Too late," and she knew that she spoke the truth, but she had no idea where that truth was coming from.

"What's the matter, child?" Mrs Dale cuddled her. She felt her forehead and was disturbed by its fever.

"You must go back to bed, darling," she said. "I'll fetch your daddy."

"No, no," Veronica pleaded, even as she had pleaded with Dr Bruton, not so very long ago, not to summon her mother home.

"Then I'll take you upstairs myself." She picked her up and carried her, anxious of the heat of her small whimpering body. She laid her gently on the bed, then went quickly to the medicine chest for Calpol.

"This will make you sleep," she said, spooning it into her mouth. "You'll be all better when you wake up."

She did not fight it. She wanted to sleep and not only to sleep, but to sleep never to wake again. She was smelling smells that no one else noticed and hearing sounds that no one else heard. She wanted to slip into a kingdom of odourless silence and never, never wake again. She heard Mrs Dale close her bedroom door and she turned her face to the wall.

189

She did not hear her fearful footsteps as she ran outside to get her father. Nor did she hear her frightened calling of his name. "Mr Smiles, Mr Smiles," echoed through her sleep, having little to smile about. Nor did she hear the frantic pulling of the garage door and afterwards poor Mrs Dale's stifled cry as she reeled from the fumes. Nor the telephone call to Dr Bruton. None of these she heard, but she slept and slept almost the day through, safe in that protective twilight that cushions the shock of a terrible awakening.

In the late afternoon, she stirred and saw the gathering darkness outside her window. She went to it and saw that the garage door was open. The car was still inside. Perhaps her father had never taken it out, or had been and gone wherever he was going while she was sleeping. She listened but all was silent. She sniffed but smelt nothing but fear. She went to the door and listened, and heard footsteps on the stairs. A man's tread, but not her father's. She hurried back into bed and watched her doorknob slowly turn. Dr Bruton, his misdiagnosis on the tip of his tongue. But he was pale, as if he himself were sick. Mrs Dale was supporting him on his arm and her father nowhere in sight, as if the two of them had conspired to send him away.

Dr Bruton sat on her bed. He took both her hands in his. "I have to tell you something," he said. "Something very sad."

"Mummy's dead," she said. "I know."

"It's not that," he said. "It's something more."

What more could there be than that? How dead could a mother be, and how often could she die?

"Your father," he whispered.

"He's dead too?" She laughed. Then seeing his crestfallen face, "I was only joking," she pleaded.

Mrs Dale sat beside her on the bed and held her. Tightly. Too tightly she thought, as if holding her down. Over her head, Mrs Dale nodded to Dr Bruton.

"Your father's dead," he said. "This morning. In the garage. A heart attack. A natural death," he added.

She'd heard that one before and she knew exactly what it meant.

"Did he die in mortal sin?" she asked.

Dr Bruton looked at Mrs Dale. His mouth was quivering.

"I don't know what that means," he said.

"Does mortal sin run in the family, Dr Bruton? Will I die of it, too?"

He held her hands again. "Your father's dead, Veronica," he said. She stared at him, then looked around her room. Her Victorian doll sat on the lace cushion on the settee. As it always sat. Ever since she could remember. Her books were on the shelf with the monkey-statue as a book end, that grinning alabaster that she acknowledged each morning on waking. Her clothes were on the chair, *her* clothes, those that she wore to school. All were hers. All were of this time. All was real. Then Dr Bruton must be real, too, and the words that belonged to him and which he had given to her. Those too were real.

"Where is he?" she said.

"He's dead," Dr Bruton said again, a little impatiently, as if her father's whereabouts were irrelevant.

"I know," she almost screamed at him. "But I want to see him."

Dr Bruton looked at Mrs Dale. Clearly neither of them had expected such a request.

"I never saw Mummy," she said.

"It's better that you shouldn't see him," Mrs Dale said, and again put her arms around her. "He doesn't look well."

"Of course he doesn't look well. How could he look well if he's dead?" she shouted, disentangling herself from the embrace.

She leapt out of bed and out of her room and into her father's room at the end of the landing.

"Where is he?" she screamed, seeing the empty unmade bed and hoping for one moment that it had all been a cruel joke.

"I'll take you to him," Mrs Dale said and, despite Dr Bruton's protestations, she picked up Veronica and carried her downstairs.

"If he's dead, why isn't he in bed?" Veronica said. Then she remembered that her dead mother too had been far from a bed, and she supposed that both of them had chosen to die before bedtime and against God's will. Then she was angry.

"Why didn't he tell me?" she shouted. "Mummy didn't tell me either. Nobody tells me anything."

She was screaming by the time they reached the dining room door. Mrs Dale, for some reason, had locked it and now she took out the key from her apron and turned it in the lock. As the door opened, Veronica smelt that smell again, but it was silent now, yet, in the silence, more pungent. A garage smell, a car-on-a-cold-morning smell, and she knew then that, like her mother, her father had died in mortal sin.

He lay on the dining room table, like a Sunday joint ready for carving. And today only Saturday. Mrs Dale put her down and she walked towards the table. His head lay where her mother usually sat and his bare feet touched his own place setting. Veronica would sit where his elbow lay and at this point she placed herself now, knowing that she was the only one left at the table. From this angle she looked at him and sniffed the smell on him, that smell which had turned his face black. Then she tickled the soles of his feet, just to make sure that he was dead. Dr Bruton had made mistakes before. She turned away, satisfied. She had seen her father and he was dead. His body was the only concrete proof of her orphanhood. The rest was hearsay. Mrs Dale locked the door after they'd left.

"I'll arrange everything," Dr Bruton said, as he made to leave.

After he had gone, Veronica asked, "What's everything?"

"He means the funeral," Mrs Dale said.

"When will that be?"

"In a week, I suppose."

"Is Daddy going to lie on the table for a week?"

"Yes," Mrs Dale said. "But in a box."

"Will we have to eat in the kitchen then?"

"Yes," she said, glad to be back on a domestic footing. "And you're going to eat right now. You've had nothing to eat all day."

Mrs Dale was surprised at the meal Veronica managed to put away. She ate as if starving.

"When will the box come? she asked.

"Tomorrow, I suppose."

"Is he going to be in it for a whole week?"

"Yes."

"Can I sleep with you then?"

"Of course." Mrs Dale too was glad of company.

The box came the following day and the dining room door was opened. But locked again as the men went to work inside. Veronica hung around outside the door until Mrs Dale swept her away and gave her things to do in the kitchen. Veronica didn't cry. Even when she had been told of her father's death, there had been no tears. She had simply screamed, dry-eyed. All through the week she behaved as if nothing untoward had happened. But she would scurry past the dining room door. "I wish he were buried," she said one day to Mrs Dale. "Then we could have proper suppers again."

Aunt Cissy came from Scotland. Her father's sister. And the dining room door was unlocked once more. Then, on the day before the funeral, the door stayed open and people came and went, muttering. Then came the day when the table could at last be cleared.

By the time Veronica was nine years old, she had been to three funerals. Two of them by way of memorials. At the age of four, she had toddled to granny-underground's commemoration. Four years later she had attended the same for her mother. Now, at the age of nine, she went to a proper funeral, one that sported a real live dead body. And even though the body was barely recognizable, it was the only one the family could muster between them. Children are born to bury their parents. The reverse is the extremity of grief. To follow a parent's body lies in the natural order of things. But in pigtails? In white socks? Rather a decent greying hairbun and support hose. And, above all, if one is a woman, a striated stomach, mother-of-pearled, token of those who will follow you yourself to your grave. But at the time, Veronica found nothing odd in this unnatural procedure, nor would she rue it for many years to come. At the time, sitting in the front pew with Aunt Cissy, and Mrs Dale on her other side, she felt something of a celebrity with everybody staring at her. Her father was in the box in front of her, covered with beautiful flowers, so much nicer than he had looked on the dining room table. The music was playing and, although it was sad, it was all a little bit like a treat. There was even a party to follow. She herself had arranged the sandwiches. She giggled.

They were whispering behind her.

"What did he die of?" a woman's voice asked.

Veronica turned round. "Mortal sin," she said, determined to get it in before the priest, who no doubt would make it the text of his sermon. But she did not turn around again to face the coffin, for her eye had caught sight of a lone figure in the back row. The pram-lady, though forever pramless now, sat there, but unlike at her mother's party, dry-eyed, tearless, with no claim this time on succession. Instead her face was swollen with anger and frustration and when she saw Veronica, she focused it like a poisoned arrow into her eye. Veronica was on the point of sticking out her tongue at her, but there were too many witnesses between them, so she satisfied herself by slipping it gently out of her mouth, slowly and with a sharp tip, then quickly turned it back to lick her lips in order to cover for herself.

The music stopped and the priest entered, that same priest who had given a send-off to her mother and granny. The Smiles departures were becoming a nasty habit. This time there was no speechifying. Just the ordinary straightforward funeral service that allowed no opportunity for opinion on the cause of the death of the departed one. The congregation was asked to stand for the final psalm and, as it proceeded, the organ struck up again and her father danced partnerless across the floor. And then disappeared.

"Where's Daddy gone?" she asked Mrs Dale.

"To heaven," that good lady promptly responded, though hell would have been more appropriate considering the fire he was approaching.

"Our Father which art in heaven . . ." the priest was droning, and Veronica smiled at Mrs Dale. The priest, too, knew where Daddy was.

"Can we have the party now?" she asked.

Mrs Dale took her hand as Aunt Cissy led the way out of the pew.

As chief mourners they were given right of way into the gardens that surrounded the crematorium. The sun was shining brightly and Veronica was satisfied that her father had gone into the sky.

The congregation stood in line waiting to shake Veronica's and Aunt Cissy's hands. They moved slowly. The men from her father's office and their wives. Others Veronica had seen before at her mother's memorial. Some of them she even remembered from her granny's. She wondered what they would do with their time now that all the Smiles were buried and gone. And then, for the first time, she realized that she was the only one left, her first taste of mortality. "I must live forever," she told herself.

Out of the corner of her eye, she saw the pram-lady approach and she grew afraid. She looked at Mrs Dale, who had seen her too, and that old disgusted look passed over her face. Mrs Dale put her arm around Veronica as if to protect her. The pram-lady was getting nearer. Three more "I'm so terribly sorrys," and she would be upon them and God knows what was on her lips. And whatever her words were, she was chewing them even as she approached. She left a gap between herself and the last condoler. She clearly wanted to make an entry. Her eyes were fixed on Veronica. She had no other target. After an interval she stepped in front of them. Then, ignoring Mrs Dale and Aunt Cissy on the other side, she bent her mouth to Veronica's ear. She was decent enough to say whatever she had to say in a whisper, out of earshot of Mrs Dale and Aunt Cissy, and thus out of range of their outraged defence. But she was decent only for decorum's sake. It would have been less cruel had she shouted it aloud so that others could have borne the burden of her accusation. But it honed in on Veronica's ear alone.

"Murderer," she hissed. "Murderer. Three times over." Then she lifted her head, smiled at Mrs Dale and passed on. Her words pierced Veronica's ear, settling there, to ring, buzz and echo there, like tinnitus, for the rest of her days.

"What did she say?" Mrs Dale asked.

"Nothing," Veronica said quickly. She was stunned. Not so much by the woman's message, but by her strange arithmetic. Three times over? She was vaguely aware of one and that had to do with the pram, but who were the other two? She wanted to ask Mrs Dale, but she sensed that it might result in a bloody battle, so she held her tongue.

The condolence line had come to an end. She wondered whether the pram-lady was coming to the party. She hoped not. She might elucidate her sums and Veronica didn't want to know. Such knowledge, she sensed, would not be good for her.

"Who was that woman who whispered to you?" Aunt Cissy said as they were walking towards the car.

"A friend of Daddy's."

"What did she say?"

"She said she was very sorry." Suddenly Veronica felt very grown-up. She had told her first outright lie and she had got away with it. Then she caught sight of the pram-lady as she got into her car. It was a very old and battered thing, and Veronica suddenly felt sorry for her. She watched her start the engine and heard how it failed. And how she tried again and yet again, until it caught in a roar of achievement and sent out black fumes to proclaim itself. Then Veronica smelt the smell again and now she sniffed at it once more, standing at the third drawer almost thirty years later, the pram-lady dead and gone, but her arithmetic loud and clear.

Veronica took out the last of the file. Soon, she thought, it will all be over. The last entry was multiple and clipped together. As she removed it, she saw the drawer lining and it shone like the merciful end of a tunnel. She left the drawer open and took the file to her desk.

Two sheets of paper. She unclipped the top sheet and placed the other, without looking at it, face down on her desk. She had to take it slowly. Pain by searing pain. There was no heading on the paper. It boasted no formality. It was a faintly ruled sheet, torn from a child's exercise book. But the giveaway was that it was yellow, that colour that her mother had used for her notes on her books. She always kept a pile of such notebooks and often Veronica had asked for one. But instead her mother would give her the ordinary white-ruled one. The yellow seemed to be inalienably hers. Now, as she stared at the colour, she knew that it had been stolen, her mother's back irrevocably turned. Whatever the sheet contained in matter of words, she resented it before reading. But when she saw "My darling Veronica" at its head and the signature of "Daddy" over the yellow page, her heart filled with sudden forgiveness for both of them even though they had both gone away without telling her.

"My darling Veronica," her father had written. "You are not to blame. You are not to blame. You are not to blame."

Three times he had written it and it echoed that old triplicate of the pram-lady so many years ago. She read it once more, and aloud.

"Remember that all your life," he wrote. "Guilt is a terrible burden to shoulder. Even the innocent are guilt-laden. They, perhaps, more than others. But for this letter, my dearest, you are not to blame. But know why I have written it and forgive me if you can. The unhappiness that I have wrought in other people, as well as in myself, is too much for me to bear. That is the whole story."

That sentence marked the end of the first paragraph and she knew that that was all he had to say. The rest would be a coda. But it was enough. It explained everything. But it explained nothing too. Her father's life was his and it was his to do with what he wished. As was her mother's. She had to believe that, otherwise she could not read further. Once again she read it over, to give herself strength to proceed, for she could see that there was much more to follow. She wished that God would come and read it to her. Or anybody, as if another reader who shared the words could share her burden. She laid the paper on her desk, distancing herself, so that her hands were free to clench themselves, and she read on.

"Of all the turtledove stories that I told you, there was one that I was saving. I give it to you now. I think it comes from Ethiopia but I'm not sure.

"It is told that in the beginning, all feathered creatures sang like angels. And so they should, for were they not the children of angels? Even the raven and his kind sang like a nightingale and this story tells how the raven forfeited his voice.

"On the seventeenth day of the seventh month, Noah rested his Ark on the mountains of Ararat. And he sent forth a raven to see if the waters were abated. But the raven never returned. Then after a while, Noah sent out a turtledove and she flew in search of land. And the dove caught sight of an olive tree rising above the waters. She alighted on a branch and knew that the waters had returned from off the earth. With her beak she plucked a twig and, turning, saw the raven still swirling in his search. And the raven was very angry for it was he whom Noah had first sent. The olive branch must be his if he wished to find favour in Noah's eyes. And he fought with the turtledove, thrusting his long beak down her throat. But the dove clove to the twig and flew back with it to the Ark. But when she tried to sing again, a song of joy for God's forgiveness, no sweet sound came from her throat. Only a plaintive gurgle. And the angels wept for her, but for the raven they were full of wrath. So they punished him and his kind for the injury he had done, and they condemned them to hoarseness and minced their voices to a croak. And that is why to this day, they haunt empty and ghostly places, where their croaking echoes threefold. And the angels took the turtledove and poured a magic oil on to his gurgling, so that all who hear the turtle's voice and hearken it well, will receive the gift of loving.

"That is the gift I pray for you, Veronica, as you grow. Do not abuse it as I have done. And do not confuse it with being loved. That, too, is good. But there is no art in it. It requires no talent. It entails no risk. Know the difference. Always. And choose loving if you can. All the rest follows. All I leave you, my daughter, is a heavy burden, made heavier by the love I bear you. Take care little one. Aunt Cissy will look after you. Your loving Daddy."

She put her head in her hands. The pain of the letter quickened her heart. Her father had only been able to guess at what age she would read it, so he had fashioned it for both a child and an adult. And she read it as both, and both readings left her desolate. It must all be over now, she thought, and wondered why God didn't come. She put her father's letter into her own file.

The last sheet of the collection lay face down on her desk. She turned it over. It was the photograph of her mother's mountain grave. A small cross in the snow, and Dr Fisher and the mourners beside it. It was the only item of the record that was not chronologically filed. And yet, for her father, that had been its harmonious placing. In its proper chronology, it had been too painful. But coupled with his own farewell, it had achieved a certain symmetry.

She put the photograph in the file and closed it. Then quietly she closed the third drawer, that funeral parlour of all her dead. Now they were buried and there were no secrets any more. Now she need never come home again. She looked around the house for the last time, bidding farewell to each room in turn, but only in the spare room lay the pain of nostalgia. She tarried there for a while, then drove to the local estate-agent and put the house on the market. She was relieved to take the road back to London.

Though her mood was melancholy, she had a small sense of achievement. A long-lasting and perilous task had been accomplished, and she wondered why her baby didn't give a small kick of applause. She adjusted her driving mirror and, in it, she saw the face of God, and she wondered why He was wearing a safety-belt, for surely He had no chance of mortality.

"Is it time yet for my release?" she asked.

"The stork in the heaven knoweth her appointed hour; the turtle, the crane and the swallow know the time of their coming."

She resented his reference to the turtle and she feared His mention of the stork.

"But is it *my* time?" she asked impatiently.

"To everything there is a season and a time for every purpose under the heaven. A time to be born and a time to die . . ."

"I *know* all that," she shouted at Him.

"A time for atonement, too," He whispered.

"But my father said I wasn't to blame."

He didn't answer for a while. Then He said, "But what do *you* say?" She shivered and looked again in the mirror, but it was clouded.

So it was not yet over. And she dreaded now what terrible price she would have to pay for her release. God was infinitely cruel, whatever his advocates pleaded. She comforted herself with thoughts of her future motherhood. She caressed her stomach but the baby did not stir. It must be sleeping, she thought. Yes, she would call it Oliver, or Olivia if it were a girl. It would be in memory of two of her dead. With her next child, she would remember her mother.

When she reached Eaton Square, Margaret gave her a message from Edward. He had telephoned to say that he would be held over in Bordeaux for a week. He had left his telephone number and sent his love. This last part of the message, Margaret had passed on in a mumble, her eyes fixed on the floor.

"Thank you, Margaret," she said, and went quickly to her room. She was glad of the respite. She looked forward to an Edwardless week and felt ashamed. She recalled her father's story of the turtledove. Her poor father. Of them all, he was the only one who had had the talent for loving. And he had died of it.

Chapter Twelve

Something was wrong. The baby hadn't moved for two days. She didn't know whether, towards the end of a pregnancy, such stillness was normal. And she was too afraid to enquire. Nevertheless, she drove herself to Harley Street wondering whether or not she should be worried. She would not go to Dr Truelove, fearful of the grapevine to Jonathan's club. So she rang the bell of another obstretician and declared herself an emergency. She did not live in London, she said. She had just arrived from France. The doctor saw her at once and at once arranged for her to go to hospital. He said little more than the fact that she needed to be thoroughly examined and she did not press him for further details. But she asked to use his phone and she told Margaret that she was going to the country for a few days, in case Edward should call. The doctor sent his porter to drive her to the hospital and, as she left his consulting room, he shook his head.

In the hospital they put her on a trolley and wheeled her into the scanning room. Nobody said a word and each of them relied on her fear of asking any questions. Then, when they were done with her, they wheeled her into a small room and put her to bed. "The doctor will come soon," the nurse said. Then she fled. Veronica waited. She would not think of what could have happened. She dared not. Instead, she thought of the desert, her own simple element, that wasteland with little feeling and less tenderness, but somehow secure. She recalled the Tuareg nomads who lived on the southern edge of the desert where she was camped. And the great windstorm that blew and threatened the camels and the tents. The orange dust that swirled in the air and the miraculous wind-patterned sand in the morning light. It soothed her, this vision, and she was dwelling in it when the doctor, without knocking, came into her room. It took her a little while to refocus on her present reality and suddenly she recalled that something was very wrong, a fact confirmed by the solemn look on the doctor's face and doubly confirmed by his solicitous taking of her hand.

"It's not good news, Lady Boniface," he said. "I'm afraid your baby is dead."

Her childhood rang in her ear.

> *Dead said the doctor,*
> *Dead said the nurse,*
> *Dead said the lady*
> *With the alligator purse.*

"An air-embolism."

She caught the word out of his embarrassed flow of explanation.

"A chance in a million."

She smiled to herself. As the baby had presumably been conceived, in the same manner had it miscarried.

"What's to be done?" she said, and as she said it she realized that her chances of motherhood were gone for ever.

"You will have to go into labour," he said. "We'll give you something to induce it. Don't worry," he said, squeezing her hand. "You'll recover. You'll bear another child."

The nurse came in then and gave Veronica some tablets.

"How long will it take?" she asked.

"You should go into labour in a few hours. We've given you something to help you sleep. You must try and relax. Tomorrow it will be over." He patted her head. He seemed generally sorry for her. Far more sorry than she felt for herself. She was more angry than sorry and in her rage, looked for someone to blame. God was the only candidate. This is what He must have meant by atonement. This desperate extreme. She hated Him with all her heart. She

202

planned revenge. But she knew it was futile. In His own perverted way, He had won. Not because of her own weakness, but because He was invincible. As long as you believed in Him, there was no other way but to join Him. With such an ally, so punitive, so priggish, so bloody holier-than-thou, the future was not rosy. But at least it would be in the desert where she had other allies and other gods, and behind their backs they could make a mockery of all of them. There was a small solace in such a thought and she fell asleep on it, knowing that that she would wake only to pain.

Which woke her shortly afterwards and she screamed. But no one came. In the hospital corridors they were familiar with such screams and knew from long experience that the screamings would cease. And then, after a while, would start again, in ever decreasing intervals. They would not disturb themselves until those intervals were short enough to signal ripeness. And, as they expected, the first interval of silence followed. And then the screams again. In her study, the door ajar, Matron looked at her watch and continued with her work. But Veronica was as much in anger as in pain and in anger there is no interval. She strove desperately to leave her bed and go herself in search of help. She reached the door as it mercifully opened. But it was only God.

"In pain shalt thou labour," He said.

"Fuck off," she screamed at Him.

It was the proximity of the call as well as its strange cursing that stirred Matron from her chair.

"Now what's all the fuss about?" she said, helping Veronica back into bed. "I'll get you down to the labour ward," she said. "But we're nowhere near ready yet."

"Will it get worse?" Veronica dared to ask.

"A little," Matron said, "but the worse it gets, the sooner it will be over."

On her way to the labour ward, the pains came again.

"It won't be long now," Matron said looking at her watch. "You're lucky. Usually it's much longer."

"This is lucky?" Veronica asked in a painless interval.

Matron was sorry for her. All the pains of labour and no pay-off. It would be an embarrassing delivery.

For another hour Veronica lay in the labour ward. Nurses

came occasionally and examined her. Then finally the doctor was called and the birthing, in earnest, began.

"Now you know what to do," the doctor said.

"How should I know?" she gasped. "I've never done it before."

"Have you had no instruction?"

She shook her head, remembering all the pamphlets which Dr Truelove had pressed upon her and which she'd never read; all those weekly ante-natal classes that she'd never attended, those classes that required a husband's participation. But she had drawn the line at involving Edward in the birth. It would have been tasteless to ask his help in birthing a baby that was not his. Even more tasteless now, knowing what she knew. Edward had nothing to do with the child but even less to do with the child that would be her Oliver, the cruel equalizer for her father's loss. No, she didn't know what to do and even less what to expect, except that the sorry fruits of her labour would have no life at all. She started to cry and was grateful for a sudden contraction which gave an excuse for her tears. They put a mask on her face and told her to breathe deeply. She panted, gasping for relief.

"Deep breaths and slow," a nurse said, then took the mask away when the pain had ceased.

And so the process continued as the pains intensified and the intervals between were of less and less duration, until there was no respite at all. Just the pain and the promise of empty deserts. And at last it came, in all its terrible silence.

They cut the cord that linked the quick and the dead and they laid the baby on her stomach.

"It's a boy," the doctor said. "Touch it, know it and mourn for it. And then you will recover."

Her hand covered its whole body. With her fingers she felt each part of it, until she knew it as well as she knew herself. And then, when her blind exploration was done, she dared to look at it.

"You must name it," the doctor said.

With both hands she held it in front of her and put it to her cheek.

"Oliver," she said, "Oliver Smiles."

Then she kissed each part of its body, while in her heart,

she heard the voice of the turtle. And she listened well, as her father had told her. And for the first time in her life, she was filled with loving.

They took the baby away and wheeled her back to her room. God had been with her, she knew. In every searing pain and in its ripeness. She knew, too, that He had been in her granny's earthquake underground. He had been in her mother's avalanche. He had been in her father's fire. And he had been in her own labour that she had laboured so in vain.

God came towards the bed.

"Is it all over now?" she said.

And for the first time, He touched her.

"An eye for an eye," He said. "It is given."

They kept her in hospital for two more days. Then sent her home, empty-handed. She let herself into the house in Eaton Square in order to avoid Margaret. She would have to prepare herself for that first post-natal encounter. But Margaret was passing through the hall at the time.

"Miss Veronica," she said, noting immediately her sudden lack of girth. She paled and steadied herself against the hall table, knowing in what kind of country her mistress had spent the last few days. But she made no comment on it.

"Would you like some tea?" she said, suddenly sorry for her.

"Thank you, Margaret. I would love that. Has Edward phoned?"

"Last night," she said, "He'll try again this evening."

That left her half a day to prepare what to say to him.

But by the time he phoned that evening, she had prepared nothing. Nor even tried. For she knew that there was nothing to tell him. For that which they had lost had never belonged to him. Instead she invented her few days in the country and when he asked after the baby, she patted her shrivelled body and said that all was well.

In the morning, she took the train to Surbiton.

A sense of unfinished business drove her there. When she arrived, she went to the station flower stall and there bought three separate bunches of chrysanthemums. She chose them for their smell of the earth. Each bunch was of the same colour and quantity, for atonement in all quarters had to be equal. She intended to walk to the churchyard and to make certain detours on the way. It was to be a nostalgic journey and by way of farewell, for she knew that she would never come to Surbiton again.

Dr Bruton's house was her first port-of-call. It was a surgery no longer. But she could see the four screwholes in the brick beside the door, site of the plaque announcing his name and his letters. That master of misdiagnoses, however numerous his diplomas. Dr Bruton had only one prognosis, a pronouncement that would do for every known symptom. A heart attack. And that accounted for a fifty-foot tumble on a mountain, a baby smothered in goose down, and a body charred by carbon-monoxide fumes. All were happy heart attacks. Dr Bruton was more in the business of cover-up than medicine and, in memory of his loyalty to her family, she took a single chrysanthemum bloom and stuck it in one of the screwholes that had once held his gold-plated name.

From the end of Dr Bruton's road, she could see the gates of her old school. She ran towards them like a child. The playground was pre-lunch empty and she could hear a faint and inept choir singing from the music room. Soon the bell would ring for lunch and mothers would gather at the gates for those children who could not stomach school dinners. And amongst them Mrs Dale, trying so hard to look like a mother and, on seeing her, enveloping Veronica in an embrace that protested her own sad lack of children.

"You look so pale, darling," she would say.

"I've been sick again."

Always sick. Sick at her mother's departure. Sicker still on the point of her return. Then back home to bed and Dr Bruton, and the look of disgust on Mrs Dale's face as Dr Bruton got it wrong yet again.

She heard the bell ring and she waited for the children to pour into the playground. She hoped that the sight of them would hearten her a little, but when they came, laughing and singing, it only served to sadden her as she felt the aching hollow in her body and knew that it would never be filled again. She turned away, leaving a flower, and walked in the direction of what was once home, not for nostalgia's sake, but as if from habit. As she passed her house, she noticed the newly-erected *For Sale* sign and it pleased her for, although her pilgrimage into her past was painful, that notice was a small sign that, in some senses, it was over and that, in a small part, she had come to terms with it. She passed the house and laid a flower on the wall, and without looking back she made her way through the back streets and alleys to the market-place, a site of a more recent past which she would visit more for nostalgia than for accommodation. For it was in that place that God had first teased her, leaving her in the lurch. Standing now in the market square, she thought of Him again, posturing between the loaves and fishes, but she knew it only as a vision, for now God had ceased to trouble her. But she recalled her fevered hysteria as she had chased Him, through the stalls and into the arcade, where He had hidden Himself, and how she had shouted her declaration of love after His retreating figure. But it was not love that He had wanted. He had enough of that. Perhaps He, too, with all His mercy, cruelty, and sheer bloody-mindedness, perhaps He too lacked the gift of loving. He, who had made the turtle, had not listened to its song.

She passed a flower stall and bought more chrysanthem-ums. One of them she gave back to the flower girl as her market place memorial. She left the square and walked about the streets for a while, postponing her next port-of-call and when, in the distance, she saw the gates of the park, she stopped short, fearful of entry. Yet she had to make that journey, too, for the past is a pilgrimage both joyous and sorrowful and there can be no cheating bypasses on such a journey. She steeled herself and made her way to the iron gates.

It was lunchtime and the park was almost empty. Old men, whose appetites no longer obeyed time-honoured meal schedules, who were hungry all the time, or never perhaps, walked with their dogs, old too, and at a leisured pace. One sat on a bench near the sandpit and with his stick he traced concentric circles in the sand, his own diminishing geometry. He did not look up as Veronica passed him by, unnerved perhaps by the shadow that she cast across his cycles, for he shivered, although it was not cold. She made her way to the swings. She noticed that one of them had caught on the crossbar, as if from a vicious swing, and it hung itself there, still trembling. It was at that high point that, as a child, she had soared to heaven, and that very point too that she had dreaded the inevitable downward curve and the sight of that unnatural friendship on the ground. She tugged at the swing and dislodged it from its crossbar hold. One could not freeze one's childhood, stop-frame it on its way to heaven. The swing came hurtling down and rocked drunkenly, like an idle gallows.

She left the playground and walked across the grass towards the bandstand. That too was deserted, witnessless, as had been her crime. She took the same route as she had taken all those years ago, looking back now and then to catch sight of her father and the pram-lady in their embrace. At the back of the bandstand, out of their sight, she sought that exact spot where, unknowing and singing, she had extinguished a life. And there she stood for a while, whilst an acrid guilt pierced her songless heart. And, turning again, there was no snow or snowman, nor father, nor pram-lady. It was another season, another time. She laid a chrysanthemum on the grass. She put a hand on that part of her body where, so lately, a child had lain and, quickly and sobbing, she left the park.

There was only one more chrysanthemum station to her cross and her body grew heavy as she approached it. It was to be her final assault on her past, the last post of homage, the final proof that the past was irreversible.

And there it lay, in its tombs and sepulchres, beyond undoing, beyond recrimination and fit now only for forgiveness. She went first into the church, unbothered by God or His son. She stared at the Christ, safe in the knowledge that it could not disturb her. For her the church was merely a floor for pews and a wall for an altar. A place to baptize, to marry and to bury. It was the latter which had brought her to this place, though none of her remembrances had lain inside. Her father had gone to the fire in the crematorium down the road, her mother to the snows and her granny to the shallows. She did not know about Oliver. But all of them, in memorial, lay outside. She sat in a pew for a while. For her the church was the house of the dead and the graveyard its garden.

She went outside. She had no order of remembrance in mind. But as it turned out, her calls were chronological.

Her first encounter was with her grandmother's plaque, headstone to no grave, but a simple message of memorial. "*Flora Kempsey, 1886–1952,*" and in gold-embossed brackets, "*(Granny-Underground). Loved and respected by all.*"

Veronica knelt. Of this death, she was wholly innocent. She had not even wished her granny dead. She was one of those on the headstone who had loved and respected her. Respected her for her life and for her death, for she had chosen the manner of both. She kissed the cold headstone and laid flowers at its base. As far as she knew, granny-underground was the first of the family to dabble in mortal sin and it seemed to have become the accepted way of life as well as death. It was almost something to be proud of. One had to be. For any alternative was shameful.

She moved along the paths. She did not remember where her family lay. The encounter with her grandmother's memorial had been sheer chance. She wandered amongst the stones, glancing at their names. But there was no familiarity even from her childhood and it was in those steps that she now walked. Then she sighted another graveless stone. The family tended to shun the body, so she guessed that it was probably her mother's.

She approached and read:

"*In memory of Priscilla Kavanagh, 1918–1955. Beloved by Oliver and Veronica. Sadly Missed.*"

Oliver and Veronica, she read, over and over again. Unknowingly she had shared with him his sorrow, though he had known of those tears she had never shed. Now she knew that it was guilt that had stemmed them. She had had no hand in her mother's death, but often she had wished her never to return from the mountain, because of the pain that would ensue. And finally her mother had granted that wish. Yes, I am guilty, Veronica thought. Her mother was the first murder of the pram-lady's arithmetic.

She sat on the spot where, by all Christian rites, her mother's body should have lain. She laid the flowers at the foot of the headstone. She hadn't expected that call of remembrance to be so painful and now all the tears that she had stocked over so many years ran freely. But, as she wept, she felt it as a purge. This was the true emptying of the third drawer. She sat there for a while until her sobs abated. Then she kissed the headstone.

"I've missed you, Mother," she whispered. "I miss you terribly."

She rose from the grass and went on her stationed way. Wandering through the gravestones, she almost missed her next port-of-call. For not only did it boast a headstone, but a proper grave as well. It's true the grave was small, child-size, but it was ample enough to evidence the presence of a body beneath. She read the inscription, though her heart had read it many times before.

"*Oliver Smiles. Died December 1956. Aged 18 months. Deeply mourned by his heartbroken Mummy and Daddy.*"

She gave Oliver his flowers, laying them amongst those with which others remembered him. She reckoned his growth. Now he would have reached his thirtieth year. Though her crime was heinous enough, that reckoning seemed to magnify it, enlarging beyond measure her father's loss, and she readily understood and forgave him for leaving her.

She knew by instinct that her father's grave was not far off. And shortly she found it, lying directly behind his son's, as sire of that issue. She knelt by the small stone urn. Again there was no body, except the premature remains of one. And behind it a memorial stone.

"*Oliver Smiles. 1916–1957. Dearly beloved father and friend. Sadly missed by Millicent Wayne*".

Brazen, Veronica thought. That which had been clandestine in life had been loudly advertised on the grave. But she was not hurt by it, for she knew that, if her father had had any say in the matter, he would have included her own name in his remembrance. She gave him his chrysanthemums.

"I have atoned, Father," she said. "My Oliver was taken for yours."

She stood. She had said all she had to say. She had been about her father's business and it was all over. God had left her alone at last and she didn't need Him to come and tell her so. She walked out of the graveyard and never once looked back. She had killed and she had herself buried her dead. It was over.

She took the train back to Victoria and then a cab to Eaton Square. As she let herself into the house, she felt like an intruder. The house, and all that it entailed, had never been part of her. At most it had been a resting place while she made up her mind. And that she had now done. She went to her desk and penned a letter to Edward.

"My dearest," she wrote. "I am leaving. The baby miscarried. I know this will grieve you, but would it help if I told you the truth? The baby was not yours, Edward. There was no miracle. Your mother was right. I think in your heart you knew it, too. But it is over now. As is all that part of my life. That past of mine that I never shared with you. But it is buried now and I am leased to start afresh. In time I will write to you. I loved you as much as I was able. The shortcomings of that love are my frailty. I never hope to meet a kinder man, nor one so loving. It is that loving that drives me away, ashamed. My own love, such as it is, I leave with you. I am going to listen well to the song of the turtle and then perhaps I shall return. Veronica."

She did not read it over. She knew its exactness and it was all that she could say. She sealed it in an envelope and left it on his desk. She collected the letters that had come for her during her absence, then went to her room and packed her rucksacks. She did not know where she was going. But she knew it would not be to the desert. She no longer needed that loophole of escape, that oh so respectable postponement of the third drawer. If one listened carefully enough, the song of the turtle could be heard anywhere in the world. So where she went was of little relevance. She buckled the last strap on her rucksack and picked up her post. A couple of magazines and a letter. The handwriting on the envelope was pleasantly familiar. Mrs Dale. Veronica tore it open with the excitement of a child who, after a long absence, was going home.

"Dear Veronica," she read, "Harry, my brother, died a month ago and, though it was very sad, it was a blessing, too, for towards the end he suffered greatly. I think about you so often. It's many years now since we met and I think sometimes how lovely it would be to see my little Veronica again."

She read the letter over and over, marvelling at its superb timing. She would go to Worthing and they would be together for a while, with no talk of the drawer, for each would know that the other had unlocked its secrets.

Margaret was out, probably shopping, so there was mercifully no need for farewell. Out of courtesy she left her a note on the kitchen table. It simply stated her departure and wished her well. She left the house with a sense of freedom she had not felt since her last sojourn in the desert.

She took a cab to Victoria. She had to wait a while before the next train to Worthing, so she went into the buffet and ordered a pot of tea. Though she took no sugar, she dawdled her spoon in the cup, an act that reflected the ease that she felt with herself.

And then she saw Him. He was walking towards her, but without purpose of encounter. It seemed that He didn't even see her. He carried no bag. He wore no passenger's disguise. He was as she had first seen him in the desert. In the oneness of Himself. He was nearing her and when He was but a few steps away, He raised His eyes to her face. But He did not linger. He did not tarry. He simply passed right through her. Like a whisper.

BROTHERS
Bernice Rubens
Winner of the Booker Prize

This is a heroic and powerful novel, spanning four generations of brothers from the same family, and a hundred and fifty turbulent years of Jewish history. Against the background of Tsarist Russia, with its persecutions and pogroms, the story of the milk brothers Benjamin and Reuben unfolds. Their descendents Aaron and Leon leave the Old Country to start a new life in the Welsh valleys; and Leon's attempts to cut himself free from his Jewish culture have far-reaching effects on future generations. The brothers David and Benjamin are drawn together in Hitler's death camps, whilst Aaron and Jakob understand very little of each other, as Jakob attempts to escape the repression of the modern Soviet Union, and Aaron strives to conform . .

'Powerfully told, unremitting in tone, BROTHERS is an impressive work, a profound reflective exercise for anyone born gentile and free.' *Financial Times*

'A narrative so complex and so sweeping remains a considerable achievement of the intelligence and the will.' *Spectator*.

'Enthralling and terrifying.' *Standard*.

FICTION   0 349 13013 2

GLASS-HOUSES
Penelope Farmer

Grace is a glassblower. A taciturn farmer's daughter from Somerset, she is able to set up her own glasshouse with the legacy left to her by her old mentor, Reg. Accompanied by her young apprentice, she moves to Derbyshire. But when Jas, once both a glassblower and her husband, and Betsy, Grace's ghostly and goading alter ego, appear, the characters, in their obsession with glass and each other, are slowly brought to explosion point.

Glass itself is the heart of the novel, the focus of its narrative, its symbolism, its elusive, illusory magic. Wrought from the earth by fire, cooled by water, it determines and describes not only the characters, the landscapes they move in, the society they are part of, but also the way the story progresses, hypnotically, through each of its stages, to a terrifying climax.

Also by Penelope Farmer in Abacus:
AWAY FROM HOME
EVE: HER STORY

0 3491 0109 4   FICTION

GRACE

Maggie Gee

Grace is eighty-five, was once loved by a major painter, and now deplores the modern evils that rampage across the world. To escape the tyranny of silent phone calls that plague her, she goes to the seaside. To Seabourne where nothing ever happens except quiet deaths and holidays. Paula is her niece. Also a victim of mysterious harassment, she lives near the railway line that carries nuclear waste through the heart of London. She feels curiously, constantly unwell. Bruno is a sexually quirky private detective who attacks daisies with scissors, germs with bleach, and old ladies for fun.

A novel of towering stature, with all the stealth and suspense of a thriller, *Grace* is written in condemnation of violence and secrecy, in praise of courage and the redeeming power of love.

'Full of poignancy and power'
JEANETTE WINTERSON

'Heart-stoppingly exciting'
TIME OUT

'Controlled and highly imaginative . . . this exceptional novel should be read everywhere'
LITERARY REVIEW

'Magically, I finished this book with the almost cheerful feeling that things are still hopeful as long as people answer back and write as well as this'

GUARDIAN

0 349 10103 5   FICTION

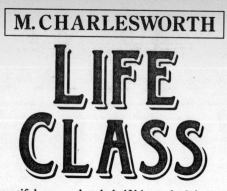

M. CHARLESWORTH

LIFE CLASS

Marriage to a beautiful woman barely half his age hadn't seemed fraught with hazard until Jack Ruffey took Annette on a belated honeymoon in Java. There, on the slopes of Mount Bromo, they encountered the enigmatic John Ridinghouse – a figure from Annette's past, an obsession for Jack's future. A tantalizing intrigue developed; a voyage – like Jack's paintings – of discovery, but with the twisted threads of jealousy, a hilariously egotistical misogynist philosopher and eerie Javanese spirits teasingly playing their parts.

'The reader is completely entranced . . . a masterpiece of perplexities'
Literary Review

Also by Monique Charlesworth in Abacus:
THE GLASS HOUSE

0 349 10101 9   FICTION

A
CAPOTE
READER

A Capote Reader contains virtually all of the author's published work – including several short pieces that have never before been published in book form. It is divided into six parts: *Short Stories* (twelve of them, all that Capote ever wrote); two *Novellas*, *The Glass Harp* and *Breakfast at Tiffany's*; *Travel Sketches* (thirteen of them, mostly around the Mediterranean); *Reportage*, including the famous Porgy and Bess trip to Russia *The Muses Are Heard*, and the bizarre murders in *Handcarved Coffins*; *Portraits* of the famous, among them Picasso, Mae West, Isak Dinesen, Chaplin, André Gide, Elizabeth Taylor – who radiated 'a hectic allure' – and 'the beautiful child' Marilyn Monroe; and *Essays* (seventeen of them, including *A Day's Work*). Each section is in chronological order of publication, demonstrating the evolution of the author's style and interests.

Also by Truman Capote in Abacus:
ANSWERED PRAYERS
MUSIC FOR CHAMELEONS
IN COLD BLOOD
BREAKFAST AT TIFFANY'S

0 3491 0095 0   FICTION

Abacus now offers an exciting range of quality fiction and non-fiction by both established and new authors. All of the books in this series are available from good bookshops, or can be ordered from the following address:

Sphere Books
Cash Sales Department
P.O. Box 11
Falmouth
Cornwall TR10 9EN.

Please send cheque or postal order (no currency), and allow 60p for postage and packing for the first book plus 25p for the second book and 15p for each additional book ordered up to a maximum charge of £1.50 in U.K.

B.F.P.O. customers please allow 60p for the first book, 25p for the second book plus 15p per copy for the next 7 books, thereafter 9p per book.

Overseas customers including Eire please allow £1.25 for postage and packing for the first book, 75p for the second book and 28p for each subsequent title ordered.